Shiloh Walker
Mary Wine
Lora Leigh

a Wish, a Kiss, a Dream

Ellora's Cave
Romantica Publishing

What the critics are saying...

"Ms. Wine did a wonderful job of keeping the sexual tension high while the love story quickly unfolded, and when that sexual tension builds to culmination, Christina and Shane's firery passion for each other nearly explodes off the pages." ~ *EcataRomance Reviews*

"Be it the angsty torment of Ms. Walker's tale, the intense seduction of Ms. Wine's, or the wild passion of Ms. Leigh's, *A Wish, A Kiss, A Dream* is one book not to be missed, taking its place firmly on the keeper shelf." ~ *Romance Junkies*

"*A Wish, A Kiss, A Dream* is a beautifully written anthology by three incredibly talented authors who have taken A Wish, A Kiss, A Dream and turned each of them into their own beautiful masterpiece." ~ *Ecataromance Reviews*

"*A Wish, A Kiss, A Dream* is sweetly romantic and sizzling hot all at once. Sighing is not optional it is required when you get your hands on this one." ~ *A Romance Review*

An Ellora's Cave Romantica Publication

www.ellorascave.com

A Wish, A Kiss, A Dream

ISBN 1419952323, 9781419952326

Edited by Pamela Campbell and Sue-Ellen Gower.
Cover art by Syneca.

This book printed in the U.S.A. by Jasmine-Jade Enterprises, LLC.

Electronic book publication February 2005
Trade paperback publication August 2005

A WISH, A KISS, A DREAM

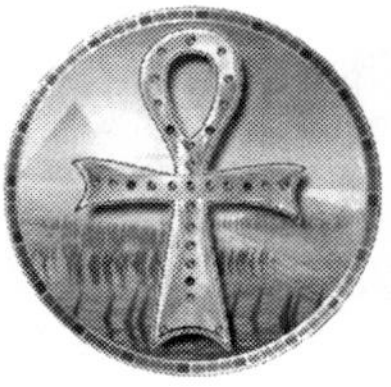

DJINN'S WISH

Shiloh Walker

Dedication

To my friends, Mary Wine and Lora Leigh… Luv you guys.

Trademarks Acknowledgement

The author acknowledges the trademarked status and trademark owners of the following wordmarks mentioned in this work of fiction:

Rolex: Rolex Watch U.S.A., Inc.

Vanilla Musk: Coty Inc.

Prologue

Centuries Past…

ℰ𝒮

His name was Tamric. Young, arrogant and headstrong, Tam wanted nothing more than the excitement of walking the mortal realms, the *Djinn* magick that would let him grant wishes, and the prestige that came when he returned to the land of Jinari.

Eying the rich, carved wooden urn with envy, he closed his eyes, trying to picture the mortal realms. They had mountains there. Mountains, rivers, oceans…

The dry hot winds of the desert blew in through the window, stirring his thick hair, bringing with it the ripe scent of *gesan* trees and *vandri,* the plump purple fruits that grew from those trees.

Tam ran a hand down the outer curve of the urn, feeling the hum of residual magick. This had been his mother's vessel once. For three hundred years, she had been gifted with the chance to walk among mortals—three centuries. *Lucky lady,* he mused, shaking his head as he rubbed his thumb over the raised carving of the *egasi,* the symbol of *Djinn* magick.

Nearing the end of her third century, she had met the mortal who had returned the urn to her, without claiming his wish, giving her leave to come back to Jinari, where she was adored and revered by all.

His lip curled in a scowl.

That was what he wanted. But when he had been all of fourteen, she had conscripted him into service. *Sentenced*—that was more like it. Enslaved for five decades.

Bleeding sands, I don't want to be a priest. Spinning away from the urn, he paced the room, the loose material of his pants rippling around the strong muscles in his legs, his jewel-adorned belt winking in the light that emanated from the walls.

A priest… "I'd rather freeze in the lowest levels of hell for fifty years."

He wanted the power of *Djinn,* wanted to experience life in the mortal world, experience mortal women…and come back here a free man, out from under the shadow of his mother. Wanted to see people look at *him* with awe.

He spun around, reached out his hand and cupped the urn's curve. The urn pulsed under his touch, oddly warm. Narrowing his eyes, he stepped closer and touched it with both hands. The throb of life seemed to course through his hands as they lay against the urn. Unusual…

He never saw the blue mist that seemed to flow up out of the floor behind him. As he ran his hands along the surface of the urn, he never realized he was being watched.

It was the gentle clearing of a throat behind him that had him whirling around to stare into the unfathomable eyes of one of the Guardians. His jaw dropped as he sank to one knee, mouth going dry with fear, his heart slamming against his chest.

"So, young Tamric. You wish to be *Djinn*?"

A female voice cried out and Tam flinched as his mother came rushing into the sacred peace room, her amethyst eyes flashing with fury, glinting with tears. "No!" she shouted, flinging out her hand at the Guardian. "He will *not* be *Djinn.*"

The Guardian smiled and Tam thought he looked kind of sad. "Isma, he wishes it. He has wished it for a long time."

"He is a fool! A child. He doesn't know what he wants," she insisted, shaking her head so that her long black braids danced around her shoulders.

The Guardian slid Tamric a glance and he felt as though the being could see straight through him. "He does not wish to go into service to the temple," the Guardian murmured, shaking his head. "Bound forever to a life of loneliness. Such a burden to place upon one who doesn't feel that calling."

Isma shook her head. "No. The Temple is a fine calling. He must learn to appreciate what I can give him," she snarled.

"I do not want it."

Both of them stilled, turning to look at him. Deep black eyes and pale purple eyes stared at him with varying degrees of surprise. "You are a boy!" Isma said. "You do not *know* what you want."

Tamric glared at her, enraged. "I am *not* a boy. I'm twenty years old. Next year, I would have been able to leave this household and set up my own. Except *you* gave away my freedom. For fifty bloody years!" he snarled, his voice dropping to a low growl as he fought to contain his fury. Damn it, he knew she loved him, wanted what was best… But it had to be *her* definition of best.

"I do not want a sexless existence where I do nothing but live in silence and ponder the meaning of the universe and pray until my knees bleed from kneeling so long on the floor," Tam said coldly, shaking his head. "You see only what the priests become after servitude. I know what I must endure to ever attain what you wish for me to have. Fifty years of slaving for the priests, fifty years without the touch of a woman, fifty years of living on little more than bread and water."

"Those fifty years teach you control, discipline," Isma said, her voice level, her eyes unreadable. "After that, you will have *everything*, your pick of lands, of brides, of everything you could ever want."

Tam shouted, "I do not want it!" Slashing at the empty air with his hand, he gritted out, "That is what *you* want for me. I've always done what *you* wanted. Now, I am doing what I want."

Turning his eyes to the Guardian, he said, "What must I do?"

The sound of his mother's denial echoed in his ears as a funnel of blue smoke enshrouded him.

Chapter One

Trapped in the dream, Kat shifted restlessly on the bed, shaking her head, muttering under her breath.

The roads didn't seem that slick. Her eyes tracked the gentle snowflakes as they fell from the sky. Their flight left in two hours. She wondered idly if the snowfall would stop their flight to New York. She'd been so looking forward to this trip. But she couldn't care less about the snow falling, whether the flight would be delayed—cancelled. After all, what did it matter?

Nothing mattered anymore.

She was living a lie. With a man who claimed he loved her. But he was fucking her best friend.

Flipping down the visor, she looked into the lighted mirror on the reverse side, staring into her own eyes for a long moment. She couldn't believe this was happening.

Feeling somebody watching her, Kat shifted her eyes in the mirror and met Jenise's reflected gaze. That dark, chocolate-brown gaze jumped away from Kat's with a nervousness that made her belly roil. Damn it. How could they do this? But she never doubted it was less than the truth.

Mara wouldn't lie.

In her mind's eye, she could see it. The lush, textured ivory wallpaper, the gold trim, the rich, plush burgundy of the carpet. The luxurious colors made a perfect backdrop for Jenise's dark beauty, her coffee-colored skin, her thick curls that she wore hanging loose down her back.

And Brian—her gut clenched as she pictured them together. Not just in the hotel hallway, where Mara had seen them.

But in the bed beyond that door. Brian's chestnut hair—thick and wavy—secured in a tail at his neck. Those broad, strong shoulders and the muscles in his back flexing as he drove his dick inside Jenise's toned body.

Damn it!

The pain inside her gut exploded into a supernova, tightening her throat, her belly clenching, the tears blinding her. Pressing her temple to the frigid glass of the window, she fought to breathe past the pain.

Slowly, she closed her eyes against the tears that burned so badly. Forcing air past her constricted throat was agony. She couldn't do this. She couldn't.

With rapid blinks of her eyes, Kat cleared the tears away. She cleared her throat gently and her voice was just slightly husky as she spoke.

Lifting her gaze, she again met Jenise's in the mirror. Jenise licked her lips, her rich, ruby lipstick gleaming faintly. Behind her, she heard the soft whisper of silk over leather as Jenise shifted her position. With a cool, brittle smile, she shifted also, turning so she could stare at Brian.

He flicked her a glance and smiled—that slow, warm smile that always heated her blood. Now it made her cold. That smile wasn't for her. Wasn't all hers.

"So…honey," she purred, batting her lashes as he looked at her again, a longer, lingering glance. "How long have you two been fucking each other behind my back?"

Jenise closed her eyes. Kat saw her from the corner of her eye, but she was still focused on Brian. His eyes stared into hers for a long, unblinking second, jaw dropped in shock. "Kat…sweetie—"

Kat turned away from him, staring out the window. The tears were back. Stinging her eyes, blinding her, so that for a long moment she couldn't see. Brian's startled voice was loud in her ears. She reached up, dashing away the tears.

Just in time to see the car go flying off the road.

Scenery flew past her eyes. Everything was spinning.

And then there was pain, sharp, vicious pain that stole her breath.

Kat woke up screaming from the dream. She sat up in the bed, pressing her hands to her eyes, feeling the wet tracks of tears.

She shuddered, sobs racking her body. Distantly, she heard a soft whine and she opened her arms, unable to speak past the sobs that choked her. A warm, furred body leaped into her arms and she closed them around Zeb's body, feeling a gentle lick on her face as he nuzzled her, trying to comfort her. She held him tighter as she gasped in air, trying to quit crying, trying to move past the dream.

She couldn't. Damn it, she couldn't keep doing this.

Long hours later, she had finally pushed the dregs of the dream aside.

A smile lit her face as she stroked her hands down the frame of the mirror, listening to Mara talk.

"It's beautiful," Mara murmured.

Kat smiled tremulously. "I know. But where did it come from? Who sent it?"

Bemused, Mara said, "Honey, I don't know. There's no card…no return address. Just this mirror."

* * * * *

Djinn, with the power of granting wishes. But only to women, and only if they shared a kiss. Needless to say, Tam had been kissed by a lot of women. Once they discovered him, hiding in the shadows of the mirror, they summoned him out, kissed him well and good, and then he was gone.

As he strolled down the crowded street in New York City, he stared at nobody, met nobody's eyes, looked at nothing, except what was directly in front of him.

He wasn't imprisoned within his vessel, which was good. Some awful people had owned that mirror, and he was glad he wasn't trapped there with nothing more to do than stare out at the activities of some the degenerates his mirror had belonged to over the years.

No, Tam was able to walk among people, live among humans, and had for quite some time. When the mirror was activated, he was pulled back to it, but other than that, he was free.

Since he couldn't claim his mirror unless its bearer gave it to him, though, he preferred to stay as far away from it as possible when he could. For more than three decades, it had been stored in some vault in England and hadn't been activated. Now, it was back in the States, in a small tourist town in Tennessee, in the hands of a woman who had the power to summon him to grant her a wish.

After she wished, she'd try for another, although he could only grant one. Sooner or later, she'd sell it or give it away. But until she called him, he was free.

Tam scowled. Not free. Never free. How could you be free when every time a woman kissed you, you knew it was because she wanted something? *Damn it.* Maybe his mother had been right. Century after century had passed, and long ago Tam had given up the hope that someday he would have his freedom, as his mother had been given hers so long ago.

Maybe service to the Temple would have been the wiser choice.

But the idea of five decades of servitude, of kneeling on bloody knees and praying, of serving the Elders in silence… *Damn it.* At least here he lived in relative comfort.

But he was trapped in a life of servitude, nonetheless. Damned forever to grant wishes, give kisses to women he had no feelings for. And wish that someday he'd be free.

"That's why you never kiss them anymore," a laughing voice said beside him.

Tam barely glanced at Jaydie, the impish *Djinn* he had known for years. Her kiss granted wishes to men—and she loved every moment of it. After several centuries, many of the

Djinn tired of their lives, bound in the mortal world, except for that brief time between masters and mistresses. For brief moments in time, they could return to Jinari. Or roam the mortal world unencumbered. Whatever they chose, for those hours, they had no mistress, no master. Tamric loved every moment of it.

Jaydie, on the other hand, hated being without a man to entice, to tease, to tempt. In fact, the moment she granted his wish, she often used her magick to find her next master and took herself there, before the old master realized she was gone.

"What are you doing here?" he asked, one brow winging up as he sidestepped somebody trying to sell him a Rolex rip-off.

"Oh, nothing. Just in the city, sensed you were near. I've been looking for you for a few days," she told him, her ink black hair floating around her shoulders as she spun around and started to walk backward in front of him, so that he could actually *look* at her when he talked. "I saw your mirror."

He arched a brow. "And?"

She shrugged. "Pretty lady, that one. Quiet. Different."

"None of them are different," Tam said flatly.

"Really? Then why didn't I feel a wish?" she asked, her dark green eyes wide and innocent.

Tam slowed to a stop, moving out of the middle of the crowded sidewalk, dragging Jaydie away from the flow of traffic. "She doesn't seem to realize what she did," he said, with a shrug. "I stood there, waiting, wanting to get back to my life, but she never even looked at me. So I left."

"You left? You can't *leave* when you've been summoned," Jaydie said, her jaw dropping, shock in her eyes.

"Well, I did," he said levelly, shrugging. "I went to her. As required. If she chose not to try to claim her wish, that's her choice."

He moved back to the sidewalk, walking on, intent on reaching his destination. Jaydie trailed along behind him, silent, thoughtful.

Heaven help me, he thought, sending a glance skyward. *Jay is trying to think.*

The steps of the museum loomed in front of him and he jogged up them, sliding inside the door and then leaning back against it for one brief moment, smiling in pleasure. He could feel the age around him, in the masterpieces of the past, and the energy from some of the more modern pieces, their power all but crying out to him.

"You didn't go home this last time. Not for even a moment," Jaydie whispered. "Don't you miss it?"

He slid her a narrow glance. "No. I didn't go home. I have no desire to go there." Jinari hadn't been home to him in ages. Realistically, he knew that. Even though he was forced to remain in the mortal world for long stretches of time, he didn't hate it. He wanted to be here.

The only thing he hated was not being completely free to roam this wondrous world with no one to answer to. No master but himself.

Staring at the brush strokes of the masterpieces he knew as well as he knew his own hand, Tam let the silence and peace soak into his soul, quieting his rioting mind.

"You have an obsession with this place," Jay said quietly.

He shrugged. "We all have them." He pushed away from the door and paid for himself and Jay, narrowing his eyes at her when she made a move to just go through without paying. Of course, since *Djinn* were only seen when they wanted to be, nobody would have raised an alarm. The pretty lady with green eyes would have just faded out of sight, and *Djinn* magick kept people from thinking about it, wondering what they'd seen.

As they moved inside, he said quietly, "They have cameras here, pet. Your magick works well on humans but do we want to test it against electronic security equipment?"

She wrinkled her nose at him, sighing. "Modern civilization can take all the fun out of being *Djinn*," she said melodramatically as she slowed to a stop in front of a canvas that was almost as tall she. Cocking her head, she studied it, and then shrugged. "I don't understand what you see in this place."

Glancing up at her, he smiled a little. "I see everything," he murmured.

* * * * *

Nothing. Katlin could have screamed as she repeated to the doctor, "I see nothing."

Literally. For the past three years of her life, everything had been darkness. The wreck that had killed her husband and her best friend had taken her vision as well.

The last thing she could remember seeing was the spinning landscape as Brian's car went flying off the road. Now she saw nothing but darkness.

"Ms. Dixon," Dr. Merkin said softly from just in front of her. "There is simply no anatomical reason I can find for your blindness." He sat too close. She could smell the garlic on his breath, feel the hot wash of it on her face.

"I've heard that line before," she said tiredly. Her guide dog, Zeb, whined in his throat, laying his head on her leg. She smiled down at him and said, "It's okay, boy."

It wasn't, though. Not really.

Damn it. She had hoped— Merkin was the best in the state, one of the best in the country. She had hoped… Shaking her head, she stood, cane in one hand, holding the other out for him to shake. "Thank you."

She ignored his comment about a possible hospital in Sweden as she slowly and steadily walked out of the room, tapping her cane back and forth in front of her. No more hospitals. She wasn't going to endure another CT scan, another MRI. No more. Especially when the doctors couldn't even tell her a reason for her lost eyesight.

Mara met her at the door—Katlin smelled the soft vanilla of her body lotion and the faint scent of Vanilla Musk even before Mara said, "Hey. Anything?"

Before the doctor could try to interrupt, Katlin shrugged. "Same old, same old." She reached out, and Mara was there, her arm out for guidance, as it had been nearly every day since the accident. "You know, you didn't have to bring me here. You do have a life," she said as they started out of the office.

"Yes, and you are a very important part of it. Besides, I wasn't going to subject some stranger from the taxi company to your tongue," she said teasingly. "Want to go get a bite to eat?"

"No," Kat said softly. "I want to go home, just home."

A soft sigh drifted from Mara and Kat fought the urge to hunch her shoulders in defense. "Baby, when are you going to start living again?"

A bitter smile curved Kat's mouth. "Why bother? There's little left to live for—except you."

* * * * *

Late that night, Kat stood in front of the unfinished canvas. With gentle, searching fingers, she ran her hand over its surface, feeling the familiar ridges where she had made her brushstrokes, years earlier.

"Why can't I throw this away?" she whispered to herself, her throat tight, her sightless eyes burning with tears. From his spot under the window, Zeb woofed softly. She ran a hand through her hair, muttering to herself. She had to stop this. Seriously had to stop this.

She was blind—*face the facts, girl.* She would be blind for the rest of her life and the colors and textures that had filled her world for years were now nothing more than memory.

She had been trying to finish the painting the day of the wreck. The day she'd discovered the truth…

Her husband and her best friend were lovers. Mara had called, tears in her voice, as she'd told Kat that she had seen them together at the Regents Hotel. They had been kissing—not a friendly little peck on the cheek but a torrid clinch. Mara had been there to pick up a business colleague and she had seen them.

They hadn't realized they had an audience as they'd broken apart to step inside the elevator.

Now Kat wished she hadn't answered Mara's phone call, hadn't listened to her, hadn't even gotten out of bed.

"Why was I so blind?" she murmured, closing her eyes as a tear rolled down her cheek.

Brian had said that he had to work for a while that day. "Pick me up on the way to the airport," she'd whispered, thinking back. He'd said he could pick up Jenise since her condo was on the way, and then they'd come get Katlin. She hadn't thought anything of it.

Tears poured down her cheeks. Not a thing.

The silence in the car had wrapped around her like a fist. Though Brian hadn't realized anything was wrong, Jenise had. Kat had seen the tension in her eyes. Maybe it was the other woman's guilty conscience, but there had been a look there. Fear. As Kat had studied her from the car's vanity mirror, she'd tried to figure out what to say. Whether to say anything at all.

Of course she said something. The pain was burning a hole in her stomach. There was no way she could say nothing. That incapacity to remain quiet had destroyed her life.

Blinded her. Cost her everything. For one tiny moment, Brian had focused on her, taking his eyes off the road. And when he hit the ice, he'd lost control.

Her words had killed them.

Kat's mind rebelled at the thought. Logically, she knew the wreck had been an accident. But the guilt was eating her alive. Guilt, hurt, dismay… She still didn't understand how they could have done that to her.

Turning away from the canvas, she walked out of the studio, walking the fifteen steps from the studio's doorway to the front door, checking to make sure it was locked. Tired, exhausted, she wanted to go to bed, but something besides her painting and her wrecked life, was calling her.

The mirror. Ever since she had first touched it, she had been drawn to it. It seemed to whisper to her, summoning her near, asking that she touch it, speak to it.

The mirror was old. Mara had described it to her in vivid detail and Katlin had run her questing hands over it, searching it. There had been no return address.

Kat had no idea who it had come from. Seemed rather wasted, sending a mirror to a blind woman. But she'd *wanted* it. The need had torn through her, becoming stronger and stronger as Mara had described it, and when she'd touched it herself, running her hands over it, seeing it in her mind's eye, she had whispered, "I wish…" But she'd stopped talking before she could finish her wish.

Wishes were useless. She wished she had never said anything to Brian, wished she'd never answered the phone call from Mara, wished Mara had never seen them. And nothing ever changed. She'd give all she had to undo what had happened that day. Wish… *I wish…* And it did no good.

The surface of the mirror had felt oddly warm under her hand, the oak frame almost seeming to pulse, as if it were alive.

Her fingers rubbed the carving at the top, a marking that Mara had said looked almost like a Celtic knot, but different. More rounded, flowing, with odd markings carved into the raised ridges. "Kat, this is some ancient kind of alphabet," Mara had whispered. "This mirror is about two hundred years old but something about the frame, the wood, feels older. I know that doesn't make any sense but I know old. And this is *old*."

* * * * *

Two days later, her fascination with the mirror had dimmed…a little. But every time she passed within ten feet of it, she felt it—a warmth emanating from the surface of the mirror, calling out to her.

And tonight was no different. She ran her hand over the smooth surface, feeling its warmth seep into her bones.

With one last, lingering stroke, Kat walked away, a bitter little smile on her lips. She was going insane. For some bizarre reason, she felt better. The mirror had felt oddly comforting.

Chapter Two

Tam stared at the woman as she walked away, her movements slow, graceful, a tiny smile on her pretty mouth. She was dressed much as she had been two days before, when she had summoned him to her with the softly whispered words, *I wish.* A short, midnight blue, silky chemise skimmed her thighs just below the rounded curve of her butt. A delightfully round butt, at that. Not some skinny coatrack there, but a real woman.

Thick, straight, fiery red hair fell past her shoulders, nearly down to the butt that kept drawing his eye. Her eyes were dark, he hadn't gotten close enough to see the color. That pretty cupid's bow mouth had seemed so sad—everything about her was sad. His jaw clenched, eyes on her retreating back.

Those eyes, whatever the color, were odd. Almost fey-like.

Hell, *she* was fey, walking on feet that barely seemed to touch the ground and eyes that looked at everything and nothing. He recalled how she had stroked the mirror, the odd look of peace that had come over her face for a moment. She'd sensed the mirror's importance. You didn't see that kind of joy and peace in somebody who thought it was just a pretty trinket.

With a tight scowl, he started to pace, wondering why in the hell she hadn't tried to use her wish. "What are you waiting for?" he muttered, not concerned with her hearing him. Mortals couldn't, unless he wanted them to.

A movement caught his attention. She had stopped in the hallway, turned around, and was staring toward where he stood with her head cocked, as though she had heard him. But that wasn't possible.

So why was she standing there, with that odd, almost frightened look in her eyes?

He thrust up his arms and in a burst of light only the *Djinn* could see, he was gone.

* * * * *

Automatically, Kat looked back over her shoulder, even though she wouldn't see anything. Then she turned, listening, head cocked. Quietly, she said, "Zeb." His wet nose poked into her hand as she nervously licked her lips. She hadn't heard anything, she didn't think, but she had the oddest feeling that she was being watched, that she wasn't alone in the house with Zeb.

"Go search, boy," she said, moving to press her back against the wall, trying to stay as out of sight as she could in the hall. She heard Zeb's nails clicking on the floor as he walked around. Her heart slammed brutally against her ribs, making breathing almost painful, as she waited, fear zinging through her system.

Blind, alone, helpless –

Then she heard a soft bark. Everything was fine. If something was wrong, Zeb would have sounded an alarm. He padded back to her and she stroked his head after he licked her hand. Shakily, she whispered, "I'm going crazy. Really, really crazy."

Just imagining things—nothing was wrong.

But she had Zeb jump up on the bed and lie down with her as she slept.

* * * * *

Every morning, as her eyes opened and she drifted out of sleep, it took a few moments before she remembered.

Sometimes, she panicked, her breath locking in her lungs as she tried to see in the darkness, but there was nothing there for her to see. Not anymore. Not for more than three years.

Today was no different.

For long moments, the blackness was oppressive, nearly suffocating as it pressed down on her. Air wheezed in and out of her lungs for endless moments as she huddled in the bed, her mind spinning in useless circles.

But after a few minutes, her mind adjusted. Her ears picked up the normal sounds that assured her she was home, her nose catching the scent of potpourri and the soft, musty smell of Zeb.

The dog watched her—once her eyes opened, he woofed softly and inched over to nuzzle her hand. She rolled over and spent a few minutes scratching his head.

"Hey, boy, did you protect me last night?" she asked him, smiling as he inched closer, his big, furry body pressed against hers, his head resting on her shoulder as he surrounded her, leaving her feeling safe and protected.

Zeb yipped.

Kat laughed and rolled into a sitting position, drawing her knees to her chest. "I don't have to work today. So, what do you want to do? Pace the house? Stare at the four walls? Listen to the TV?" she asked dryly. Sighing, she dropped her forehead to her knees and whispered, "I have to get a life."

Her belly rumbled and she smirked. "Maybe I'll put off getting a life—while I eat." Ten minutes later, she was eating oatmeal and drinking orange juice while Zeb happily scarfed down his dog food—very happily—if the sounds were any sign. He ate his food as through it had been a month since he'd last been fed, instead of just last night.

Kat smiled softly as he finished and gave a happy little bark. "You're welcome," she said.

Setting her bowl in the sink, she rinsed it out, feeling along the counter for the dishwashing liquid. There had been a time when she would have just left the bowl there. If she didn't get to it that morning, then the housecleaner would get to it later that afternoon. The housecleaner was something she'd had to give up. As much as she loved Dorrie, the lady had kept leaving little things out of place, or moving her stuff around.

Kat's life demanded strict organization now—something that she had taken a while to accept. But after banged knees, various bruises and general frustration when she couldn't find things without calling Mara, she'd accepted it. She'd rather become a neat freak than look like a victim of abuse.

So once a week somebody did come in and do basic cleaning, but it was somebody who could actually remember not to move things around instead of the chipper, talkative, but somewhat absentminded Dorrie.

Drying her hands, Kat left the kitchen for her office, her fingers seeking out the radio and flipping it on before she sat down at the computer. At least she had learned how to do this. Going back to school had been awful but she caught on quickly, and last year she had gotten this specially modified computer.

Now Kat could go online, she could read, she could have contact with a world outside her own condo and outside the faceless, nameless voices she talked to on the phone during her job. The job kept her from feeling so isolated, so useless. The contact on the web helped to keep her sane, letting her visit the world she had once traveled so freely.

A soft little voice whispered, *You could do that if you just left the condo.*

"Shut up," she whispered, reaching up to rub her temple. "Just shut up." Once the computer had finished its little humming noises, she touched her fingers to the touch-sensitive Braille keyboard, sending the command to open the cable internet connection. She listened to the news, rolling her eyes as it seemed like a repeat of the past day's events.

Hell, today was going to be a repeat of pretty much every other day.

* * * * *

Tam folded his arms over his chest as he watched the woman sit down at her computer. There was something kind of odd about that computer, especially the keyboard. His computer didn't look anything like that. Granted, he had gotten one simply because he was curious about why so many people insisted on their importance. Once he had one, he had to admit, it definitely had potential—especially the games. He really liked the games.

Narrowing his eyes, he studied the computer more closely, watching as she stared blindly at the screen...*blindly.*

The telephone rang and he watched as she jumped slightly, her head whipped up, that pretty red hair floated around her shoulders. She stared toward the phone, and Tam dismissed the passing idea as she stood up.

She walked over to the telephone, with that smooth, floating grace she possessed. Her hand reached for the phone and passed right over it. She patted the surface of the console table, finally landing on the phone.

She's blind... His eyes moved back to the computer, to more closely study it. The buttons of the keyboard were modified, each with a series of small raised dots. There was also a long slender strip below it, which he had seen her touch—made of a series of tiny little rods that shifted and moved.

Slowly, he turned back to stare at her.

That was why she hadn't said anything that night when he had drifted out of the mirror in a fog of blue smoke that solidified to form his body.

The woman hadn't seen him.

She's blind…

His eyes narrowed thoughtfully. It was possible, wasn't it? After all, if she had known a *Djinn* would appear at the activation of the mirror, then wouldn't she have said something? She hadn't said anything because she hadn't seen him, hadn't realized what she was doing when she'd touched it and murmured, *I wish…*before her voice had broken off abruptly.

An idea started to blossom in his head as he watched her, not paying any attention to her conversation, just studying that ethereal face, that soft rosebud mouth. She still wore her chemise, that deep midnight blue that glowed against the ivory of her skin. Her mouth curved into a smile as she listened to whoever was on the other end of the line. He listened to the musical sound of her laughter, watching as she shifted to one foot, idly rubbing the back of her calf with the other foot.

Tam found his eyes drawn to those legs, lids drooping low as he formed an image of those long legs wrapping around his hips while he buried his cock inside the snug, wet confines of her pussy.

Hmmm… Wasn't expecting this…

But the hunger that had appeared so suddenly now tore through him. It shouldn't have come as such a surprise, this raging, gnawing hunger.

She smelled sweet, female. He'd noticed that last night—her scent had lingered in his mind, in his blood. Her skin glowed and he imagined it felt like silk.

His cock stiffened and started to throb as he studied that sleek, softly curved body. Her breasts rose and fell under the silk of her chemise and he wondered what her skin tasted like, what color her nipples were, how she would feel beneath him.

Touching her would be a pleasure—it wasn't very often that he found a woman he actually would *enjoy* taking to bed.

Not that he'd never tried using sex to convince women to give him what he wanted. He had.

But now—maybe—he had a chance at complete freedom. Not having to slide from that mirror every time some woman stroked it and whispered, *I wish…* Not having to endure kisses from any and every woman, whether he desired them not.

Freedom.

But to get that, a woman had to wish him free or give him the mirror before she made her wish. Since he granted one wish, and one wish only, how likely was he to get that? In more than three thousand years, he had yet to meet the woman who would give up her wish.

But it was entirely possible that somebody might *give* him the mirror, if she didn't realize what it was.

As she hung up the phone, he threw up his arms, disappearing in an explosion of light.

Chapter Three

She tugged the headset off when a knock at her door caught her by surprise. She didn't have visitors. Well other than Mara, and occasional visits from people she had met at the School. And they never came without calling first. Mara wouldn't come while Kat was working.

With a soft whistle, she called Zeb to her side before she walked over to the door. Kat wrapped her fingers around the cane that rested by the door, sliding her wrist through the strap before pushing the button on the speaker. "Yes?" she asked quietly.

The voice that came through the speaker was unlike any she had ever heard. Deep, hypnotic, faintly accented...*sexy*. It stroked over her skin like a warm hand and it took a moment for her to assimilate what he had said. "Hello...I've moved into the condo across from you. Just wanted to introduce myself."

Gnawing on her lip, she sank the fingers of her free hand into the soft, thick fur of Zeb's crown. Well, how did you answer that without being totally rude? Finally, she said, "It's nice to know the place finally sold. It's lovely. But I'm working—now isn't a good time for me. Sorry."

Then she moved away before she could give in to the temptation to open the door, just to hear that amazing voice in real life, instead of through an electronic speaker. The telephone rang, the different tone signifying that it was the work phone and she went back to her desk. Sliding into the chair, she reached out until her fingers brushed the headset. Sliding it on, she hit the line and said, "This is Kat."

* * * * *

Tam scowled as she dismissed him. Completely and totally. This wasn't something he'd planned on. Tam had planned on knocking, charming her a little, introducing himself, at least making a *little* headway.

But she hadn't even opened the damned door.

Blowing out a frustrated breath, he started to turn away but then he reached out, resting a hand on the door.

Inside, he could feel her. Focusing his refined senses, he could feel her as she moved away from the door, those pretty almond-shaped eyes staring sightlessly in front of her.

They were gray. Deep, storm cloud gray. Almost pewter in color. He had slid inside her condo last night, unable to resist looking at her again. From the shadows of the room, he had stared at her—silent, unmoving—just watching her as she ran her long agile fingers over the book in her lap.

Nerves had jangled inside her. Nerves, fear, hesitation…*fear*…

Narrowing his eyes, he let his hand fall from the door as he backed away. All right. He had not been prepared for that.

And now he felt more the fool. Why wouldn't he have been prepared for it? The woman was blind. How frightening must it be not to be able to see what stood right before you? Not to be able to face anything that came at you? Even the simplest of things?

No wonder she hadn't opened the door.

Damn it. Tam felt the disappointment well inside him as he turned away, his mouth tightening in a scowl. Okay, so he wouldn't be meeting her right now, wouldn't see that sweet face up close, wouldn't stare into her stormy eyes or try to uncover the secrets that made her so sad.

At least, not today.

Stalking back to the condo he had purchased just that morning, he slammed the door and flopped onto the couch. "I'll just try again."

And he did. The next day, and the next. Same answer—*Now isn't a good time for me.*

Finally he just settled by the door in the hall, unseen. Sooner or later, she would come outside. And he could go for days—weeks—without food, water, or sleep. So that was what he would do. But he only had to wait until late that third afternoon.

A long, sleekly built blonde stepped off the elevator, strolling toward him with a brown paper bag in hand and a determined glint in her eyes. As she knocked purposefully on the door, Tam smiled slowly, rising and moving through the wall into his own temporary home, waiting until the count of five to open the door. He conjured up a black jacket that he threw over his shoulder just as he was stepping out, and the look on his face would have done the finest actor in the world quite proud.

The blonde glanced at him but she finished talking into the small speaker before she turned to look at him, a curious expression on her face.

"Hello," he said. "I hope you have better luck than me. I've tried several times to introduce myself but it's always a bad time."

The blonde arched a brow at him just as the door swung open. With a slow smile, she said, "Well, that's normal for Kat, isn't it?"

"Ummm... What?" his shy neighbor asked, touching her tongue to her lips. A tan and black dog with big intelligent eyes, poked his head around his mistress, and stared at Tam curiously.

He watched as her hand landed on the dog's head, trailed down his neck in an automatic gesture, her fingers closing around the odd handle on his harness. The dog yipped softly and Tam held out his hand, letting the dog sniff at it as he raised his gaze to the lady he had been trying to meet for three days now.

Stepping forward, making sure his boot heels sounded on the floor, he cleared his throat gently, and spoke quietly, "I was just telling your friend that I hadn't had much luck meeting you." A soft pink flush stained her cheeks.

Her fingers clutched the cane so tightly he could see her knuckles turning white. The small notch in her throat bobbed as she swallowed, then forced a tight smile. She reached out, and Tam saw the familiarity between the two women as the blonde stepped forward, catching the hand her friend had stuck out. "Sorry. You kept catching me while I was working," she said, her voice quiet, hesitant. A blush rose over her cheeks and he had the feeling that she felt rather sheepish.

"I'm Katlin," she said, holding her hand out. The dog remained at her side, sitting on his haunches politely, never once taking his attention from his mistress.

Her eyes stared straight ahead, which was about in the center of his chest. She was delicately made—this close it was impossible not to notice. Her fragile appearance, with her slender arms, swanlike neck, and subtle curves, all contributed to her fey appearance.

"Tam, Tam Jones," he said, folding his hand around hers, holding it for a minute as he stared at her. "Glad I finally got to meet you."

"Kat Dixon," she said faintly. A pink tongue slid out to wet her lips as she shrugged nervously. "I… I don't get much in the way of company—not very good at playing the hostess."

Her friend chided softly, "You are a fine hostess, Kat." Her penetrating hazel eyes met Tam's and she stuck her hand out. "I'm Mara. Kat's best friend. I'm usually here three or four times a week."

He shook her hand but his eyes were drawn back to Kat. She was so damned pretty. "I was just going to go try and find someplace to eat," he said softly. "I don't suppose I could talk you two ladies into joining me, could I? I'm new here—up until early this week, I've never stepped foot in Gatlinburg and every time I go out, I get caught in tourist traffic."

Kat's mouth turned down and he saw the refusal in those pretty blank eyes.

Apparently so did her friend but she didn't let that stop her. "Sure, we'd love to. Come on in while I put this stuff away for Kat. Kat, why don't we take him to the steakhouse at the end of the parkway? We can take the bypass and miss most of the traffic."

"Mara—"

He watched as her friend cheerfully ran right over her, ushering her back into the house. He followed slowly, eying the large German shepherd as he trotted back inside, his eyes lingering on his mistress for a moment.

Tam scowled as that canine gaze swung back to him, those deep eyes watching, his tongue lolling out of his mouth.

Tam watched, listening as Mara dragged Kat down the hall. Though they spoke in low whispers, he had no problem hearing as Mara said, "Come on! Get dressed."

"Why? I'm not going anywhere," Katlin said, and he could hear the scowl in her voice.

"Yes, you are. That guy is gorgeous, and he's staring at you like you are the hottest thing he's ever seen," Mara said.

He grinned as Kat gave an indelicate snort. "Yes, I'm sure he'd love to go out with a blind woman," she said dryly.

Now it was his turn to scowl. So she couldn't see? He'd met plenty of women who were incapable of *thought*. So what if her eyes didn't work? Her mind obviously did. Turning away, he started to pace the rather sparsely decorated apartment, his eyes flickering past the mirror that was now hanging by the door, forcing himself not to go and stare at it obsessively.

He *wanted* his mirror back. With a passion that robbed him of all thought, he wanted it back. Wanted that total freedom that came with it. Scowling with frustration, he turned away from it, trying to focus his attention on something else.

If stealing it would have worked then he would have done so ages ago. Anything to get his mirror back.

His hands closed into fists as he shoved his greed back inside. *Soon. Soon,* he told himself.

At the far end of the living room, he saw a pair of French doors, both pushed open so that he could glimpse a large, nearly vacant room just beyond them. Beyond that, he could see the parkway and the many shops, all still decorated with greenery and Christmas lights.

Fat snowflakes fell from the sky, already piling up in little drifts against the window. The sky was a leaden gray and Tam could hear the wind as it whipped through the town.

Something caught his eye and he cocked his head, moving forward to study it closer. It was a painting. His expert eye moved over it, studying the unusual swirls of color with a thoughtful frown.

He knew art. A love of art had kept him company through the centuries as he'd watched civilizations rise and fall. But art remained. Something of it always survived, whether in drawings on a cave wall, the decaying statuary and architecture in Rome, or the masterpieces you could view only from behind a velvet rope at museums throughout the world.

Art survived.

Even when the artists faded away.

He knew this artist. She had been a gem—young, American, versatile, with a unique vision that was revealed in her work. Then, just years after appearing on the scene, she had disappeared, and nobody ever spoke of her now.

Kat…Katlin! Katlin Dixon. Bleeding hell! Damn it. He stared in blind shock at the unfinished picture, his throat going tight. He'd seen her art in a museum in France, in art shops all over the world as her popularity had grown and her paintings were reproduced for those who couldn't afford the originals or the limited editions.

The faint echo of footsteps touched his ears and he whirled around, retreating from the empty studio before Kat or Mara realized that he had left the living room. That empty studio stung his heart, images of her work flashing through his mind. What must it be like? To have such talent, such a driving need, those images burning in her mind, and then the outlet for them destroyed?

As she came walking back into the room, a grim look in her sightless eyes, Tam suspected he knew, exactly, what she would wish for, if she had the chance. Scowling, he shoved it out of his mind. This was his best chance…the best chance he'd had in hundreds of years, and he'd be damned if he'd blow it.

Chapter Four

Oh, he was charming. She had to admit that. Tam Jones was one of the most pleasant, amusing men she had ever met in her life. And that voice was every bit as sexy as she remembered. He smelled…rich, exotic—of sandalwood and incense. She couldn't define it but as she sat next to him in the restaurant, waiting for the waiter to bring her Braille menu, she inhaled deeply, her head flooding with that sexy scent of his.

The waiter approached and she held out her hand, waiting, as he said in an overloud voice, "Here's the menu, ma'am. Just let us know if you need any help ordering."

With a blank expression, she raised her voice a few notches as she replied, "Thank you." As he started to walk away, she heard Mara snickering and Kat's lips curled up in response. "Maybe I should have my ears checked. Everybody seems to think I'm deaf, too."

Mara laughed. "People don't think, sweetie. You know that."

"Well, yeah. But I always knew that," she said drolly, running her fingers over the menu. She wasn't hungry. Nerves jumped in her belly, doing a hot little cha-cha. Being out in public, being out with a man for the first time in years… She knew there was no way she could eat much.

People were staring at her. She could feel their eyes. Under the table, Zeb lay quietly, his head resting by her feet. She'd heard somebody mutter about the dog when they first came in, then the abrupt silence after the woman's companion said, *She's blind! Be quiet.*

As Tam said her name, she forced her attention back to him, trying to block out her anxiety about being away from her condo. Nothing to worry about. She'd made it here in one piece. She could handle lunch in public.

Nothing to worry about. *Yeah, right.*

Focusing her attention back on Tam, she pasted a polite smile on her face as he asked, "How long have you lived in Gatlinburg?"

She shrugged, a thoughtful frown on her face. "Off and on for more than ten years. I used to spend time in Chicago but I've been here pretty much all the time for the past few years."

"What do you do?"

For a moment, her fingers stilled on the menu. *What do you do?* It had been a very long time since she had heard that. On the rare occasion that she did meet new people, so many of them assumed she didn't do anything. "I'm a counselor. I had a double major in college...decided to use the psych one just this past year."

She had to fight not to shiver at the sound of his voice. Did he look as good as he sounded, as good as he smelled? Swallowing, she tried to block that out of her mind and focus on his voice.

"And you work out of your house?"

She forced a smile. "Telephone counselor. It's a suicide help line." Her lashes dropped. "I had a sister who killed herself when she was fourteen."

* * * * *

As Kat paced her room alone a few hours later, she rubbed her hands up and down her arms.

In her mind's eye, she could see a picture of him. Mara had described him in vivid detail, dark skin—teak colored—startling pale blue eyes, rich dark hair, a few shades darker than mahogany. Exotic, Mara had said.

Exotic, to go with that voice, with its indeterminate accent.

Jones… What a simple name, one that didn't fit the image she had of him.

Tam. It suited the picture she had in her mind of him. It sounded strong, proud, as rich as that low, husky voice.

Something inside her belly tightened as she thought of him, recalled the rich sandalwood scent of his body—sandalwood, musk and male. Her mouth watered as she remembered breathing that scent in, drowning in it.

Mara had told her, "He stares at you like you're a chocolate sundae and he's a recovering chocoholic about to fall off the wagon."

A confirmed chocoholic, Kat knew exactly the look Mara was talking about. Intense, hungry, greedy. Hot little pangs of nerves darted through her before she shoved the idea aside.

She was blind, for crying out loud. And even when she could see, she hadn't been a major prize. After all, look what Brian had done to her. Messed around on her, lied to her, deceived her. If she was anything special, her husband wouldn't have cheated on her.

Kat resisted the urge to go into the now empty studio, resisted the urge to run her hands over the dried ridges of paint on the unfinished canvas. She couldn't keep doing that. It had been her New Year's resolution to try and move past the remnants of her old life and find something else.

The counseling helped. She was making a difference there, and it didn't matter to the people on the phone if she could see or not.

It filled the emptiness of her days, but she needed so much more.

Today had been a start though.

I went outside…

And not just to go to a doctor appointment. She had actually gone out and eaten at a restaurant. One of the mundane things that she used to take for granted. She had felt the icy sting of snowflakes as they hit her face, melting away, and had felt the wind blowing through her hair as they'd walked to the restaurant.

And it had felt good. With a slow smile, she promised she'd go out again. Soon.

It had almost felt normal, after the first hour.

She stopped in front of the mirror that Mara's boyfriend had hung up for her a few days ago. Lee was funny, sharp-witted and he didn't treat her like an invalid. Once upon a time, they had all gone out together—she, Brian, Lee and Mara. Sometimes Jenise had tagged along—sometimes she had brought a date.

They'd all had so much fun. She missed that.

Damn it, she had to get back into life.

"I'm losing myself here," she murmured, reaching out with a seeking hand, touching her fingers to the surface of the mirror, lids drooping as the heat that seemed to radiate from it seeped into her pores.

Something teased her nose—a hot, spicy scent—unlike anything she could remember smelling before. Under her hand, the mirror pulsed. She flinched but she didn't pull it away. Something about this mirror—

Behind her, she heard a soft whine. Zeb had woken from his nap. She whistled to him and heard the clack of his nails on the floor as he padded up to her. Stroking his head, she said in a thick voice, "I'm pitiful, you know that? I talk to you, and to a mirror, more than I do to people."

Chapter Five

Kat squared her shoulders as she stood in front of the door. Damn it. She could *do* this. Mara was waiting downstairs. Zeb stood patiently at her side, waiting for her to make a decision.

You're being a coward.

Blowing out a frustrated breath, she grabbed the handle and stepped outside the door. Panic struck her in the chest like a fist. Zeb's furred warmth was a steady presence at her side, and as she closed the door, she buried her fingers in the short, thick fur just above his harness. "I can do this," she whispered. "I can."

A quiet voice from across the hall said, "I imagine you can do almost anything you want."

Her face flushed as she realized she had an audience. Zeb hadn't warned her—but she imagined the dog had been trying not to rattle her already frazzled nerves. Since Zeb didn't consider Tam a threat, she guessed the canine had concentrated on just helping her through the door.

She forced a tight, shaky smile and said, "I-I guess I was talking to myself, wasn't I?"

His chuckle ran over her skin like a warm hand. "A little. Are you feeling well? You seem a little distressed."

Distressed… What an old-fashioned sounding word. And how accurate. The flush that burned her cheeks deepened and she wished she could just disappear into the floor. *I'm scared to walk outside my house…* The bad thing was, a lot of people could probably understand that.

But she couldn't live with it. This fear ate at her, shamed her, depressed her. Closing her eyes, she took a deep breath and tried to still the internal tremors that had her belly tied up in knots. "I'm going downstairs," she said slowly.

"Where's Mara?" he asked, his voice neutral.

Kat smirked, a self-deprecating laugh escaping her as she brushed her hair out of her face. "Waiting for me...downstairs." Tears burned her eyes and she turned away, lifting her face skyward.

"I have the feeling that's where you wanted her to wait."

She smiled, shaking her head. "You're right. I did ask her to wait there. You know, it's exactly fifteen steps to the elevator. Two steps to get inside. I turn around and the buttons are on my right, in Braille. There is no reason I can't walk to that elevator and go downstairs by myself. Zeb's with me. This is a very safe, secure place to live. So why am I terrified?"

A warm hand cupped the back of her neck and suddenly, her fear faded away, replaced by a heat that warmed her very soul as he bent low and whispered, "I wouldn't even be able to work up the nerve to try."

His hand fell away but her skin still buzzed from his touch. Slowly, she forced herself to breathe again. Feeling his warm gaze on her, she gripped Zeb's harness. Took one step.

Then another. Behind her, she heard the steady fall of his steps as he followed her, and a tremulous smile curved her lips. *Four steps, three...two...* Taking a deep breath, she stopped and swept out her cane, hearing the little thud as it hit the door. Lifting her hand, she reached out. A wide grin spread across her face as she felt the cool metal of the doors.

Turning her head, she flashed him a brilliant smile. "Who knew a walk down a hall could be so exhilarating?" she said, feeling a little sheepish but completely overjoyed.

"Freedom is very exhilarating, I'd imagine," Tam said. His voice sounded just a little bitter and she wondered at it.

"You amaze me. I wouldn't have the courage to even *want* to try, Kat."

* * * * *

Tam heard the knock at the door but he already knew who it was. He was so acutely tuned to Kat—he could place sounds to actions, even behind the door and walls of her condo. The water would run in the morning for about twenty minutes as she showered—the woman loved her showers. Music would turn on at about 9 a.m. and then he would hear a faint electronic hum as she booted up her computer.

She'd be on for about twenty minutes and then the computer would shut down and she'd go to work. The dual ring of the telephone signaled she was working, and it would sound sporadically for seven hours. Then she was done, and he'd hear the sounds of her fixing supper, the hum of the radio, then silence as she settled down for the night.

As he heard her door open that morning, he looked up from the book he was trying to concentrate on, feeling the blood inside his body heat. Rising, he crossed to the door and opened it just as she was getting ready to knock. He watched as her hand fell limply to her side, a startled smile on her face.

"You look lovely as always, Kat," he said, forcing his eyes to remain on her face, away from the smooth expanse of skin bared by the scoop neck of her sweater. It fell beguilingly off one shoulder as she shifted from one foot to the other. Zeb wagged his tail at Tam before leaning against his mistress's leg.

Her cheeks flushed a soft pink and she smiled nervously. "Thank you." The tip of her tongue appeared and Tam had to force himself not to groan. He wanted to taste that mouth. So badly.

That endearingly nervous grin of hers appeared as she stroked her hair back from her face. "I was wondering… Have you had lunch yet?"

Eyes narrowing on her face, he replied, "No. No, I haven't. I'm starving, too." Well, not for food, he added silently. But he suspected if he told her that, she'd be even more terrified than she already was.

"I wanted to go to the Italian place down on the parkway. Don't suppose you'd like to go, would you?"

"I'd love to."

* * * * *

Over the pungent scents of garlic and tomato, he could smell the intoxicating scent of her skin. The music of her laughter died from the air but her pretty, rosebud lips were still curved in amusement.

"Do they always do that?" he asked as the embarrassed waiter quickly retreated.

The smile on her lips faded away, replaced by a pensive look as she shrugged. The mellow ivory of her shoulder caught his eye—his mouth all but watered with the need to bend over and run his tongue over that smooth flesh. As that shoulder shifted in a shrug, he forced his eyes to her face.

In her hands, she held a cup of steaming coffee. The waiter had offered her a *straw*. Tam had dryly stated, "She doesn't need to see to be able to remember where her mouth is." That was what had her giggling. He'd wished he hadn't said anything after the waiter walked away, his cheeks a painful red. Instead of the laughter in her eyes, she looked thoughtful.

"People don't understand anybody who is different from them, Tam. And not understanding makes them do or say stupid things," she finally told him. A grin tugged at her lips and she said, "One lady—somebody I knew years ago—asked if I'd be moving into a...*facility*. Like a nursing home. That made me laugh. Some people let it get to them too much. But it's not prejudice, not really. It's just stupidity."

"People are frequently stupid," he mused. He'd seen a great deal of stupidity in his life. More than Kat could ever imagine. Her wisdom, though, awed him. Very few people could have accepted that kind of change in their lives, dealt with the tragedies and gone on to forge a new one, all with very little bitterness.

"Aren't they?" she said, her tone thoughtful. "I hope they have the good fortune to stay that way. The only way they could understand a lot of their foolishness is to actually go through something that opens their eyes. After all, ignorance can be bliss."

He didn't know what to say to that. But before he could try to fill the silence, she sat back in her chair, one hand in her lap. From the slight motions of her arm, he suspected Zeb had his head in her lap and he was being stroked with slow, gentle strokes of her hand. A twinge of jealousy jolted through him and he scowled. Jealous of a damned dog.

"Zeb's been acting like a puppy," she said quietly. "He loves people, loves going outside. He even sees me near the door and I can almost hear his ears perk up."

"Maybe you should take him out for a walk every day. I'd love to go with you," he said, keeping his voice neutral. Maybe get inside her apartment...see that mirror...he still wasn't any closer to it. How could he convince her to give it to him when he couldn't even seem to approach the subject?

How could he tell her the truth? But could he lie and try to trick her into giving it to him?

Frustration ran through him. If ever a mortal woman would be willing to give up a wish, a chance of a lifetime, it would be her.

He should just get on with it. Risk her thinking he was a lunatic when he tried to explain. Or come up with some plausible story that would convince her to turn it over to him.

There isn't one... He rolled his eyes heavenward as he thought about that. There was no lie he could tell her that she would believe. And the truth...well, she'd be certain he was nuts.

But oddly, as she smiled, her eyes sparkling, he found he really didn't care all that much. After all, if she did give him that mirror, then he was gone. Out of her life.

And *that* idea settled in his gut like a lead weight.

* * * * *

Nearly a month later, Tam stood watching her as she gazed into the mirror, her eyes seeking, sightless. Those dark gray eyes were haunting his sleep. Everything about her haunted him—her eyes, the shining red swing of her hair, the curve of her hip, the scent of her body.

He wanted her—so badly that he ached with it.

She wanted him as well. He could see it in the gentle coloring of her cheeks when they met in the hall for their walks. When she stepped aside to let him into her condo, he could hear the rapid beat of her heart. Nervous lust glittered in the air around her—yet she never did anything.

Those long walks they took several times a week had definitely let him get closer to her. But he hadn't done a damn thing about the mirror. Other than hover inside its unseen depths and stare at her, brooding.

This had turned into a mess.

He should have just shared the mirror's secrets, let her take her wish and get on with what passed for his life.

Now he couldn't stop thinking of *her*.

A muscle ticced in his jaw as he watched her from the surface of the mirror, scowling. Those eyes, those warm gray eyes, saw nothing. That long sleek body, the sadness inside her, everything about her called to him. His body went hard as iron every time he thought of her. Which was all the damned time.

He couldn't get her out of his mind.

Or the sound of her voice. The soft vanilla and lavender scent of her skin.

And the sadness in her face.

The delightful curve of her ass, the long line of her legs…the music of her laugh. Everything.

Damn it, he had come here to get that mirror and here it was nearly a month later and he was no closer. The bad thing was, he had never really tried.

Every night, she would pause in front of the mirror, touch it with her hand, murmuring to herself. Her words haunted him. The first time, she had whispered, *I'm losing myself here.*

Tam wanted to cuddle her close, kiss that sad look from her face, and stroke her slender body until she arched in his hands like a kitten. Hold her close, for always.

And *that* was why he hadn't done anything about the mirror. If by some chance she gave it to him, he'd have no reason to stay. Tam was fast approaching the point where he would give damn near anything to stay with her. Always.

And if she used her wish… The mirror would be passed on, and he'd be out of her life.

For the first time in a very long time, he didn't want to get away from the woman who held his future in her hands. Tam wanted to be closer—desperately wanted to be closer.

He hated himself. He wanted to stay with her. Wanted to see the dawn break on her face as he watched her sleep. Wanted to love that sweet body until she screamed out his name.

But he had the ability to take away some of the pain he saw in her eyes.

He could take away her blindness—take it from her with a simple kiss—if she would just use her wish.

Part of him kept whispering…*tell her…let her use her wish…* He'd never seen a woman more deserving of the happiness his magick could give her. But she knew nothing about it.

And for fear of never seeing her again, he said nothing.

Chapter Six

When Tam's voice drifted through the door, Kat depressed the buzzer, hoping the hot pleasure she felt inside wasn't that noticeable as she told him to give her a minute. Last night had been her turn at the nightshift and she'd just woken up a few hours ago.

Haunted by dark dreams, her sleep had been restless.

A woman who called herself Maxie had called during her shift. Her story had broken Kat's heart—escaping an abusive father, marrying a man she had thought was perfect for her. But then she'd started having nightmares, nightmares that kept her awake, interfered with her life, with everything. Maxie had never told her husband about the abuse she'd suffered at her father's hands—until a few weeks ago. She had confided in him, told him about what had happened to her.

He should have been there for her. But instead, a week later, he'd filed for divorce. He hadn't wanted to be involved with a woman whose father had raped her. Hadn't wanted that kind of sickness in any family he might raise.

Now Maxie was caught in a morass of depression so deep that the only way she saw to escape it was suicide.

Kat hoped she'd gotten through to her.

And she hoped that bastard who had called himself her husband developed a severe problem with impotence. Jackass.

Shoving the case out of her mind, she had tried to focus on a book, on music…on anything. She'd thought about going back to bed, to maybe have some sweet dreams, not awful ones.

Kat would much rather get back to her normal dreams. Those hot, vivid dreams where she could see, where she was wrapped around Tam, and could stare up into his face and see the beauty of it. Stare at him while he sank deep inside of her.

She was glad she hadn't lain down for a nap, though. Between dreaming about him, and being with him, there was no competition.

Damn it, she wanted him. Her instincts murmured that he wanted her but fear kept her from doing anything about it.

Even when she had been whole, she had been hesitant to make a move on a man. But not seeing him... That was harder. Harder to tell if the tension in the air came from lust, or just discomfort. Or maybe the tension was only in her mind, and he felt nothing.

She moved through the condo as swiftly as she could, reaching in the closet, seeking a pair of jeans and a sweater. After she dressed, she splashed her face with cold water and brushed her hair. Palms damp, she moved back to the door and opened it, resting one hand on Zeb's head as Tam came inside.

"You look a little sleepy," Tam murmured as he closed the door behind him.

She arched a brow at him, grinning. "That's always a nice way of telling somebody that they look like crap," she said, running a hand through her hair nervously. With a wry laugh, she added, "I have a hard time telling."

She was learning to joke about it. This was a fact of life. This was her. Something about Tam's simple acceptance of it was shifting her view of herself. How knowing a man only a month could make such a change, she didn't know.

Tam came by every few days and managed, at least once a week, to urge her into going out with him. Lunch, dinner, even breakfast once. And shopping. She had gone *shopping* for the first time in a very long while. He was funny, with a quirky sense of humor much like her own.

And he didn't seem to care that she was blind. Even if they were just friends, that mattered to her.

She'd lost a lot of friends when she'd lost her eyesight. People didn't know how to deal with her, so they just faded away—never calling anymore, never coming over. Cutting her out of their lives.

But Tam didn't make her feel less because she couldn't see.

With him, she actually felt *more*.

"Now I didn't say that," he murmured, drawing her attention from her random thoughts, back to him. "If I thought you looked a mess, I just wouldn't have said anything."

His voice was closer…*he* was closer. Through her clothing, she could feel a radiant heat, and his breath caressed her face even before he reached out to touch her, lifting her chin in his hand. "I said you looked sleepy…like a tired little kitten. I've always had a weakness for kittens."

Fire jumped into her belly at that odd note in his voice—deep, intense, a throbbing edge of hunger. As his hand cupped her chin, Kat traced her lips with her tongue, skin prickling at the sudden onslaught of tension in the air.

"I want to kiss you," he whispered. "I've wanted to for a while and I can't keep ignoring it."

Any answer Kat might have formed faded away as she felt his warm, calloused hands frame her face, and then the hot silk of his tongue stroking against the seam of her lips. Her mouth opened and she shivered as he pushed his tongue inside her mouth, his hands sliding down, one cupping her neck, one going down to grip her hip and pull her pelvis snug against his.

It felt like a jolt of lightning had exploded inside her gut as the hard ridge of his cock throbbed against her belly. Whimpering low in her throat, she rose onto her toes, wrapping her arms around him, feeling her breasts press flat against his chest.

He growled. That hot, primitive sound sent shivers down her spine. Her nipples, naked under the thick material of her chenille sweater, tightened into painful little nubs, and hot cream gathered in her pussy.

Fire sang in her blood as his hands raced over her greedily. His mouth left hers, kissing a hot path from her mouth down her chin, up the line of her jaw to press a stinging, biting kiss against her nape.

Kat moaned, a low, needy sound as his hands slid under the hem of her sweater, pressing against the smooth flesh of her sides. Oh, damn…how was this happening?

His hands stroked up the naked skin of her back and she arched into his touch, just like the kitten he had whispered about. Nipples ached, tightened, stabbing into his chest through her sweater. Her skin drew tight, itchy, crying out for more of his touch. Hot…burning hot…

But then she was cold and shivering. Tam had moved away, his breathing harsh and ragged. "Damn it, Kat. I'm sorry. I shouldn't have done that," he murmured.

Licking her lips, she tried to focus on his voice, not the words…it was amazing the things a blind person could *see*. Senses were refined, heightened. She could smell the hot, male scent of his body, stronger now than it had ever been. And the rough tremor in his voice. His voice was shaking. She heard his harsh, rapid breath as he sucked in air in a manner similar to hers. All clues that pointed to one simple fact.

He wants me, she realized, dazed.

"Why are you sorry?" she asked, sinking her teeth into her lip as she felt the heat of his gaze stroke over her. His eyes seemed to have a touch all their own, because she could feel it when he was looking at her, even if she couldn't see. Forcing a small smile, she added, "I kind of liked it."

She was so damned adorable, so sexy… Tam gritted his teeth as he stared at her, trying to figure out a way to explain to her that wanting her was wrong. Sharp, white teeth bit down on her lip as she stared in his direction, her face flushed, eyes dark, her entire body almost vibrating with hunger. She was the picture of female arousal and he wanted nothing more than to slake this building hunger for her.

But it wasn't right.

He'd come to this town under false pretenses, because he wanted something she had.

And the mirror was mattering less and less… Staring at her in the dim light of the condo, the hot, sweet taste of her mouth still in his head, he started to wonder. She wanted him…had feelings for him, he could see it in her eyes.

Could he stay?

She didn't know what the mirror was. Wasn't likely to ever use her wish…if she didn't use it, then the mirror was hers. Always hers, until she used that wish. Even passing it on to somebody else wouldn't change that. The only way Tam would be forced to answer to another would be if she used the wish, and gave the mirror away. Or she could give it to Tam before she used the wish.

He *wanted* to stay. For the first time in his very long life, he thought of seeing her face again and again, watching as lines of laughter appeared around her sad eyes, deepening, the sands of time starting to change that fresh, lovely beauty into something even more lovely, a classical beauty that not even time could change.

Yes. He wanted to stay.

But there was one thing he wanted more. To see her happy.

Moving back to her, he watched her face, watched as she lifted her eyes, seeming to track his movements even though she couldn't see him. He moved closer, until his toes nudged hers and he caught his breath as she leaned up against him, her belly cradling the steel-hard length of his dick. Damn it, he ached. His cock throbbed within the unrelenting fit of the denim that cupped him. The ripe scent of her body filled his head. Kat's soft curves pressed against him, a torturous sensation that made him want to howl and drag her down to the floor, tearing away her clothes, fucking her until she screamed, burning his touch onto her body so that she would wish for nothing more than him, ever.

With a tortured groan, he bent down, taking her mouth with his, shuddering as she reached out with her tongue and traced the outline of his lips, then pushed inside his mouth.

He bit down lightly—passionate heat seemed to burst from her body in a corona of magickal colors. Her nipples burned into his chest through the layers of clothes and he slid one hand under her shirt, cupping a full, round breast, capturing the nipple between thumb and forefinger, milking slowly.

Moving his lips to her ear, he whispered, "Kat, you know this is driving me crazy."

She laughed softly as she lowered herself to stand flat on her feet. He stared down into her pretty face, the yearning in her empty eyes tugging at his heart.

"Can I ask you something?" she whispered softly.

He chuckled. "Yes—although I can't guarantee an answer that makes sense."

His heart squeezed in his chest as she ran her hands up his chest, hesitating on his shoulders, as she whispered, "I want to see you."

For a moment, his heart stopped. *She knew…this was her wish.* A bizarre sense of betrayal ripped through him as he wondered, *Has she known all this time, and just waited, trying to make me care about her?*

But then her fingers touched his chin, gently, before withdrawing. "Mara told me what you look like but it's not the same. Can I…"

Her fingers whispered over his cheek again and he realized what she was asking. The fist of pain that had wrapped around his heart loosened, while a deeper ache settled in.

He was falling in love with her.

Taking her hand, he guided her fingers to his face. "My hair is brown," he murmured as her fingers combed through it. "Dark reddish-brown, I guess."

A soft smile curved her lips. "It's soft—feels warm." Her fingertips, soft and gentle, moved down to his face, stroking over his high forehead and the arch of his brows. His lids dropped as she feathered a gentle touch over his eyes.

"Blue," he told her.

Opening his eyes, he watched, falling into the spell of her hands and the look of wonder on her face. Her fingers stroked over his cheekbones, then she ran one slow finger down the straight line of his nose. When her finger touched his mouth, he caught it between his teeth, biting lightly. "You're driving me crazy," he said conversationally as she continued her tactile exploration.

Kat laughed, a deep, husky chuckle that echoed in his head as she cupped his face in her hands, smiling in bliss. "You look almost exactly as I thought you would," she whispered.

With a pained laugh, he said, "I've never enjoyed being looked at so much."

Her eyes lit up as she grinned at him. "I've been dying to see what you looked like," she told him.

"You should have asked. There's no way I'd turn down having your hands on me, even if it is just my face."

His cock tightened painfully as she boldly said, "I'd love to look at more." A pink flush spread up from her neck, coloring her cheeks. Her teeth sank into her lip and he groaned, lowering his head and kissing her mouth until her teeth loosened their hold and then he caught the plump flesh in his teeth and bit down. "Look all you want."

This was moving too fast, he suspected. Instinct told him she didn't normally behave this way. Neither did he.

Sex was a chore, at best. A tool, something he could use to try and get what he wanted. Since he had failed to get the mirror every time, sex was becoming more and more tedious.

Hell, it had been years since he had lain with a woman. And longer than that—far longer—since he had truly wanted anyone.

But he'd never wanted a woman the way he wanted her.

Right now, Tam wanted nothing more than to strip her naked, lay her down on the floor, spread her open and feast on the banquet of her body. As her hands moved down to his shoulders, Tam's head fell back. Swallowing, he tried to rein in the demanding needs of his body, standing still as Kat slowly reached and stroked her hands along his shirt, smiling as she found the buttons.

With each button she opened, she paused, stroking every uncovered piece of flesh as a look of pure delight moved across her face. "Mara said you're dark. Like teak."

Tam glanced down, studying the deep tones of his skin against the paleness of her hands. *Djinn* were a dark race, their roots in the ancient lands of Babylonia. They had rich, dark skin tones, often matched with vibrant colored eyes. Shrugging, he said, "It's just skin. I never thought about it much."

With a warm laugh, Kat replied, "Colors used to be my life. I loved colors. Bright ones, dark ones, vivid ones…simple ones. I like having a color in mind while I touch you. Damn, this body of yours is amazing."

Tam could have groveled at her feet as she ran her hands down his chest, completely bared now. Her nails—pale, neat ovals—scraped over his nipples. He hissed, clenching his hands into fists as he fought for control. "Kat, sweet, I don't know if I can keep this up. I want you so bad I hurt," he rasped, gritting his teeth. "Ever since I first saw you, I've wanted you. And if you plan on stopping, you need to do it now. If you keep this up, and then stop…I think I might die."

A slow smile lifted the corner of her lips. She stepped back and Tam felt something wither inside him. But then her hands went to the bottom of her sweater, his breath froze in his throat. He had to force himself to exhale and it felt as though the air was made from jagged, broken pieces of glass, moving through his tight, burning throat as vicious hunger tore through him.

"Damn it, Kat, you're gorgeous," he whispered, reaching out a hand, running one finger down the center of her torso, from the hollow of her throat, down to her navel, up to circle one nipple, then the other.

His eyes narrowed as he saw faint scars on her breasts and one angry, twisted one on her side. It started just at the curve of her right breast and ran down that side, disappearing under the low-slung waistband of her jeans. "What happened to you?" he asked, his voice gritty.

Kat's cheeks flushed painfully red. She'd forgotten about her scars. She never saw them, only touched them casually as she showered. The most painful reminder of the accident was her lost vision.

Her arms lifted as she tried to hide herself, embarrassed now. "I was in a wreck—a few years ago. That's what blinded me. I hardly ever think about the scars," she said, her voice thick.

His hands caught her wrists and forced them down to her sides, leaving her bare before him. "You're gorgeous," he repeated. And his voice sounded guttural, primitive. A hungry moan echoed in the air and she shivered as she felt his breath on her breasts. A sob ripped out of her as his mouth—hot, wet silk—closed over her nipple. "These scars can't change that, can't hide that…but it makes me furious to think that something has hurt you."

His mouth cruised down the outer curve of her breast to press against the scar on her side, stroking it with his lips, kissing away pain that had passed years ago. "I just want to undo all of it," he whispered. Her skin pebbled under the soft caress of his breath as he moved to kiss another scar, smaller, just under her left breast. Glass from the windshield had caused those…the jagged one on her right side was caused by debris that had come through the windows after they had shattered from the impact. A tree branch, they had said. It hadn't hurt her though, not for a long time.

Now it felt like liquid fire as he moved back and kissed the flesh. She dipped her fingers into his hair, stroking the soft, thick locks as her head fell back and she sucked air into her burning lungs.

The touch of his mouth sent light and color streaking through her body to explode inside her mind—brilliant blues and reds and purples. Color…she remembered color. It was a torment, the memory of color in the darkness of her life. But now, the hot rainbow of colors that lit her mind were beautiful, an echo of the way his hands felt on her body. His hands, that clever mouth…

Her hands reached out and found his shoulders at her waist. He'd knelt down in front of her, and as she touched him, he reached out and pulled her body tightly against him. His tongue curled around one nipple and she shivered. His hands held her flat against him and she felt the hard wall of his chest pressing her belly.

Cool air touched her hips as he unbuttoned her jeans and pushed them down, baring her body completely.

"Tam," she whimpered. Need was a hungry ache in her belly, riding her, as she shifted and moved against him.

Her body shuddered as he cupped her in his hand, pushing one finger inside her with no preliminaries, pumping it in and out of the slippery channel of her pussy. She climaxed—hard and sudden—so many nights of loneliness disappearing with one fiery burst as she came in his hand.

"That's sweet," he whispered as he caught her against him.

The world seemed to spin around her as he rose, holding her effortlessly in his arms. She rested her head against him as he carried her down the hall and she basked in the warmth of the moment, letting him take her where he wished, not worrying about how many steps to take to the bedroom, down the hall…not worrying about anything lying in her path that could trip her.

The comforter felt cool against her back as he lay her down, his weight pressing against her legs as he sprawled between them, pushing them wide. "You're so wet," he groaned and she shrieked as he lowered his head, pressing his mouth against her with a hungry moan that vibrated against her flesh.

Brilliant hot bursts of color echoed behind her eyes as he used his tongue and his teeth to tease her flesh. Kat fisted the thick material of the jacquard comforter in her hands as she arched up against his mouth, shrieking out his name as he started to fuck his tongue in and out of her pussy.

Her heart slammed against her ribs, her skin grew tight as her body fought to contain the orgasm that was building inside her. It felt too big, too intense, all the sensations rioting inside her.

He shifted, moving up just a bit and lightly closing his teeth around her clit, lashing his tongue across it while just below, he teased the tight muscles of her pussy, circling the opening with a feather light touch of his fingers, before sliding one finger deep inside, withdrawing, circling the entrance again, then pushing deep.

Over and over, then he added a second finger just as he sucked her clit into his mouth. She erupted with a scream as the climax tore through her body, her skin vibrating, electrical shocks shooting through her veins. A volcano seemed to have formed in her womb, and now lava was spilling from her pussy, her body shuddering with the force of the aftershocks.

She was still quivering as he crawled up her body, slanting his mouth across hers so that she could taste her cream on it as he drove his tongue inside to tangle hungrily with hers.

Kat's body was alight with sensation—she hadn't ever felt anything like this in her life. The orgasm that should have drained her had electrified her, heightening her senses until even a whisper of his breath on her flesh was an agonizing pleasure.

His hands streaked over her body, cupping her breasts, palming her ass. They seemed to be everywhere at once. His knee pushed her thighs apart and Kat sobbed as she felt the thick width of his cock nestled at the entrance to her pussy. "Damn it, I want you so much," he murmured as he lifted his head. She felt the bed dip by her head, the press of his hands on the mattress as he braced his weight above her.

A long wail left her lips as he pushed through the tight tissues slowly, stroking deep inside her. Tears burned her eyes as he pushed deep, forcing her body to accommodate a man's cock after years of emptiness. The pain couldn't drown out the pleasure though, and she cried out with it, digging her nails into the muscles of his arms and tilting her hips up, trying to take more of him.

"Sweet heaven…" Tam whispered out above her. She shivered in response to the amazement she heard in his voice. *Does he feel it too?* she wondered helplessly. She wanted, so badly, to see him. "Baby, you feel amazing."

His voice sent goose bumps tingling down her spine and she reached up, seeking out the hard ridges of his torso as she murmured, "So do you." Arching her back, she lifted her hips against him and tried to pull him deeper inside.

Tam caught her hands, easing them down by her head, holding them in place, his weight crushing into her. She gasped as the movement took him deeper inside the aching depths of her pussy. "This has to last," Tam murmured against her lips. "Something this perfect can't be rushed. Hmmm…your pussy is so hot, so snug… I love it."

She cried at his words, her fingers clenching convulsively around his. "Tam, please!"

"It is," he insisted. "Like silk. So soft, so snug… You're tight, you're wet. Sweeter than anything I've ever felt in my life."

He started to withdraw and she whimpered, arching up against him, following the retreat of his hips with hers, eager to keep him inside her.

Tam laughed, a rough, husky sound, as he closed his hands around the sleek curve of her hips, holding her still as he pulled out, surging back into her with one long, slow stroke. Deep inside her, she felt his cock throb, felt the ridged head of him pressing against her womb. Something hot and hungry coiled in her belly as he pulled out and drove back in, just as slowly, just as teasingly as before.

Beneath him, Kat groaned, sinking her teeth into her lip, her head moving back and forth on her pillow, long strands of red hair flying around her head. The retreat and thrust of his hips set her body aflame, clamoring for more.

His mouth came back down on hers and she groaned greedily, hungry for more of that dark, exotic taste. She caught his tongue between her teeth and bit delicately, smiling against his lips as he growled and started shafting her with hard, short thrusts of his cock. "Witch," he whispered huskily.

"Hmmmm." She flexed the muscles in her pussy, shuddering as he drove into her again, harder, until she started to slide across the bed, the sheet bunching under her. His hands slipped under her, bracing her shoulders as he fucked her.

She could feel it, the bright, dazzling orgasm, just out of reach…his body pressed against her clit with every stroke. Just a little harder—that's all she needed, just a little more, a little harder. Kat tightened the muscles of her vagina around him once more and he bellowed out her name, stiffening above her and starting to drive into her roughly.

Tam's control shattered as she squeezed him once more with all the hot, hungry little muscles inside her pussy. Staring down at her, he pumped in and out with all the strength he had in his back and hips, muscles bunching, gleaming in the backwash of the sparks flying from his body.

Magick, uncontrolled and desperate, pulsed from him like a rain shower, in brilliant sparks of light and color that danced and played over her skin. So damned lovely, he thought helplessly as she screamed out his name, throwing her head back. She convulsed around him, her entire body tensing, her pussy so tight he had to work his dick inside her with every harsh thrust.

His climax slammed into him, wrapping a fist around his gut as he came inside her, hot washes of seed splashing deep inside the welcome depths of her sex.

She was still climaxing around his cock, those little milking sensations drawing his own climax out, on and on, until she had drained him dry. He sank into her, the soft contours of her body cushioning his. With a groan, he flipped onto his back, pulling her with him so that she draped over him.

Cupping her head in his hand, he held her pressed against his chest as he labored to catch his breath.

Her body trembled, racked with the aftershocks of her climax. Closing his eyes, he made a wish. *I want to keep her…*

But the *Djinn* didn't get their wishes granted. They could only grant them.

* * * * *

Hours later, he lay propped on his elbow, running a slow, teasing finger down her torso. Tam couldn't get over how amazing she felt next to him, how perfectly she fit him. The scars on her torso and side tore at him, wrapping a fist around his throat and robbing him of air.

Hoarsely, he asked, "How did these happen?"

As the glow in her eyes dimmed, Tam wished he could take it back, but before he could say anything, she murmured huskily, "I married the guy I fell in love with in college. I thought we had the perfect life, you know that? We rarely fought, he pampered me... I was a painter, he was a very successful lawyer. We seemed to have everything going for us. My best friend, Jenise, was my agent. I was getting pretty popular."

She rolled onto her side, away from him and he curled up behind her, rubbing his hand in small circles on her hip as tension mounted in her body. "We were all going to New York. I had a show there. Brian had to go into the office for a while but said he'd swing by and get Jenise, and then they'd pick me up on the way to the airport."

A deep, shuddering sigh left her and for a long moment, she was silent. "Mara called me. Just a little before they were supposed to be here. She and I talked every now and then, went out to lunch and stuff. It wasn't unusual for her to call me but I hadn't ever talked to her when she was that upset before. She was crying."

Kat took a deep breath, shifting around, anxiety and pain mixing in her belly as she remembered the phone call. "Mara saw them at the Regents Hotel. They came out of a room just as she rounded the corner, and she pulled back, and watched as they kissed each other. They were having an affair. My best friend and my husband."

He heard the dry click in her throat as she swallowed. "I have to wonder... What would have happened if I hadn't said anything? If I had waited? We were driving down the parkway on our way to the airport in Knoxville and I said, calm as you please, "So, sweetheart…how long have you been fucking my best friend?"

A harsh sob slipped past her lips. "He looked at me—so shocked. But I saw the guilt in his eyes, in Jenise's. He didn't see the curve ahead and he was driving too fast," she said, her voice oddly calm. "Brian lost control of the car—hit a patch of ice and skidded off the road. We crashed into a tree at over sixty miles an hour.

* * * * *

Tam opened his door, resisting the urge to slam it behind him. Now, alone, he paced the apartment, a growl rumbling in his throat. Anger and frustration ate at him, the emotions escaping his body in violent little explosions of light—purple, red, deep blue—the little sparks streaking from his body with every step he took.

Damn it.

This fucking close to the mirror and it hadn't ever felt farther away.

His heart broke as he recalled the tears on her face as she told him how she'd gotten scarred, how she had lost her eyesight. Bleeding hell, he knew who she was. Not that he was going to tell her that, at least not yet, but he knew who Katlin Dixon was. One of the most talented artists he had seen since the Renaissance, and now she lived in darkness.

How could he take away her chance to regain her life?

That woman *needed* him. Needed the *Djinn* magick that would grant her one wish.

Throwing his arms up, he let the *Djinn* magick take him from the mortal world to the "land between", where the *Djinn* dwelled when not in the mortal world. This was where they longed to be, where they came when they were granted freedom. This was where they came for answers, for rest.

He alit in the middle of a sandswept vista, throwing his head back and staring at the pale gleam of the amethyst sky overhead. "How could you do this?" he demanded. "How could you bring her into my life when you knew I'd have to lose her?"

The man who slowly formed in front of him stared at Tam out of old, wise eyes. The eyes were set in an ageless face, one Tam had always thought of as kind. His chest burning, he strode up to the winged Guardian and glared at him, his hands clenched into tight fists. "You *knew* this would happen," he growled at Michael.

"You *knew* I'd fall in love with her. And loving her, I can't *not* give her what she desires most," Tam snarled, spinning away and pacing, the soft, fine sand kicking up behind him as he moved back and forth.

The sun glittered on the Guardian's wings and Michael sighed, his blue eyes narrowing as he studied the *Djinn* before him. "I did not know. What is decided by Him isn't knowledge that I am granted," he said softly, shaking his head. The thick black hair floated around his strong face in the cool wind that rose. "But how can you be certain that you will lose her? Are you suddenly all seeing, Tamric?"

Sucking air into his constricted lungs, Tam tried to still the helpless fury inside him. "Damn it, the woman is *blind*. She lost everything! I can give just a little back to her. But when I do it, she is lost to me. The mirror will go to another. And I will follow."

Michael smiled, a sad smile as he murmured, "Often in life we are required to make sacrifices."

Tam bit back the furious words he wanted to say. Not nice to chastise, or strangle, all-powerful beings. "Sacrifice," he whispered, turning away and staring at the deepening hues of the eastern sky. Deep purple, and shades of violet and pink streaked the sky of his home world and he felt his throat tighten. "Yes. Often sacrifice is required."

He flicked the guardian a narrow look and then just shook his head as he let the *Djinn* magick take him.

Chapter Seven

Kat snuggled against Tam's chest, stroking her hand down the hard muscles of his belly. Satisfaction warmed her bones and had her wanting to curl against him and purr.

"I'll have to leave soon."

She felt his words strike her in the heart, a cold splash of water. *Leave*… Swallowing, she whispered, "Going back home?"

His words sounded odd as he said, "Yes. Time for me to go back to work."

Kat felt him move, then she was being rolled under him. She could feel his eyes on her face as he lowered his mouth and whispered, "This has been one of the most amazing weeks of my life. I… I wish I could stay."

Tears burned in her eyes but she blinked them away, forcing a shaky smile as she replied, "Me, too." She reached out and felt his hand catch hers, guiding it to his lips. After he kissed her palm, she cupped his face and murmured, "I'm going to miss you."

His mouth pressed against hers, and his kiss tasted bittersweet, like the ache in her heart.

You didn't really expect it to last forever, did you? a soft voice whispered inside her head.

No. But she had found herself wishing it would.

"Damn it, Kat," he groaned against her lips and she gasped as he pushed his knee between her thighs, mounting her and driving the thick length of his cock deep inside her with no preliminaries. His tongue pushed deep inside her mouth, his hands cupping the soft curves of her ass and lifting her for his thrusts as he took her quickly, savagely.

She shuddered, crying out under the hungry touch of his mouth as he scraped his teeth across her neck, kissing his way down to her breasts. His tongue circled around the nipple then his teeth caught it, tugging on it.

Kat buried her hands in his hair, shifting so she could wrap her legs around his hips, her heels digging into his spine as she pumped up to meet his thrusts, taking him as deep as she could.

Heat spread through her body and she would have screamed with the pleasure of it, if he hadn't taken her mouth again in just that moment. The rough caress of his tongue in her mouth robbed her of breath and hot pinwheels of color burst behind her eyes as the climax loomed closer.

"No," he grunted, pulling his mouth away and pulling out of her, flipping her over until she was on her belly. "Not so fast. This must last..."

His words echoed in her mind, and she felt his cock against her ass as he pulled her until she rose to her hands and knees. Tossing her head back, she panted for air as he pressed his cock against her, the plum-shaped head spearing deep inside her pussy. Her muscles clutched greedily at him, and she pushed back, trying to take his sex completely inside her.

But his hands held her hips, kept her from sliding completely back. With slow, measured strokes, he fucked her, his hands spread wide on her hips, his fingers curling into her flesh.

"You're so bloody perfect," he whispered, and she shivered, feeling the caress of his eyes on her body. "Making love to you is the most amazing thing in my life. I can't believe I'm walking away from this."

"Then don't," she pleaded, tears burning her eyes as pain tore through her heart. She was in love with him... How had it happened so fast? Why did it feel as though she had spent her whole life waiting for him?

He surged harder inside her and she cried out, feeling the fat head of his cock butt against her womb. Hot streaks of pleasure lanced through her and she keened, her pussy tightening around his dick as he pulled out.

Over and over, harder, he stroked into her, until sweat broke out on her body and the hunger was a vicious living thing inside her, like an animal was striving to take over. "Damn it, Tam! Please!" she sobbed out, her fingers clenching in the sheets as she tried to push back against him.

He growled out something as he bent over her, his voice so low and rough, she could hardly understand him. *"Sacrifice..."* and then he bellowed, his weight crushing her into the bed as he rode her down, his hips slapping against her ass as he slammed into her.

Reaching behind her, she fisted her hand in the thick silken hair at his nape, holding him tight against her as he crushed her into the bed. He throbbed inside her and she gasped when his cock seemed to swell and grow even larger. She convulsed around him, her pussy clamping down on him as she climaxed, feeling a hot wave pour from deep within her womb as she came. She moaned, the shudders racking through her until her entire body was arching against his.

He came, pumping inside rapidly, his teeth sinking into the smooth curve of her shoulder. She could feel the hot wet jets of his come as he climaxed inside her. Her heart pounded in her ears, the blood roaring in her head, as he wrapped his arms around her. Propping his weight on his elbows, he covered her and hugged her tightly against him.

Sleep loomed near, and just before she fell into its arms, she thought she heard him whisper, "I love you, Kat."

* * * * *

Moments after his foolish admission, he heard her sigh in her sleep, her fingers unlocking their grip in his hair, caressing down his cheek. His heart clenched as she murmured, "Love you, Tam."

He eased out of her, cuddling up against her, reaching out to touch her mind as she slept. He'd come over late in the evening. It had been nearly a week since they'd made love that first time. And his time was up. If he didn't walk away now, he'd never be able to. Brushing her hair away from her face, he kissed her cheek before settling down to sleep at her side for the last time.

In the morning, he was giving Kat her wish.

* * * * *

She awoke to the delicious scents of breakfast and she stretched, arching her back, arms reaching high overhead. All over, her body ached, in the sweetest of ways, and she smiled sadly as she remembered last night.

He was leaving today. In her gut, she knew. *I won't make this hard on him,* she told herself. *I won't make a scene.* Heaven knew Tam had brought a little bit of light into her dark world. She wasn't going to repay him with tears and pleas that he stay with her.

Hell, why would he want to? Even though she no longer felt so broken, she was far from perfect, far from what a man would dream about for his mate in life. With a bitter laugh, she reminded herself, not even her husband had wanted her as his one and only. And that had been before her many problems.

She rose, walking to the closet and feeling for the robe that hung on the door. The warmed silk was a gift from Tam—peacock blue, he had told her as he slid it on her the first time. *Your hair glows against it like it's on fire,* he had whispered. Sighing, she tied it around her waist. At her knee, Zeb woofed softly and she reached down, stroking his head. "I'm okay, boy," she whispered. His cold nose nudged her knee and she laughed. "Okay. I *will* be. Is that better?"

She folded her hand around his harness and walked out of the room with him at her side. "Let's go see what he's making us to eat," she said. "I'll swipe some of that bacon for you."

And she did, feeling along the plate by the stove and filching a piece for herself and him as she listened to Tam washing out dishes at the sink. He said dryly, "I saw that."

Arching her brows, she turned an innocent face to him and said brightly, "Saw what? I didn't see anything."

He laughed, the deep, husky sound bringing a smile to her face. She loved hearing him laugh. She loved him.

All the air left her lungs in a rush and she spun away from him, walking over to the counter, keeping her face averted. *I love him…*

Had she been dreaming when he pressed his face against her hair and whispered, "Kat, I love you"? She licked her dry lips, curling her fingers into the unyielding wood of the counter. Did he love her? If he did…maybe…maybe he would stay. Or ask her to come with him…or…

Clenching her jaw, she told herself to stop it. A guy didn't ask a woman such things after just one single week. Swallowing, she blinked the tears out of her eyes.

"You okay?"

His voice sounded close, too close. He moved so silently. Forcing a bright smile, she turned around and lied, "I'm fine."

His finger brushed her cheek. "You don't look fine," he whispered softly.

Kat gave up trying to smile, lifting one shoulder helplessly as she said, "I think I miss you already."

His arms came up around her and he pulled her against him. Burying her face against his chest, she breathed in the rich male scent of his body, reveling in the simplicity of his touch, the beauty of it. He did care. Maybe he even loved her. And if he did, maybe sometime, he'd come back.

His lips brushed her temple and he whispered, "I feel the same way. Kat, how did you get inside me this way? So fast. I can't even go an hour without thinking about you..." His fingers dipped into her hair and she lifted her mouth to his, holding him tightly as he kissed her gently. Sweetly.

"I've got a present for you," he whispered against her lips before pulling away.

"A present?" she asked, forcing a smile. "What for?"

He laughed and said, "It's Valentine's Day, isn't it?"

A real smile curved her lips as she murmured, "Valentine's Day? I forgot."

His hands stroked down her arms and he caught her fingers, drawing her along behind him. She felt him push a box into her hands and she stroked her fingertips over the cool, slick texture of the wrapping paper. Finding the edge of the paper, she slid her finger under the flap and tugged, pulling the wrap off and setting it aside.

Tissue paper rustled as she lifted the lid off the box. Reaching in, she felt out the silky material inside, lifting it up, stroking her hands over it, a slow smile curving her lips.

"It matches the robe," Tam said gruffly.

"Blue," she murmured, lifting it up and holding it by the narrow straps to her chest, smoothing one hand down its length, feeling his eyes on her.

His hands came up, stroked her sides, then she felt him loosen the tie of her robe and the silken fabric parted. His hand closed over hers and he held the nightgown up. The hot touch of his eyes was as tangible as if he had reached out and stroked his hands across her flesh.

"Happy Valentine's Day," he whispered just before his mouth took hers.

Tears stung her eyes but she didn't let them fall as he crushed her body to his, the heat of his chest burning her through the nightgown that separated their bodies. Against her belly, she felt the heat of his cock, throbbing within the confines of his clothes.

Cool tile pressed into her back as he took her to the floor, the silk of the nightgown still trapped between their bodies.

"One more time," he crooned against her mouth. "One more time…"

A farewell… She felt it in her heart as he moved down her body, still holding the silk against her flesh. His mouth closed over the tip of one nipple, his tongue caressing her through the silk, the sharp edge of his teeth scoring her flesh lightly before he moved on down.

The air stung her nipple, cold against the wet silk that clung to it. His mouth burned through the cloth while he trailed one hand up her thigh, pushing the silk aside as he dragged his fingers up her leg. His fingers dipped inside the hot well of her body, pumping in and out with slow deliberate strokes. She shrieked as his mouth closed over the aching throb of her clit, sucking it deeply into his mouth.

Orgasm hovered just out of reach and she sobbed as he sucked on her clit, catching it between his teeth and tugging lightly. Even as she screamed out his name, he pulled away, wedged his thighs into the cradle of her hips, and stroked his cock back and forth between her slick folds before he changed the angle of his hips and pushed inside.

A harsh groan escaped him and she felt his chest rumble against her breasts as his mouth came down and covered hers, his tongue pushing inside and mimicking the rhythm of his hips as he fucked her.

Hard, hot hands cupped her hips as he lifted her against him, deepening the angle of his strokes, pumping into her faster. Almost frantic, he muttered her name against her lips, one hand sweeping up her side and burying in her hair, fisting there as he arched her neck up.

The harsh rasp of his cock over her swollen, wet tissues, the biting press of his mouth on hers, his chest rubbing against hers through the silk of the nightgown, the contrast of his hard, rough hands, the cool, slick silk—all of it stole the air from her lungs and she fought to breathe, tearing her mouth away from his and sucking deep breaths.

Kat shuddered, the muscles in her pussy tightening around Tam's cock and she screamed as he seemed to swell inside her, a smoldering hot length of steel that caressed and pulsed deep in her sex.

His body shuddered, his hips bucking against hers and he muttered, "Damn it, you make me lose all control—I can't wait."

Hot, wet jets of seed spurted inside her and she moaned as he stroked over the bundled bed of nerves in her pussy. With a rush, she exploded, coming in one harsh, racking shudder after another, her body arching under his, head thrown back.

Whimpering, she drifted back to earth and found his hands stroking soothingly over her back as he rolled over and brought her with him, cuddling her against his chest.

"Happy Valentine's Day," he murmured once more.

A slow smile curved her lips and she said quietly, "I didn't get you anything."

His mouth brushed hers and she arched her neck, smiling as he whispered, "Yes, you have…you gave me more than you could possibly know." His tongue slid inside her mouth, moving over hers in a slow, tender stroke, and then he pulled away, hugging her against him.

She didn't try to force a smile as she pushed herself up, her hands catching the nightgown and cuddling it to her. Ducking her head, she stood, pulling away from him with her face turned so he wouldn't see the tears that filled her eyes.

Tying her robe, she carefully folded the nightgown and sought the box, laying it gently inside. Behind her, she heard him stand, then the rustle of his clothes before his hands closed around her hips, bringing her back against him. He wrapped his arms around her and rested his chin on the crown of her head.

"Hungry?" he murmured.

Forcing a smile, she said, "Hmm…I could eat, I think."

Even though she wasn't hungry, she made herself eat some of the bacon and half of the waffle he'd cooked. "I haven't had waffles in ages," she murmured, her hand closing around the cold glass of juice. Sipping, she let it slide down her dry, tight throat, then she set it down, pushing back from the table just a little. "That was delicious."

"Hmmm. That's why you ate so much," he said drolly.

With a halfhearted shrug, she smiled. "I'm not that hungry. But it was delicious."

"Come here."

Rising, she pushed back and walked around the table, resting her hand on the edge until her fingers touched his hand. Letting him guide her into his lap, she cuddled against him, stroking a small circle on his chest with her finger.

He was already dressed. She felt the slick texture of silk under her fingers. He'd worn cotton yesterday. She felt his chest expand, knew he was getting ready to speak, to tell her good-bye.

But instead, the words that came out were, "Do you ever make wishes, Kat? Real ones." His lips brushed her brow as he spoke, and she shivered slightly, feeling her nipples tighten, her body going soft and pliant as hunger moved through her.

With a slight smile, she said, "We all make wishes from time to time."

He laughed, and the sound was tired, strained. "I know…believe me, I know." His fingers combed through her hair and she sighed in pleasure as his fingers kneaded her scalp, moving down to her neck, rubbing at the tense muscles there before he started just stroking her hair. "What kind of wishes have you made?"

Wrinkling her nose, she said, "Is this a test?"

"No…not a test. I'm just curious."

Kat flattened her hand against his chest, feeling the slow, steady beat of his heart. Thoughtfully, she murmured, "What kind of wishes…"

Tam couldn't look at her as she spoke. Closing his eyes, he listened as she said softly, "I've wished I could see again. Sometimes I would wish that Mara hadn't seen Brian and Jenise together. And sometimes I've wished I hadn't answered the phone."

He swallowed, the constriction in his chest making it hard for him to breath. Wrapping his arms tightly around her, he asked gruffly, "If you could have anything you wanted, what would you wish for?"

"Anything at all?"

He braced himself, gathering the magick inside him. As soon as he granted her wish, he was gone. He'd disappear, right then and there, and he'd never see her again. Tam knew he couldn't take it, seeing her, knowing that when the urge to give the mirror away came, he'd be gone, out of her life forever.

"I wish…"

Lowering his head, unable to keep from looking at her lovely face one more time, he listened, body stiff and tense as she murmured, "If I could have anything at all… I'd wish that you could stay with me forever."

His jaw dropped. Swallowing the knot in his throat, he forced a shaking breath into his lungs. "Are you sure?" Trying to lighten his tone, he added, "That's a rather simple wish. Isn't there anything else you want more?"

Touching his fingers to her brows, he watched as her lids drooped, then he ran the pad of his thumbs lightly over her closed eyes. "Are you sure that's what you would wish for?"

Be sure… Shock swelled within him, shock and awe, humbled pleasure. But she had to be sure. She had only this one wish, and he hadn't even told her the wish would be granted.

But he knew she was falling in love with him. And he hadn't told her how much he loved her out of a need to protect her. He wanted that wish to be for what she wanted the most, not to be for some newfound love, temporary and fleeting as so many mortal loves were.

Kat smiled, reaching up and catching his wrist, drawing his hand down until she could press a kiss to his palm. His entire body tensed from that light touch. "I've adjusted to be being blind. I don't like it…but it's my life. And even if I could see again, my life would feel empty after this past month, especially this past week. Yes. If I could have anything…it would be for you to stay, for you to *want* to stay."

His eyes closed. Awe filled him, along with hot satisfaction, and hunger. But first, the wish.

The magick was building inside of him. He hadn't known what to expect. But this was different. The bond that held him to the mirror started to snap, like a thread drawn tight and cut, as he lowered his lips to hers. The bond broke as his mouth touched hers, and he felt the backlash of magick, a hot wind that wrapped around them, filling the room with a wash of color and light.

She felt it, too. He tasted the wonder, the awe in her kiss as he pushed inside her mouth greedily, seeking out her tongue with his. Never had he kissed a woman so deeply when he granted wishes. And before her, it had been centuries untold since he had truly enjoyed the granting of wishes, enjoyed the taste and feel of a woman's mouth under his.

But he would never tire of her mouth, her taste, that sweet wonder of her kiss. He shifted, surging out of the chair and taking her to the floor in a series of harsh, sudden moves. "Damn it, I have to have you," he muttered, his hand jerking open the tie that held her robe closed. Spreading the edges of the robe, he stared down at her body, seeing the fading flickering lights of *Djinn* magick explode over her body.

In the distance, he heard a crack, the tinkling of glass as the mirror broke, and he grinned, finally free at last. Her eyes, unseeing, stared up at his as he lifted his head, and he felt his happiness dim, just a little.

She'd given up her sight for him. If she had known… But he shoved it out of his head. He'd spend the rest of his life making sure she never regretted the wish she hadn't known she'd been given. With focused intent, he kissed his way down her body, the echo of breaking glass still dancing in his mind.

He never saw the silver cloud that came drifting in. Never saw the glittering bits of mirror dissolve as they forged into the silvery cloud that hung over them. As he pushed her thighs wide, lowering his mouth to her pussy, the cloud formed a ring, spinning fast and bright over their bodies.

Stiffening his tongue, he pushed it inside her, shuddering as he lapped up the sweet, rich taste of her cream. "I love you, Kat," he muttered, his fingers biting into the skin of her ass as she screamed out, arching her back.

The dark pink of her nipples stood out from the creamy mounds of her breast, and he moved up the length of her body, his mouth watering as he stared at her breasts. Damn it, he wanted to taste all of her at once. Biting the pebbled flesh gently, he listened as she gasped, then he suckled her nipple deep, using his tongue to press it against the roof of his mouth. He tore at his jeans and groaned as his cock leaped free, throbbing, aching in the cool air as he shifted his position and pressed against her, pushing inside the hot, honeyed well of her pussy. "Sweet Kat," he crooned, watching as his flesh disappeared inside her, the lips of her sex spread tight around his length. "I love fucking you, love watching you come. You're so tight, so wet..."

She mewled under his slow possession, reaching up and clutching at his shoulders. Over them, the ring of silver cloud continued to spin, starting to pulse. "Tam...please!" she sobbed out. As he slid completely inside her, he dropped down, resting his weight on his elbows so he could stare down at her face.

"I love you, Tam," she gasped, her breath coming out of her in rough, unsteady pants. "I love you so much."

Tears flooded his eyes and he lowered his head, kissing her deeply as he rocked inside of her, feeling the slick, satiny muscles of her sheath grip him so tightly.

Her nipples stabbed into his chest, hot little points of sensation. Tam gritted his teeth as he pulled out, slowly pushing back inside her as her hands cupped his ass, her short, neat nails biting into his flesh.

"You feel so good," he murmured, closing his eyes. A shudder raced down his spine and he arched his back, driving deep into the heart of her.

Their bodies gleamed under a light sheen of sweat, flesh sliding slickly against flesh, his hard, angled planes fitting perfectly against her curves.

Rolling to his back, he pushed up inside her, feeling the small stroking flutters in her sex, signaling how close she was to coming. His eyes opened slowly. He wanted to watch her—

"Kat!" he screamed as he saw the silvery cloud above them. It dropped, changing shape as it moved, forming a funnel. Kat's climax started. Tam was frozen in place, unable to move as her head fell back, exposing her face to the cloud of magick.

Her lips parted as she, blissfully unaware, rocked against him, her snug pussy gripping his dick as she came. And he had to watch, locked inside her body and unable to do anything as the funnel breached her lips. She felt it then and her body stiffened.

She tried to scream, and *finally* Tam could move, flipping her onto her back and trying to cover her. He struck out with his own magick but the funnel continued to bore its way inside her mouth. Her skin was now glowing silver from the magick, brighter and brighter.

Her lids flew open and her eyes were the color of pure silver, all silver, no discernable iris, the whites of her eyes all gone as the silver light poured from her eyes, like lights shining out of her face.

Her eyes became opaque…then shifted even more, and for a moment, they were pools of reflection in her face, like a mirror, and Tam could see his own horrified face as his magick struck ineffectually at the funnel cloud.

Her scream stopped as abruptly as it had started. Her body went limp and Tam felt terror squeeze its cold hand around his heart. Touching his fingers to her neck, he felt the slow, steady beat of her heart.

Relief flooded him as he shifted, sitting on his bare ass, the cold tile of the floor leaching into him as he lifted her, cuddling her limp body in his arms. "What in the hell was that?" he muttered, confusion, helplessness and terror all vying for supremacy inside him.

Stroking her brow, he held her close as he waited for her to wake.

* * * * *

Hours passed. He finally rose from the floor and carried her to bed, tucking her into the warm blankets, conscious of the fluffy white flakes that drifted from the sky. Tam lay next to her, staring at her sleeping profile, his arm draped across her belly.

He watched the slow, steady rise and fall of her chest, his heart a hot, leaden weight in his chest.

What had happened…?

* * * * *

Kat stretched, coming into wakefulness slowly, her lashes lifting, a smile curling her face.

Then she screamed as her mind processed the stimuli it received.

It's snowing…

Her lips parted, tears burning her eyes as she stared outside, and for the first time in three years, saw something.

"Kat?"

Her head swung around and she saw the man who had held her close while she slept.

Tam… He was beautiful.

"Oh my God," she whispered thickly, reaching out and touching her fingers to his face.

His lips moved and she stared helplessly at his mouth, not even registering his words. "Tam," she whispered, feeling the hot tears in her eyes spill out and run unchecked down her face.

"Kat, what's wrong?" he asked, rising and reaching out. She could see the movement, not just feel the shift of his weight on the mattress. But she could *see* it as he reached out his hands—long-fingered, wide-palmed hands that gleamed copper in the dim light.

She reached out slowly, her fingers shaking as she caught one hand before it could touch her.

His eyes widened and she lifted her gaze to meet his. "Kat?" he repeated, his voice gritty with shock.

"Tam… I can see you," she whispered. Then she launched herself at him, wrapping her arms around him, his weight falling back on the bed. "I can see you!"

His lips moved against her hair and she lifted her head, staring down at his face. A crooked grin lit those handsome, carved lines and he whispered, "I hope I'm not too ugly for you. I was kind of planning on staying."

She cupped his face in her hands, seeing the fine tremor in her fingers. The sandpaper feel of his early morning shadow scraped against her palms, like it had before but this time, she could actually see that sexy shadow she had only before envisioned in her mind.

"I don't understand this," she whispered, tearing her eyes from the sight of her hands on his cheeks to stare into those pale, summer-sky-blue eyes.

His gaze softened and he shifted. The world spun dizzyingly fast around her and she closed her eyes, her hands flying out to catch his shoulders as her head swam, her mind unaccustomed to the sudden shock of sight again.

"Whoa," she whispered, lifting her lashes. She was dizzy but didn't care. Staring up at him, she licked her lips.

She could finally see that intense gaze she had felt so many times. "How did this happen?" she whispered.

Tam heard the wonder in her voice. It was reflected in his own heart. As he lowered his mouth, he whispered, "Who knows, Kat?"

But he did know.

Kat had gotten her wish.

But, for some reason, the *Djinn* had too.

About the Author

They always say to tell a little about yourself! I was born in Kentucky and have been reading avidly since I was six. At twelve, I discovered how much fun it was to write when I took a book that didn't end the way it should have ended, and I rewrote it. I've been writing since then. About me now... hmm... I've been married since I was 19 to my high school sweetheart and we live in the mid-west. Up until April 2004, I worked as a nurse, but since then, I've been writing full time. This way, I'm doing what I've always wanted in life…writing…but I can also devote more time to my family—two adorable children who are growing way too fast, and my husband who doesn't see enough of me...About me now...hmm... I've been married since I was 19 to my high school sweetheart and we live in the midwest. Recently I made the plunge and turned to writing full-time and am looking for a part-time job so I can devote more time to my family—two adorable children who are growing way too fast, and my husband who doesn't see enough of me...

Shiloh welcomes comments from readers. You can find her website and email address on her author bio page at www.ellorascave.com.

Tell Us What You Think

We appreciate hearing reader opinions about our books. You can email us at Comments@EllorasCave.com.

Also by Shiloh Walker

Coming In Last
Ellora's Cavemen: Tales From the Temple IV (*anthology*)
Every Last Fantasy
Firewalkers: Dreamer
Her Best Friend's Lover
Her Wildest Dreams
His Christmas Cara
Make Me Believe
Mythe & Magick
Mythe: Vampire
Once Upon a Midnight Blue
Silk Scarves and Seduction
The Dragon's Warrior
The Hunters 1: Delcan and Tori
The Hunters 2: Eli and Sarel
The Hunters 3: Byron and Kit
The Hunters 4: Jonathan and Lori
The Hunters 5: Ben and Shadoe
Touch of Gypsy Fire
Voyeur
Whipped Cream and Handcuffs

PAYING UP

Mary Wine

Trademarks Acknowledgement

The author acknowledges the trademarked status and trademark owners of the following wordmarks mentioned in this work of fiction:

Hummer: AM General Corporation

Chapter One

Christina Jennifer Faulkner listened to her own sigh and grumbled. Life was being difficult today. She leaned forward to glare at the computer sitting in her dad's store but the machine seemed less than impressed with her temper.

Well…she was going to win!

"Are you still messing with that order?"

"Yes, Dad, the satellite link isn't responding."

Again. She curled her lips back as the screen flashed her a broken connection message. She lifted her head as the open window let a low rumble in. The faint sound of a helicopter's blades made her push away from the computer. The dish wouldn't work right until the military aircraft was over the ridge.

Her order would have to wait. Her frustration dissipated along with the aircraft noise. Funny how just knowing a little information made stuff easier to deal with. Most of the residents of Benton County assumed the helicopters used the area as a training ground.

She knew better. It was knowledge she just might be healthier forgetting but she wasn't stupid either. She'd seen the coal black military machines with her own eyes. Watched the men who commanded them, lived in the foreign bustle of a military compound that sat right up over the next ridge.

Looking around her father's shop, she smiled and a silvery giggle rippled out of her throat. Her dad ran a clothing slash winter stock store. Heavy boots and thick jackets along with propane space heaters and snow gear.

Now, the real truth was, her dad just liked the woods in the winter. The shop was his personal sandbox and he enjoyed playing in it. The computer age was a menace as far as Tomas Faulkner was concerned. He liked a good magazine to order from.

"Where are you off to tonight?

Her dad looked up from a pile of magazines to run his parental eye over her clothing. Her short skirt didn't miss his attention.

"Cynthia is nursing a twisted ankle. Mick needs some help tonight." The only bar in town was home to the best barbeque in Benton county. Known as The Pit, it was the center of Friday night in Benton. It was also Valentine's Day week. Mick Trunal was too good of a family friend to leave at the mercy of a howling room full of hungry men and no waitress to shuttle beer in between the replays of tonight's baseball game.

Her dad grunted and raised his finger at her. "Call me when you get there."

"I will, Dad." Standing up, she placed a kiss on his leathery cheek before she felt a sharp tug on her skirt.

"Jacobs know you're wearing that short a skirt?"

"I don't really care if he does." Shane Jacobs hadn't even dropped her so much as a phone call in over two months. Who cared if she wanted to show a little thigh?

"Your attitude needs adjusting, my girl."

She blew her father another kiss as she grabbed her purse and headed for the door. Her dad thought Shane Jacobs walked on water. There was no point in debating any opinion she might have of him. The man had returned her to parents who believed her dead.

She stepped out into the Benton night and smiled as the stars lit up the road. She lifted her shoulders as she began walking the short distance to the pool hall. It was only two blocks and the streets of Benton were perfectly safe to walk at night.

At least that was what she'd like to believe again. This time her sigh was bitter. How did you resent knowing the truth? The world wasn't a nice place, and living your days under that fairy-tale assumption was a good way to get killed before you even knew there was a gun pointed at your face.

Her shoulder itched and she rubbed it out of habit. Her bullet wounds were healed now, but the scars her mirror showed her haunted her. It was absolutely terrifying the way life would just rise up in a surge of evil so thick, it devoured people before they even had time to think.

Right here in sweet-looking Benton, she and her best friend had ended up fighting for their lives. Christina had to remind herself that it had really happened. Well, the four bullet wounds covering her torso weren't the product of her imagination.

Neither was Shane Jacobs. Looking up at the mountains that made up most of Benton County, she tried to see the house that she'd shared with the man. Oh, he'd been more of a jailer than a host but there were parts of the memory that refused to dwindle in her mind.

You are so pathetic, Tina.

Really! The man hadn't remembered she was alive and here she was casting puppy dog eyes at a moonlit forest. Beyond dumb. Love was something that most men were born with the natural ability to avoid. They faked it to get sex. A woman had to be smarter than their slick words if she wanted to keep her sanity intact.

A true smile lifted her lips. Roshelle had found one of those rare men who truly loved. You just couldn't fake the way Jared Campbell followed her with his eyes. Her friend had emerged from their brush with evil and prevailed.

She would too. Picking up her feet, Christina headed toward her destination. Maybe she'd even get herself a date tonight. It was time to look forward.

* * * * *

Major Shane Jacobs took after his parents. The man was a giant. Six-foot ten inches tall just like his father. He wasn't lanky, either, instead his shoulders were broad and his chest wide.

Roshelle hissed as the man used every millimeter of that chest capacity to yell at his men. It wasn't a loss of temper explosion, instead it was a precise application of military command that shook the window behind her. The sentry guarding her snapped to attention before leaving to obey his commanding officer's order.

Her son sent out a soft whimper as the overabundance of noise startled him. Roshelle frowned at Shane but he seemed completely undisturbed by her pout.

"Is there a problem, ma'am?"

Most women would have considered that rude. Roshelle admitted she would have been one of them just a few short months ago. Now? Well, she was used to the giant and the way he ran her husband's unit. It wasn't sociable but it was polished in its deadly efficiency. Her mountain home was more of a military base most of the time. The Army Rangers that made up her husband's unit were always ready for any threat that might show up. Here, security took precedence over niceties, manners and even privacy. It was something she accepted as part of the man she'd married.

"Did you have an answer to that, ma'am?"

Her son jumped and filled his month-old chest before wailing in that glass-cutting tone of a newborn. Shane froze in his tracks as he looked at the one person on the premises who wasn't going to be impressed with his authority. Her son turned red as he screamed out his displeasure.

Her breasts instantly responded to her infant. Milk soaked the front of her shirt despite the fact that she'd fed Tivon only forty-five minutes earlier.

"OHHH… Shane Jacobs, you need to work off that steam somewhere away from me!"

The scent of her milk made her son frantic. His arms beat back and forth as he made loud, sucking sounds with his little mouth. She couldn't feed him now! Her breasts weren't full and that meant Tivon wouldn't end up with a full belly either. Getting a newborn on schedule wasn't easy and she glared at Shane as her son continued to demand a nipple.

"Yes, he does." Grace Campbell didn't raise her voice. The woman appeared from the side of the house and walked on silent feet toward Roshelle. Her mother-in-law still fascinated her. The woman held the most amazing will. It seemed to radiate around her.

She reached for her grandson and Tivon immediately stopped his screaming. His eyes locked with the emerald green ones of his grandmother as the baby seemed to connect with her on some higher level.

That was entirely possible. Grace Campbell was a psychic, and Roshelle had learned to respect that fact. Her husband's mind was as sharp as his mother's and the gift seemed to be part of her son's genetic code.

Grace didn't make a single sound. She didn't cuddle or rock her grandson. Instead she supported his head in a steady hand as her arm took his weight. Tivon stuck a fist into his mouth while his little emerald eyes stared into his grandmother's.

"Go shower. I'll deal with Jacobs."

Shane snorted but Roshelle had to resist the urge to laugh. Grace was a woman of few words, but she backed up each and everyone of them. Turning around she went looking toward that shower before she ended up smelling like spoilt milk. It would almost be worth the stench to stick around.

Shane cussed under his breath and waited. He was out of line and knew it. There weren't many people on the mountain who could make him listen to them if he didn't want to, but his father's operative was one of them. Despite her lack of rank, she was his senior.

Grace was busy studying her grandson and seemed to be ignoring him. He knew better. The veteran psychic was razor-sharp even in midlife. She'd lived her entire life in a unit of Army Rangers. Nothing got past the woman.

Her green eyes shifted to him before the corner of her mouth twitched up ever so slightly. She turned away from the house and walked down the front steps as she continued her mental connection with the baby.

Shane fell into step beside her. She sent those sharp eyes sideways at him before raising an eyebrow. "Lonely, Jacobs? Sorry, but I don't need any company."

"I thought you were going to deal with me."

She stopped and glared at him. "The only person who can deal with your problem is you. It would be nice for the rest of us if you got around to doing that before that girl goes and marries some other resident of the county. Then I might have to consider shooting you."

Shane halted and watched the woman head toward the trees. Grace wasn't much on civilization. She preferred the forest to the walls of a house and had raised her three sons among the trees.

He was used to that, actually more comfortable with rugged harsh edges opposed to civil niceties. He lived his life surrounded by military bluntness. His problem was the fact that he had an itch for the soft, delicate female he'd met right here on his mountain.

Another curse rolled out of his mouth as Shane considered lighting a cigarette. The problem with that was he didn't smoke. The habit seemed to have become attractive just about the same time he'd met Ms. Christina Faulkner.

If he lit up, his mother just might kill him. If he didn't, Christina's memory might make him wish for that death. Discovering someone else saw right through him didn't help. Grace had more than her fair share of insight but with his luck, every damn man under his command knew what was eating him.

Shit!

Turning around he headed back across the front drive that separated his house from Jared Campbell's home. A dry laugh escaped his throat. Jared did in fact have himself a home now. It was funny that a woman had brought about that change.

Jared had found himself a rare gem in Roshelle. Damned if Shane had any clue how the woman did it, but she managed to balance out her life among the military element that surrounded her. Civilians didn't transplant well into the classified realm that he and Jared lived in.

A silver laugh rose from memory as he recalled just how Christina tossed her blonde head of curls. Her blue eyes sparkled every time she giggled. His mouth wanted to twitch up into a stupid grin every time he heard that voice, even in his memory. No woman should be allowed to keep a man company in his dreams if she hadn't discovered what kind of sheets he slept between. For Christ's sake, he hadn't even slapped her bottom.

No, you idiot, all you did was watch her.

Maybe that was the trouble. He'd watched the way she walked and the way she worried her lower lip as she contemplated trying to outwit him. She cuddled up with a pillow as she slept and always kicked the covers off her feet so that her little painted toenails peeked out.

The details of her sultry walk were embedded in his mind, the motion of her hips as they swayed back and forth. Even the soft feminine scent of her hair seemed to be recorded like classified data in his mind. He'd made the mistake of touching her just one single time and the feel of her bottom across his legs still made his cock itch.

The word idiot wasn't strong enough. Shane looked at his house and turned toward one of his helicopters instead. He was inventing work to avoid going into his house. Somehow, the place was uncomfortable without his guest in residence. Yup, idiot wasn't the word.

It was fool.

* * * * *

"I've got an order for you."

Christina felt a chill run down her neck. She'd been serving customers all night but she knew that tone of voice. It was deep and hard as steel. The shiver shaking her collided with her temper. She turned on her heel as she refused to shrink away from the man sitting in the corner of the pool hall side of The Pit.

Half the place was a bar and dance floor and the other side a pool hall. Rourke Campbell was leaning against the doorjamb with one booted foot crossed over the other. His arms were crossed over his chest giving him the lazy look of any Benton County resident looking for a little kick back fun.

She knew better. He was Jared Campbell's brother and as lethal as a cobra. Her time on their mountain had been filled with whispers of psychics. It wasn't something they told you about, instead she'd witnessed it firsthand. This man, just like his brother, was an operative with the black forces of the Army. They lived on the edge of life and melted into the erased pages of classified operations.

His lips curled back to show her an even row of teeth. His eyes were the same emerald green as Jared's and seemed to cut right into her soul. She stomped her foot into the wooden floor as the urge to scurry off to the kitchen filled her immediate thoughts.

She stood in place and let his eyes inspect her. It wasn't the first time since her return from his secret home that she'd noticed someone watching her. She'd kept her word to his father, Sheriff Brice Campbell. Not a single word had passed her lips about the compound over the ridge. But that didn't mean his family had any intention of letting her memory dim. They watched her and made sure she knew it.

Sometimes the sheriff just dropped in to her father's store, other times it was just that tingle on her neck that called her attention to some musclebound man sitting in a car outside a shop she'd stopped into. Their eyes set them apart from other civilian men. She'd never understood why military men said the word civilian like it referred to another species than their own.

Now she understood.

"Don't worry, I haven't bitten anyone all day."

"Oh, well, I think that means you're about to snap any second. We have a leash law in The Pit. All animals must be secured in the patio area."

He laughed at her. Tipped his head back and let a rumble of male amusement hit the ceiling. His eyes sparkled when they caught her again. A sharp glint of appreciation made her shift in her shoes. Rourke Campbell was certainly every inch a solid hunk of male but she didn't want him to start looking at her like a woman.

One dark eyebrow rose in response to her reaction. His lips settled into a grin that was just a little too sympathetic. Confusion hit her but she kept her lips closed. This family didn't answer questions, they bred them.

"If you've got some coffee back there, bring a mug back for me. Black, double strong if you've got it."

Oh, they had it. Double black was regular stock at The Pit. For that matter, most establishments that had a bar doubled as a coffee house. It was just the little fact that Rourke Campbell was planning on staying around long enough to drink that coffee that made her frown on her way to the kitchen.

It was like she was stuck somewhere between her kidnapping ordeal and her real life. Yes, she was home but she wasn't living her life. Instead she felt a rope attaching her to the life and death struggle that had ended with four bullets hitting her flesh.

You couldn't go back in life. Maybe that was the lesson she needed to accept. Once innocence was gone, you had to make your way as best you could. Using her hip, she pushed the door open while balancing a tray with Rourke's coffee on it. She lifted her chin as she walked back toward the man. She did know about his life—so what? She'd keep her promise and somehow find the courage to stop worrying so much about the possibilities of the hard world out there.

* * * * *

"Dr. Roshelle Campbell, you look remarkably domesticated this evening."

Roshelle didn't jump. A little smile lifted her lips as she managed to control her need to react to Jared's brother's games. Rourke enjoyed appearing out of a shadow almost as much as her husband did.

"And you look like someone I've repeatedly asked to knock on the door."

Rourke showed her his teeth in response. "Why? You can feel me if you pay attention."

His words sparked a rise of pride that spread over her face. Roshelle enjoyed it as Rourke continued to grin at her. She could feel him. Her empathic senses were gaining focus every time she made herself understand them. It was something that took practice and her husband's family was quite willing to help her get all the practice she needed.

"Guilty. I was half asleep."

"Well, I'm not. I stopped and had some coffee tonight. That friend of yours makes a mean cup of double black and delivered it in a skirt so short, I'm still thinking about it."

Now that she was paying attention, Roshelle felt the unmistakable rise of heat in her living room. She looked around the room but the men held their faces in calm masks that didn't give her any clue as to who found Rourke's statement so offensive.

Her husband jerked his head up to catch her eyes. Jared had entered her mind the night they met and the link was strengthening every day. Their son was chewing on his father's finger and looking impossibly tiny next to her large husband. Tivon wasn't small either! The baby had arrived at nine and a half pounds and ate like a wolf cub.

Jared suddenly looked at his brother and raised an eyebrow. "I didn't know Christina was working at The Pit."

"Me either, but I'm making a mental note to start having coffee there more often. She's got legs that reach to her rib cage."

This time Roshelle felt that emotion turn into anger. Her eyes moved to Shane Jacobs without conscious thought. They went where her mind was centered. Shane was always around. He was her husband's partner so she was comfortable with the man's company now.

Tonight, jealousy bled off him like a vapor. His face was a mask of military control but his eyes simmered with the heat her mind told her was nearing an explosive level.

Roshelle pulled her eyes off Shane. Rourke knew exactly what his words were igniting in the man. Unless she missed her guess, he was baiting Shane with that comment about Christina's legs. All of the men surrounding her were hard. They lived their life on the edge and played just as hard. Even something as common as friendly advice was handed out differently between them. In this case, Rourke was reaching for a piece of meat and daring Shane to claim it.

A naughty little grin played with her lips as she considered just what would happen if Christina had any idea that she was being talked about between the men. Angelic looks aside, her friend would transform into Satan and make every last male hormone suffer.

Boy, did she miss her friend!

* * * * *

"Are you off to The Pit again?" Tomas Faulkner wasn't happy about her skirt—again. A daughter just knew her father's eye. The urge to squirm was building as she watched her dad's forehead crease into even deeper folds.

"Daddy, it's a sprained ankle, she can't just get over it in one night. Mick needs the help and it's not like I don't know every person who comes into the place."

Her dad grunted but raised a finger at her. "We do get strangers, my girl. You tell Mick I said to have one of his boys take out the garbage. I don't want you out back in the dark."

"Yes, Dad." She rolled her eyes and her dad used his finger to tap his cheek. Rising onto her toes, she gave him his kiss before she felt the tug on her skirt hem again.

"We are going shopping on Sunday. You've grown out of your skirts."

Her dad stood in the doorway and watched her walk down the block.

"No, Dad, I grew into my skirts." But how did you tell your father something like that?

The Pit was two blocks from her father's store. Up one and across the next. Turning the corner, she walked out of her father's sight and The Pit came into view.

A man stood in the barbershop doorway, leaning against the brick façade. He was facing toward her, his face masked by the shadows. Her feet froze as she considered him. Unless he was asleep on his feet he could see her but no greeting came from him.

Her father's warning was fresh in her mind. They did get strangers in Benton and any of the locals would have said hello by now. There was nothing open on the block of small shops, only The Pit at the end of the sidewalk. Music drifted on the night breeze from the open front door, along with laughter.

Fear tingled along her spine as she recognized the perfect setting for another abduction. Her blood turned icy as every muscle she possessed tightened almost unbearably. Terror was trying to capture her completely and reduce her to a screaming animal that reacted instead of thought.

She refused to do that! Clutching at her courage, she fought against the tide of remembered horror. She found her cell phone in her pocket and opened it without looking before using her sense of touch to slip up to the number five. That would speed-dial her dad in a second and he'd be grabbing his shotgun in another second.

Her feet had already taken one step backward as she felt the number five under her fingertip. Headlights flashed over her as a truck came up the street, and its brakes squealed as it stopped next to her. The passenger window was already down, Web Nelson grinned at her across the front seat.

"Care for a lift to the end of the block?"

Christina sent Web a smile as she reached for the door handle. Relief hit her as she climbed into the truck and away from the stranger in the doorway. Her eyes flickered back to the shadow in the doorway and found it empty. Her fingers shook as she tried to control the fear eating away at her. It twisted her stomach with nausea as she climbed into the truck. Her head turned as they drove past the doorway.

It was completely empty.

* * * * *

"I might have to kick your ass." Rourke's words were too quiet. Shane shrugged his shoulders as the man jumped from the limb of a tree.

"You can try, but I'm betting on me tonight."

Shane felt the other man scan his thoughts lightly. It was a feeling he had grown up with. Tonight, he was sort of glad Rourke Campbell was a psychic—maybe he'd get the hell away from him before he had to explain to Colonel Jacobs, his father and superior, exactly why he felt the need to smash one of their operatives in the face.

Shane didn't want to talk about Christina with anyone and he wanted Rourke Campbell at least three states away from her, too. Rourke suddenly lifted his hands in surrender.

"Fine, I get it. But..." His hands lowered and hooked into his belt. "You scared her, buddy. Bad." A row of white enamel flashed at him in the night. "And if I didn't think that fact was going to hurt you, I'd be happy to let my fist do the job."

Rourke dissipated into the night as Shane cussed. He hadn't meant to frighten her. Training had a way of merging into instinct. Hiding his face was practically bred into him from a lifetime of military training.

He looked down the street at The Pit and thought long and hard about a cold beer. That short little skirt just teasing her thighs made Shane forget about the beer. There wasn't a red-blooded man in Benton who wouldn't be enjoying the view and he just might end up in jail if he had to sit there and watch them looking at his woman.

Potato sack dresses suddenly gained appeal.

Chapter Two

"Girl, something is eating you!"

Sandra, the cook for The Pit, shook her head as she handed over another order of buffalo wings. She split her lips with a smile that displayed a silver crown, and shook her head again. A spatula was brandished at Christina like a wand.

"You are too young to be so troubled."

"No troubles here."

"Shut your mouth, girl, I see it in those eyes." Sandra looked back at her grill and Christina took her chance to escape. She caught herself looking around The Pit with suspicious eyes and almost screamed.

That was it!

Her temper arrived to banish her demons. Better late than never, she supposed! Delivering the appetizer to a couple of truckers, she cleared away their empty mugs. The Pit was quiet now, the people hanging around were shooting pool or just watching a replay of the game on the big screen television.

She could go home. Mick didn't promise service at all hours in his bar. Once the place quieted down for the night you had to grab your own order from the kitchen window. She had been inventing reasons to stay away from her walk home.

Her temper simmered as she chewed on that fact. It was so easy to think you were over something until you had to face it. The more she thought about it, the madder she got.

"Hey, Mick, I'm heading home."

"Thanks, Chrissy." He sent her a wink over the bar and turned back to the man he was talking to. Half the town still called her Chrissy. Yeah, Shelly and Chrissy, the ponytail twins! Sometimes she wondered if Mick ever noticed that she traded in her hair ribbons for a bra.

On second thought, maybe she didn't need to know. She stepped out into the February night and shrugged into her coat. The chilly air slapped her cheeks making her smile.

The expression faded as she neared the doorway of the barbershop. A shadow filled the doorway. Setting her teeth into her lip she forced her back straight and walked by it. Nothing moved or materialized from the spot. Whoever he was, the man was long gone now. Picking up her pace she headed around the corner toward home.

"I didn't mean to scare you."

"You didn't scare me." Christina had to drag a huge lungful of air into her chest to make up for the acceleration of her heart. The muscle was beating frantically as she looked at the man standing in a doorway. He looked lazy and relaxed but the sheer size of him could easily overwhelm even the most confident of people.

"I didn't mean to."

Shane Jacob's voice kept her heart racing as she looked at the moon-bathed features of his face. There was a surge of some emotion bubbling through her that made her frown. It felt like she was happy to see him.

"That helicopter you fly has messed up your hearing."

His lips parted to show her an even row of teeth.

Her little nipples were hard enough to cut glass. Shane couldn't stop staring at the twin points of tattletale display. Fear was another form of stimulation—desire was almost its twin and the two were incredibly closely related. The breasts on a female were hooked into her sensory receptors, the nipples responding to any stimulus that was strong enough.

His mouth suddenly watered at the idea of those little nipples responding to him stimulating her body. His body sent up a surge of need that made his skin itch to be bare. Watching wasn't going to satisfy him anymore. Needs surfaced from his mind that he'd never allowed himself to examine too closely.

Tonight it was crystal clear. His cock slowly stiffened as he looked at the pair of blue eyes that had been keeping him company.

"So, your nipples get hard for any man you meet?"

"What?"

Shane pushed away from the doorway and moved closer to her. She stared at him in shock as her eyes tried to read his expression in the poor lighting. Raising a hand he gently stroked one little point and listened to her gasp of outrage.

"These little points say you are experiencing a rush of sensation. Either that resulted from a shock, or you and I have been sharing the same dreams about each other."

Her palm hit his cheek. Shane turned his head with the blow to keep the energy from hurting her arm. He grabbed her hand and held it prisoner in his larger one.

"Tsk tsk, what a temper." Shane rubbed the flat of her hand as she tried to jerk it away.

"Let go!"

"I don't think so."

He continued to rub her smarting hand. Christina jerked her arm again but he simply lifted an eyebrow at her and moved his grip up her arm one hand length.

"Is that your idea of a warning?"

He shook his head and stopped rubbing her hand. Two fingertips gently traced the delicate skin of her inner wrist. Pleasure raced up her arm making her shiver. The hand holding her arm in place tightened as his fingers made a second pass before he lifted her hand and pressed his lips onto her palm. Fire shot up her arm at the hot brush of his male lips. For some reason she was acutely aware of the fact that he was a man and she a woman. An insane desire to drop her eyes to the crotch of his pants made her heart double its pace again.

"For every action, there is a reaction. When you touch me, Christina, I get to touch you back."

"You touched me first." She yanked on her arm because she just couldn't control the impulse. Her skin seemed to become one single point of sensation. It raced from her wrist to her nipples where the tight nubs contracted even further and began to ache. A slow flow of fluid eased down her passage as she battled against the idea of turning her hand to touch the solid muscles of the arm holding her.

"Right after I scared you."

"You did not frighten me, Shane Jacobs!"

"Then I aroused you."

His voice was rich and dark. It challenged her to admit to either emotion. Both put her at a disadvantage. Instinct warned her to run, but temptation begged her to stay. She licked her dry lips before pulling her brain into focus.

"Well, I'll remember not to make the mistake of touching you again. Now, let my arm go!"

He did and her jaw fell open in response. Shane ground his teeth together as he held his body in position. The need to flee was racing across her eyes. The tip of her tongue passed over her bottom lip making him groan. He wanted to taste that lip, lick along its surface and find out what her mouth felt like under his.

"Sure about that? I think you'll be the one touching me first next time, Christina."

"When tarantulas are lovable."

He flashed those pearly white teeth at her and, lifting his huge hand, spread the fingers out and mimicked a large spider crawling. "You appeared to like the way these fingers felt on your delightfully soft skin." His voice dipped even lower as the edge of it roughened. "I love the way you feel. I can't wait for you to pay your debt."

His voice was pure temptation. Her body begged her with little jerks to move closer to that rich, deep sound of male promise. Her logic screamed to be heard over the clamoring of her skin. Both sets of impulses got mixed together as she just stood there trying to understand but her eyes dropped to the front of his pants. The thick bulge pushing against the fabric made her body ache. Her passage suddenly felt empty as it sent a rush of fluid down its walls. His cock was swollen and thick inside those pants and her body wanted to get much, much closer to its hard length.

"What are you talking about?"

"Our bet. You look nice and healthy, so I won." He stepped up next to her and tipped her chin up with his hand. The warm scent of his skin surrounded her, making her belly tremble with need. Her lungs deepened their next breath to pull even more of that male scent into her body. Heat erupted in her womb and bled down the walls of her passage. The hard muscle of his body bushed against her making her yearn for a tighter embrace that would bring that hard cock into contact with her. Her thoughts seemed centered on the idea that she had caused his arousal. Excitement poured from the thought that he had come to see her and his cock was hard in response to her.

"That means you owe me a kiss."

His mouth captured hers as his arm snaked around her waist and held her against his body. Her hands landed on his shoulders to shove him away but instead sent her the realization of how delightfully powerful he felt beneath her fingertips. There was hard muscle packed onto his shoulders making her hands shake as they flattened and pressed against him.

His kiss wasn't soft. His mouth moved over her lips in a smooth conquest as the hand cupping her chin pulled her jaw open to admit his tongue. He thrust it deeply into her mouth as she moaned around the hard male taste of him. She was intently aware of how aggressive his body was. His strength seeped into her body setting off a wave of need so powerful she slumped against his frame and clung to his shoulders.

The tip of his tongue traced the length of hers. Slow and deep, he stroked her tongue until hers twisted with his. The arm across her waist slipped down over her hips to her bottom. His fingers stroked each cheek before curling around one half and pressing her hips forward. Her hips thrust forward and found the hard bulge she'd admired. She was acutely aware of her mons and the passage inside her body heating and moistening for his hard cock.

Fluid flowed down the walls of her passage as his tongue thrust deeply into her mouth. A whimper escaped her throat as her blood raced too quickly through her veins. It all moved too fast! Her body was too hot! She pushed frantically against the wall of male animal that held her. The need to escape made her tear their mouths apart as she twisted in his grasp.

Shane spun her loose. His breathing was harsh as he looked at her nipples. Christina slowly backed away from the raw passion blazing from his face. The man was always so composed, his face a mask that never hinted at his emotions. Tonight it was harshly cut with the primitive need to take. His nostrils slightly flared as she stepped back even further. It wasn't the look on his face that frightened her the most, it was the huge bulge under his fly that told her he was on the edge of control. The thick rod straining against his fatigues promised her that he wanted more than a kiss. The swollen folds of her sex screamed at her to invite his need closer so that it could feed her own hunger.

The animal in the man wanted to mate with her. Spread her body and thrust into the wet channel between her thighs. Leave his mark in the most basic and primitive of ways. She shook her head as she backed away. Shane forced his feet to stand in place. The sweet scent of her pussy drifted on the night air making him battle against the urge to capture her. Instead, he watched her struggle against the wave of desire flickering across her body. She would be his, just as soon as she got used to the idea.

Her body was a jumble of impulses that slammed into a brain that frantically tried to sort them into understanding. The only idea that rang through her brain was the certain knowledge that once this man took her, she would belong to him. It would be irreversible and her surrender viewed as unconditional. Her pride rebelled against that truth even as her passage wept in agreement.

"I am going home now."

He nodded his head as he crossed his arms over his chest. It made the muscles of his arms bulge out even more. Her eyes slipped over his strength and her lips softened with feminine need for that strength.

"Then go, but I'll be back for my kiss."

Her heart jumped as her eyes widened. "You just took it."

He shook his head and grinned at her. "You bet me a kiss and that means you still owe me one, freely given kiss. You're welcome to come back over here and pay up right now."

She turned around and ran instead. Shane moved after her. He picked out the details of her bottom as she scurried away from him. The full, sultry shape of her hips that seemed to be swaying just for his eyes. They were like a neon sign that was aimed at his cock. The thing jerked and pulsed in his pants making him cuss as each step sent pain through his hard-on.

He followed her until she shut her front door and turned the bolt. A harsh grunt of approval hit the night as he walked the perimeter of her dad's shop. Everything was secure but his eyes picked out the weaknesses in the structure's defenses. All the ways someone might gain unlawful entry.

Shane felt rage boil up inside him. He actually enjoyed the emotion as it took the bite off his hunger. His cock still throbbed but it was a dull steady ache that mixed with his rage giving him the balance to walk back to where he'd parked his

Hummer. He slipped behind the wheel and punched the accelerator to the floor.

The winner in any battle was the man who took the time to prepare. A true warrior never faced off in a struggle without planning his attack. The aching cock in his pants was his reward for facing Christina without a plan.

He wouldn't be making that mistake again.

Shane pulled into his driveway and simply walked right into his house. The ranger on duty issued him a salute that he barely returned. There was no such thing as off-duty for him. He ran a classified ranger unit that didn't exist. That meant his personal life and his military one were a single entity.

If his men didn't know where he'd gone tonight, they would know where he was headed tomorrow. A low snarl of approval came from his lips as he considered that idea. Good. He wanted every male on the planet to think of Christina as his. He wanted them to believe he'd snap their necks if they even thought about looking at her long legs.

He marched into his bathroom and turned the shower on. Shane left the light off—the dark fit his mood as he stripped. Moonlight streamed in through the bathroom window. He folded his clothes as he took them off, out of habit, and his boots were lined up against the wall, his gun slipped on the top of the shower stall on a small corner shelf that he'd installed just for his sidearm.

The weapon never sat out of his reach, ever. It was his life. He stepped into the shower and bared his teeth as the icy water coated his hot skin. He'd only turned on the cold water, craved the contrast of temperature against his raging blood.

His cock stuck out from his body, refusing to slacken as the taste of Christina's lips lingered on his. Her scent was deep in his lungs as his cock gave another twitch at the idea of the hot arousal he'd smelled on her. She'd been wet for him. So wet, he smelled it right through her clothing. His erection stood firm in the cold water as hunger chewed at the logic that had sent him away from her bed.

He curled his fingers around the swollen rod, slipping up and down its rigid length. Pleasure joined the ache as he worked his hand faster. His seed splashed onto the tile as his lips curled away from his clenched teeth.

His mind sharpened as his body's demands quieted. Stepping out of the stall he reached for a towel and began to plot.

Chapter Three

Christina woke up tired. Her sheets were pulled and twisted from her bed and her hair was a nest of knots that pinched her scalp as she forced a brush along the strands.

She looked at her reflection like the body in the mirror belonged to a stranger. Those couldn't be her breasts. The globes looked swollen. The nipples drawn into little puckered nubs that still hadn't returned to the flat state they normally lay in.

Her skin seemed almost flushed and it was ultra-sensitive too. She lingered over the details of her makeup and hair because the bra she'd removed from her dresser looked like a torture device. Her breasts were still pulsing with little zips of feeling that screamed against the idea of anything containing them except Shane's hands.

She didn't want to put her jeans on. The folds of her sex felt too crowded already, and the idea of stepping into her panties made her mad. All she wanted to do was put on the lightest of cotton sundresses and leave her skin free to feel the air.

Christina hissed with frustration and pulled her clothing on.

Shane Jacobs had done this to her! She didn't know how but somehow he'd pushed some button in her brain that turned her gender against her common sense. Interrupting her normal morning thinking were flashes of his face, images of the way his arms bulged with muscle and the feel of his hard erection against her belly.

The stack of work she had waiting for her battled against her mental fantasies. She made mistakes and forgot details that were so practiced in her routine, she would have laughed if the cause wasn't so frightening.

Oh, she was scared. It made her furious but Christina couldn't very well lie to herself. She'd been kissed before. On a hundred dates that she couldn't seem to remember faces from. All she saw was Shane and the way he bared his teeth at her.

The boys she'd dated had kissed her but Shane had taken her mouth and tasted it like a man. Her body blossomed with the memory as her sex actually heated and sent its lubricating flow down the walls of her passage just from the memory.

Yeah, she was scared. Right down to her virginity. She had never gone past first base with any date and never let them see her breasts or touch her nipples. Maybe she had known that her body would tumble into insanity like this. Perhaps that was the reason she had clung to her resolve to deny the offers of love that had been presented as reasons to yield her body.

Her body shivered as she recognized the basic fact that Shane wouldn't be thinking about getting to second base with her. That man was going to strip her body and take it through the entire game, pitch by pitch, without missing a single inning.

Her only chance was to refuse to take the field and leave him on the pitching mound alone.

* * * * *

"Dad, can I drive a truck to The Pit?"

Her father immediately stood up. His eyebrows slated over his eyes as he aimed sharp eyes at her. Christina offered him a smile she hoped was normal. Her stomach was working itself into a huge knot as the sun set and the time for her walk to The Pit neared.

She didn't own a car anymore. When she'd been kidnapped it had been right out of the front seat of her own car. Out on one of Benton's mountain roads. Two trucks had forced her to stop or collide with them. She still had no clue what became of the car. Her kidnappers had been well-funded and a tow truck came with her abduction. They had hauled away her car just as they had taken her hostage. There hadn't even been skid marks to tell anyone where she'd disappeared from.

Her parents came up with excuse after excuse to keep her away from a car dealership. She had just let it slide because her father owned all three trucks that he'd ever bought in his lifetime. In the four months she'd been home, she'd spent three of them attempting to get her insurance company to pay a settlement on her previous car. With no wreckage, it was proving to be an uphill climb.

But she wasn't walking to The Pit tonight. She'd rather face her father and ask for a ride before risking another run-in with Shane in the dark.

She would overcome her urges, her gender was not going to control her. Her kidnapping ordeal was just making the connection with Shane more intense. That had to be the reason her body leapt under his touch. He was part of that cloak and dagger world that had swallowed her up and spat her back out, barely clinging to her soul.

As long as she avoided the man, her body would return to normal. That shouldn't be too hard. Shane didn't belong in her world. He stuck out like a lion at a cat show. Sure he might prowl around the dark edges but he'd stay away from the bright lights.

"Sure, take Betty."

"Thanks, Daddy."

He pointed to his cheek and she ran over to give him his kiss. He had a name for each truck and seemed to like them all just about the same amount. "Betty" was the smallest of the three and the one he knew she liked to drive the best. But since they were each her daddy's babies, she always let him choose which one to loan her.

After all, she was well past the age of being in the nest. That was another thing her parents kept finding reasons to delay. Moving out on her own once again. But she needed a job for that and her position at the courthouse had been filled while she healed from her gunshot wounds. It wasn't exactly fair to discharge the current employee since everyone had believed she was dead at the time.

She needed a car so she could drive to a better job that would give her the means to set up her own house. Instead, she unlocked her dad's truck and drove it toward The Pit.

Tomorrow she was going to buy a car. She needed to get out of Benton and back on track with her own life. Shane Jacobs was part of the things she needed to move beyond.

That meant he had to be retired to her memory as well.

* * * * *

Instead he was sitting at a corner table waiting for her. A mug of double black coffee was already resting in his hand like he knew she wouldn't serve him if she could avoid it.

His lips offered her a grin as his eyes watched her. Those sharp eyes followed her everywhere for hours. Her stomach turned into one solid mass of tension that wouldn't let her drink a glass of water.

The grin melted off his face as the strain bled through her cheerful mask. But he kept his eyes on her. She fumbled her third set of mugs before lifting her head to stare at him. Somber eyes returned her gaze. Shane had the most amazing eyes she'd ever seen on a man. They were hazel but so calm and steady she could find peace while staring into them. She had forgotten just how much she enjoyed looking into his eyes. It seemed so completely right.

He stood up and walked straight toward her. The place was quiet and almost empty. His eyes held hers the entire way until he leaned over the bar to whisper next to her ear.

"I have a question for you. Answer it and I'll leave."

A tiny wave of disappointment surfaced as she considered him leaving.

"All right."

"Are you a virgin?"

His eyes sliced into hers as he watched her face while asking his question. He was making certain he caught her honest reaction. It sprang up as a blush that stained her cheeks crimson. Her jaw dropped open but she couldn't find any way to conceal her innocence from him. The look that sprang into his eyes made her shiver.

"Answer the question, Christina. Have you ever taken a man's length?"

"You can't just ask me a crude question like that," she hissed under her breath and looked around the room quickly. No one was paying them a bit of attention but it felt like everyone could tell exactly what they were talking about. Her face burned so hot, she was sure the couple in the dark corner could see her blush. "I don't have to listen to this."

His hands landed on top of hers to keep her in place. His thumbs eased under her wrists to stroke the skin of her inner wrists once more. This time her body jumped to attention. It didn't heat up in stages like last night, it jumped into full arousal with just the first touch. Her nipples instantly hardened. His eyes lowered to her sweater and found the twin points before rising back to her face again.

She gasped at the hard glitter staring back at her this time. There was nothing friendly about him, not a single shred of peace in his hazel eyes. Pure male aggression aimed its way into her head.

"You don't want to push me, honey. The way you look at my crotch drives me insane and the smell of your wet pussy makes me want to rip you open but I don't want to hurt you. So answer my question, have you ever taken a cock into your sweet little body or any kind of sex toy?"

"No." She hissed the word and hoped he'd choke on it! "Bet or no bet, that won't be changing either." She pushed off the bar forcing him to let her go or have her body jerk to a halt like a freshly caught fish. His hands lifted in a split second as he curled his fingers into fists.

"I answered you, so leave."

His eyes lowered to her nipples instead. They lingered over her breasts and wandered up the curve of her neck.

"When you make a bet with me, Christina, you'd better plan on paying up." His eyes turned hard as he leaned back across the bar. "Or I'll hound you until you die." His hazel eyes softened as he stroked the side of her face with a warm hand. "But I won't hurt you, so don't be mad at me. You want me, honey, I can smell how wet you are right here. Maybe that isn't warm and flowery but it's honest and I don't play little boy games."

He stood up and straightened to his full height. The hard cut of his body screamed at her to invite him to do everything a man did with his woman. A hundred dark whispers from her fantasies urged her to indulge his whims. He suddenly grinned at the look in her eyes and leaned toward her to whisper once again.

"I see your face when I close my eyes at night. Every night since I took you back to your father my house has been empty."

He was gone a second later. A silly smile covered her face as she thought about his admission. He hadn't come back for their dumb bet.

Shane had come back for her.

* * * * *

He was watching her when she left The Pit. There was no mistaking that the Hummer parked on the curb was Shane's. Oh, it was plain-looking, not really even military-looking. The dull brown all-terrain vehicle could have belonged to another resident.

It didn't. The huge form of the driver, even in the dark, was Shane and she just knew it. It was almost like she felt his eyes on her. The Hummer wheeled away from the curb the second she drove past. It made a U-turn and followed her truck around the corner. He pulled over again to watch her park in front of her dad's store.

The bottom floor was the store and the upper floor the family residence. Her dad owned a small cabin up the mountain but she had been raised above his shop. Unlocking the door, Christina slipped inside, closed it and peeked through the curtain.

Shane had moved. The curb was empty almost making her question whether or not the man had really been there. She shook her head and turned toward the stairs. He wasn't like the men she'd been raised around. Even her dad.

Shane was some kind of predator that had been trained to deadly perfection. Just normal everyday things were done differently than she'd always seen. Things like walking. Shane was always watching his surroundings, his eyes moving and recording anything that moved. Tonight, he'd sat with his back to a wall and both doors clearly in sight. He didn't sit behind the table either. He angled his chair away from it and left his mug on the edge. He could have sprung out of his chair in a second flat. No fumbling around chairs or the table, the man made certain of that before he sat down.

He always expected something to happen and made sure he could respond when it did. Standing in front of her mirror she looked at the evidence that said he had the right to live that way.

Four bullets had ripped through her body in a split second. Shane hadn't been there. He and Jared had left her and Roshelle under the guard of their men. The attack had come so quickly, it was over before she realized her life was in danger.

Everything had gone silent as she listened to her own heart beating because she expected it to stop forever.

Instead, she'd looked into those hazel eyes of Shane's and discovered exactly how much she liked them. Hope had stared back at her as he tended to her wounds, and despite the fact that she'd told him she thought she was dying, somehow he'd made her believe she wouldn't.

And she had lived, so she owed the man a kiss. A shiver shook her body. She watched her nipples tighten in the mirror as warm liquid heat slipped down the sides of her passage. She felt so needy with an ache in her womb that clamored for her to answer her needs.

Instead she crawled into her bed without her clothing. Her skin refused to be covered and that was the only desire that she seemed to be able to answer.

Chapter Four

"Damn lovers' holiday." Two dull thuds hit the floor as her dad muttered some more. Standing up from the small desk in the little office of her dad's shop, Christina looked at her father as he scowled at whatever he'd dropped on the floor. Her movement caught his attention and he gave her his disgruntled male expression.

"Your mother has booked us a romantic getaway."

"I'm really sorry, Daddy." She held the corners of her lips down because her dad considered fishing in a remote cabin romantic. The very fact that the two-room structure had indoor plumbing was his idea of luxury. How he had ever married her fashion plate mother was a mystery.

"I'll run the shop, Dad, no worries."

"Aw, forget it! No one came in on last Valentine's Day. Leave the door locked."

"Tomas! Ready or not..."

That was her mother's normal warning before unleashing her newest shopping trip look. There was the tap-tap of high heels on the wooden stairs before Terri slipped into view. Her father's face almost glowed as he looked at her. Suddenly it wasn't so hard to understand what drew the two together.

"Young lady, you appear to be lost, want to get into trouble together?"

"My papa might make you meet me at the church first and make me an honest woman."

Her parents sent each other looks that no daughter wanted to be reminded they knew how to give each other. Her dad grabbed Christina in a hug as he winked at her.

"Hey now, I married her, didn't I?"

"Have fun, Dad."

Her dad twisted his face into a crooked smile before he picked up their luggage and followed her mother out the door.

"If you need us, dear, just call the cell phone." Her mother blew a kiss as she climbed into the front seat of a truck. She seemed out of place in the utility vehicle, as pristine as she looked, but the glow on her face said she was right where she wanted to be.

* * * * *

"You are saving an old man's life tonight."

Mick rolled his eyes as his hands continued to mix a drink while he spoke. The Pit was wall-to-wall people. Even Cynthia sat at the register with her injured ankle propped on a crate as she ran the register. Valentine's Day weekend and no one wanted to stay home. The actual lovers' holiday wasn't until tomorrow, but Friday night was a good enough reason to begin the celebration.

Christina was enjoying the night. Her feet ached and there was a pinch between her shoulder blades but the excitement of the place just made her happy. The only thing waiting for her was a dark house. Here, there were friends and a few extra tips to help with that car-buying expedition.

Her parents' unannounced trip was going to be her opportunity to step back into the world. Tomorrow morning she was heading out of Benton and toward a car dealership.

It was midnight when Mick kicked her out. The band was playing a smooth love ballad that stuck in her head as she drove home. She was still humming as she turned her key in the lock.

"Are you ready to pay up?"

* * * * *

She hit him this time. Christina didn't make a single sound as she curled her fingers into a little fist and sent it flying into his face.

"Ouch." Her hand exploded with pain as she connected with his oversized jaw. Pain traveled down her hand, up her arm and right into that pinch that was between her shoulder blades.

Her memory reminded her of his reaction the last time she struck him. She jumped back but not quickly enough. Her hand ended up a prisoner in his as she glared at him.

"Better, honey, but you need to use your shoulder if you want to make a punch worth anything. Especially when you're dealing with someone twice your size." Shane began rubbing her hand, his fingers sending little ripples of delight shooting down her smarting arm.

"What are you doing in my dad's shop? The door was locked." A sarcastic grin split his face as Shane raised a single eyebrow at her. The cocky expression made her want to try using her shoulder and make her next swing hurt. The giant hadn't even grunted. "You know, my dad likes his shotgun. Trespassing in his shop just might get you shot."

"Guess it's a good thing your dad isn't home tonight."

Shane's face went blank with his statement. A shiver raced down her backbone as she watched his eyes cut into hers. He was watching her with the intent look of a hunter. Her nipples suddenly tightened almost unbearably as she considered being his target.

Shane released her hand as he let her take a few steps away from him. Nervousness flickered in her eyes but the blue orbs also moved over his chest and down his length before returning to his face. Desire shot through his bloodstream like fire. Arousal wasn't something you planned—it was either there or not. The twin points of her nipples lifted her shirt making his cock harden with need.

"Come here, Christina."

Shane was used to being obeyed. His voice was edged with authority. The order was some sort of test of her will. Her body suddenly insisted she do as he wanted. Walk the three paces that would place her back within his embrace. Heat seemed to radiate from her skin in waves that made her clothing too hot.

She understood the rush of sensation now. Knew without a doubt why there was the smooth flow of heat from her breasts to her womb. The folds of her sex became ultra-smooth as fluid eased between them. Tossing her hair back, she looked at the man standing in front of her. Running her eyes over his shoulders, she looked at the pure strength displayed by their wide width.

Every cell in her body seemed to hum with approval for him. Her body demanded a closer inspection of his and her temper reared its head. She wanted to wrap her thoughts around the idea that he'd come back to her for some reason beyond their bet.

"All right, Shane, I did bet you a kiss and I'm a woman of my word." Taking another step forward she lifted her arms to reach for those shoulders.

His warm breath teased her lips before she went up onto her toes to complete the kiss. Her fingers wandered over his chest as she opened her mouth against his. His male taste teased her. The tip of her tongue couldn't resist the temptation to journey toward the center of his mouth, delve into him and stroke the length of his tongue.

His hands closed over her waist as he lifted her higher. Their bodies connected as he thrust his tongue deeply into her mouth. Desire contracted around her womb as the hard length of his cock burned into her belly. His lips left hers as he continued to lift her up, until his lips found the smooth column of her neck and she gasped as pleasure rippled down her body.

Shane placed her on the shop counter and threaded one hand through the silken strands of her hair. Tipping her head up, he nipped the skin on her neck and groaned. Moving lower he found her shoulder and gently bit the spot where her neck began. A little whimper rose from her chest as he let her head go.

Every button on her shirt went flying toward the floor. A quick jerk from his hands snapped the threads before Shane separated the front of the garment. Her bra had a front clasp and he growled approval as his fingers separated it. The cool night air brushed against her overheated flesh making her purr with satisfaction. His fingers gently smoothed over the twin mounds of her breasts before rolling each of her nipples between a thumb and forefinger.

A cry filled the dark store. Christina wasn't even sure it was hers. It was too feminine, too full of primitive pleasure. Her back arched to offer her breasts to him like some mating ritual. Moonlight bathed them both as he stepped forward and nudged her thighs apart.

"I've been thinking about tasting these nipples for far too long, honey." The look on his face fascinated her. It was pure male appreciation, hard and cut with a primitive edge that made her tremble. His hands cupped her breasts, making her gasp with pleasure. Her back arched even further as she placed her hands on the counter behind her for balance. Her short skirt rose up with her parting thighs. She was suddenly deeply aware of her mons. Only her thin panties shielded her from him, and she was so wet the cotton stuck to her folds as his head dipped toward her offered breasts.

She cried out as he caught a nipple between his lips. Shane growled around the nub as he used his tongue to worry its tip. The hot smell of her pussy burned into his head as he latched onto her breast and suckled on it. His cock was throbbing with a need to bury its length in her.

She was a virgin, his virgin. His cock was going to wait until he loosened up her tight passage. Moving his mouth to her opposite breast, Shane sent one hand along her thigh. He pushed her skirt completely to her hip before gently touching her spread folds for the first time. She jumped but his arm around her waist held her firmly in place as he pressed his hand over her sex.

"Shane…I need you." And she didn't give a damn about anything else at that moment. Her hand found the hard bulge of his cock and tried to find the button on his fly in the dark. He captured her hand and firmly returned it to the countertop behind her.

"Shhh…I'm going to touch you first, honey." His voice was solid with determination, his eyes glittering at her as the hand sitting over her sex pressed once again. Pleasure shot straight into her womb. She arched toward that hand out of pure need. Tension began to throb directly under his hand. The crotch of her underwear was pushed aside as a single finger dipped between her folds. It stroked her length before settling on the little nub at the top of her mons. A strangled cry came from her lips as that finger rubbed and circled her clit.

"Look at me." She was twisting in his embrace, her hips bucking toward his hand seeking release. Her juices coated his hand as he pressed harder on her little clit. Her eyes flew open as she strained toward the pressure his hand applied, her lungs rose and fell rapidly as climax began to dilate her eyes.

"Come for me, Christina, let it take you."

She didn't have a choice. Her body contorted as pleasure broke and exploded across her flesh. Her fingers curled into talons that dug into his shoulders and she screamed at the fabric separating her from his skin. The smell of her own body rose thick between them as she gasped for breath. His hand was still between her thighs as she tried to form a single word to recover some shred of dignity.

His mouth caught hers instead, pushing her lips open as his tongue invaded and stroked the length of hers. The kiss was hard and deep, and he lingered over it as her body rocked on the waves of her climax.

His fingers moved down her spread sex to the opening of her body. One fingertip circled the slick flesh before thrusting gently into her channel. Her body hummed with pleasure as he pulled free and thrust two thick fingers into her body once again. Her hips bucked forward as his thumb landed on her clit and gently rubbed as he continued to thrust into her.

"That's it honey." His words came out on a groan as Shane thrust further into her. She was so damn tight it made him want to snarl. All he wanted to think about was the way her pussy would feel sucking his cock into it. Instead he pressed his fingers deeply into her and listened to the sounds coming from her throat to gauge whether or not she was in pain. Her bottom lifted for his next thrust making him grunt with approval.

He lifted her off the counter in one solid movement. She landed against his chest as his legs carried her toward the stairs. There wasn't any sound except for her breathing, his feet didn't seem to make a single noise as he moved through the house. It was almost like he was one of the shadows that had come to life to join her fantasies.

The light in her bathroom was on, and it spilled into the hallway as Shane carried her toward her bedroom. His jaw was set in a hard line as he angled her through the doorway. He let her feet down as she took in her bed with a shocked gasp.

The covers were turned down. A green and brown, camouflage fabric, duffel bag stood on its end in the corner and a pair of huge black boots was lined up against the wall next to it.

"Just because my parents are out of town doesn't mean you just get to move into my bedroom."

"Christina, honey, it's time for you and me to finish some business. Now take that skirt off if you value it."

Her retort died on her lips as he stepped back and opened his shirt. His chest was magnificent. Every inch of it sculpted to pure feminine perfection. Her fingers itched to run along the ridges and explore the strength that radiated from him.

The box of condoms sitting on her bedside table made her temper explode.

"I swear you must be the most presumptuous male on the planet!" She didn't take her skirt off. Instead she jerked it back over her thighs as her face flamed with embarrassment. She'd just stood there with the thing around her waist like a simpleton.

"You are not sleeping in my bed."

Shane popped a button on his fly open in response. She didn't want to look, but her eyes disobeyed her brain and dropped to his hand as he unlatched another button and then another. He wasn't wearing a stitch under those fatigues either. Hard male flesh fell out of the open fly and thrust forward with clear intent.

"And *that* is not coming anywhere near my body!"

Shane laughed at her. He tipped his head back and roared with male amusement. His open pants dropped to the floor and he simply stepped out of them. She stared at the erection his pants had held. His cock was thick and long and crowned with a ruby head that had just a single drop of fluid shining at its slit. The insane desire to touch him crossed her mind as her palm itched to see what that monster felt like.

"Spoken like a true virgin."

She lifted her eyes and Shane sobered. Hurt crossed her face as she tugged on her skirt hem with nervous fingers. She had forgotten that her breasts were bare. They stood out proudly, crowned with little pink nipples.

"I didn't mean to hurt your feelings, honey."

She felt like denying that he had but his eyes were too sharp. She simply shrugged and tugged her skirt down into place again. "I don't want to be a notch on some guy's belt." Christina watched his face as she said that. Just because she had a pretty face didn't mean she was dumb and too many men had made the mistake of believing just that. If you were pretty then you were shallow enough to believe they loved you on a second date.

Shane's face suddenly went hard. His eyes were cold with rage as they focused on her shoulder. Standing close to the bathroom door, the light spilled over her body. The scars from her bullet wounds stood out clearly on her skin. The urge to cover her body made her turn around.

"Turn back around." That was an order. His voice was hard and edged with rage. "Right now."

"It's my body."

"Wrong." His hand spun her around as his large body crowded her against the wall. "You belong to me now. Don't hide from me, honey, I already know about those scars. Seeing them just makes me want to kill those bastards all over again."

It was such a brutal statement but she turned into the protective shelter of it. Shane's face was harsh with anger but his eyes moved over her scars with a firm resolution that told her it would not be happening again. He had made certain of that in a brutal way but there was also a deep sense of caring that came from the knowledge that he would defend her so—permanently.

The hard length of his erection brushed her bare leg making that heat flame across her skin and flow down her passage. The little nub hidden in the folds of her sex throbbed with the desire to be touched once again. Shane's eyes were glued to the scar on her chest where her sternum had stopped a bullet intended for her heart.

"They're ugly."

"Nope, they're the proof that you aren't a quitter." His fingers smoothed over the red skin before catching her chin to lift it to his hard gaze. "The fact that you didn't give up and die makes you the most attractive woman I've ever met."

His mouth caught hers with a gentle kiss. His lips were firm as they pushed hers open and took a long taste from her mouth. The bare male skin beckoned to her fingers. She had to touch him and feel the pulse of life she could actually smell. All her body wanted was him in whatever way he might demand. Shane was going to take her and she shivered at the raw idea of his body possessing her.

He lifted his head from hers and grinned at the passion-drugged eyes. His cock was throbbing harder as the smell of her hot pussy made it nearly impossible to maintain any kind of control. Shane ground his teeth together and resisted the urge to rip her little excuse of a skirt off her. He was not going to fall on her like an animal…even if he currently felt like one.

"If you want a shower, you have ten minutes."

"Do you know how to talk to a person without giving orders?"

He curled his lips back into a grin. "No, ma'am."

Ask a dumb question and you get an even dumber answer. She did want a shower but the fact that Shane was once again a step ahead of her made her mad. Discovering that he seemed to understand her body as well as she did was too exposing.

"Nine minutes and the clock is ticking."

"I don't belong to you."

This time his smile was predatory. He stroked one of her flaming cheeks before running his eyes down her almost bare body. He caught her chin when she would have tossed her head, and held her jaw with iron strength that was completely unyielding. "If you want your shower, you'd better take it now. You stand here teasing me with the scent of your wet pussy and we'll get right down to seeing just where I think you belong."

Determination blazed from his eyes. A little gasp escaped her mouth as she saw the certainty of his possession on his face. This man was going to have her and her body was going to help him do it.

* * * * *

Eight minutes was worse than a death sentence. Shane paced and stared at the bathroom door. He cussed and prowled the perimeter of the room once again. Want and need were both trying to break down the wall of his self-control and smash every sane idea in his head into kindling.

He took a deep breath and forced the idea of Christina's spread body out of his mind. A man didn't fall onto a woman like a fresh kill—that sort of rutting was left behind in his youth when all his adolescent body could do was fuck.

Especially a virgin. Shane looked at the bedroom and snorted. This wasn't a girl's room, there were hints of womanhood all over it. Midnight blue satin sheets on the bed and a little silky nightdress that matched them. Short skirts hung in the closet and there were killer high heels to set off the bottom that made his mouth water. Yeah, Christina had bid farewell to little girl things some time ago. Instead there were subtle cosmetics, delicate perfumes and hip-hugging thong panties.

Those things just made him look at her virginity with more respect. Shane clamped his control solidly in place over his raging cock. The damn thing was going to have to wait.

But he would have her. The scent of her climax was still on his fingers, the little sound she'd made as he brought her to that first peak echoing in his ears. They weren't a pair of kids who needed to play dating games.

No, they were two different genders that had circled each other in the most ancient of rituals. Maybe he was a harsh man, but Shane wasn't going to call it some soft, girlie-man name. He wanted to spread her thighs wide open right in the middle of her bed and let her feel his weight as he thrust into that tight pussy.

The water turned off in the shower making him grin. Christina wasn't a coward and that made him want her that much more.

She didn't have to do anything she didn't want to. Christina looked at her beaded nipples and considered the way her blush seemed to bleed all the way down her neck and over her breasts. Every sense seemed acute. She swore she could almost smell Shane in the next room. It was like she was tracking him with her senses. Her body going into some kind of surveillance mode to search for signs of her male.

But that didn't mean she was going to do anything that would land her in the clutches of despair tomorrow morning. Shane Jacobs had to be the worst man for her to decide she wanted so badly. The man didn't exist! He emerged from shadows and he walked through a world that had almost snuffed out her life.

But he'd come back to her. That was a fact her heart clung to. She didn't even have the means of placing a phone call to him but he'd shown up in her life without any invitation from her. The action spoke louder than any rule about how a man and woman ended up in bed together.

Need moved through her in a hot wave that melted every other thought. Her skin became a network of receptors that seemed to only function to transmit pleasure to her core. She wanted him, and that box of condoms on her nightstand told her Shane had planned to spend the night in her bed. A condom in a man's wallet would serve his lust when any available woman was at hand. The duffel bag told her Shane was planning on more than just a quick round of lust.

Flipping the water back on, she stepped back into the shower. If she was going to delve into the greatest mystery of life, there was one little detail she intended to see to first. A shadow moved into the doorway and she opened the glass door.

"Stay out there, Shane Jacobs! I'll shower at my own pace!"

* * * * *

His cock was still ramrod straight. Her eyes fastened onto the erection with amazement. The weapon hadn't slackened at all.

Christina shrugged and forced one foot onto the carpeting. She didn't know what she was doing, only that she'd regret not tasting this man completely before he left her life again.

"Drop the towel."

She batted her eyelashes instead. Shane blinked his eyes and looked again to make sure that was what he'd seen. He'd never seen a woman actually do that sort of thing. She trailed a single finger over the top of her towel and fluttered her lashes again.

"You mean this towel?" Her finger traveled over the swell of each breast as she looked at him far too innocently. "You know something, Shane Jacobs? Your mother should have taught you how to ask a lady for what you want." Her finger tapped the center of her bottom lip as she lowered her lashes and watched him through them. The pit of his stomach knotted with anticipation. She sucked just the very end of that finger between her lips making him groan.

"You see, Shane, I'm not too sure why I have to point this out to you, but I am not one of your men." She turned around and looked over her shoulder as she unhooked her towel and held the ends open. The blue terrycloth dipped lower across her back. "In fact, it's somewhat insulting that you haven't noticed I don't look anything like a man at all."

"I noticed, all right."

"There you go again." The towel went back around her body and she turned to show him that she'd tucked the ends back over each other. "Scowling and hollering at me. That's really no way to get what you want from a girl."

Her game restored her balance. Christina was suddenly having fun instead of shivering in pure response to the man. His eyes roamed over her body before he curled his lips back to show her his teeth. He looked every inch the commanding officer as he aimed his hard eyes at her.

"Lose the towel, now."

"Would you like to know a secret?" Her fingers lingered over the tucked edges of her towel as she fluttered her eyelashes again. Shane felt that knot in his stomach tighten.

"Sure."

"I shaved in the shower…everywhere."

"Please drop that Goddamn towel."

* * * * *

Gravity was his best friend. Christina plucked the end of her towel free and let it fall to her feet. His eyes targeted her mons and his mouth almost fell open.

Every last strand of golden hair was gone. Her cleft was open to his gaze as she stood and let him look his fill.

"You are so stunning, honey." It was more than her creamy skin. The relaxed look on her face made her the most beautiful creature on the planet. She was embracing their need for each other and simply enjoying her body. That was a confidence most women never found, the ability to accept who they were. It went beyond surface beauty and traveled into the deep attraction that took root in the soul.

No man had ever looked at her the way Shane did. He saw through her practiced responses and forced her to reveal her true nature to him. It was so very freeing in that moment. She was just a woman who was going to share her body with a man. Nervousness tried to sneak into her head but she resisted its lure. Instead she looked back into the hazel eyes that were filling with the heat of conquest. Shane Jacobs was done playing. He was ready to be fed.

He lifted one hand and beckoned to her with the crock of a single finger. "Come over here, honey."

It was less than a step but being asked made her smile. Her body shivered as she lifted one foot and stepped into his embrace. His hand cupped her chin and raised it to be inspected by his eyes.

"Relax, honey, I won't hurt you."

He tightened one arm around her waist and finished closing the gap between them. Her skin erupted with sensation as it meshed with his. The crisp hair covering his chest felt so right against her. He lifted her from the ground as his mouth covered hers. Christina lifted her arms to clasp the shoulders she'd spent so much time coveting. Her fingertips traced the ridges and ripples of hard muscle as Shane carried her to her bed.

Her back touched the sheets as his mouth pushed hers open in a deep kiss of intention. His hands slid down the sides of her body in a slow motion that began at her chest and curved along her waist and then out again over her hips. His body didn't follow her onto the bed. Instead his mouth lowered to her breasts as he sat back on his knees and used his grip on her hips to pull her toward him. Her thighs were forced to spread as she got closer to his body.

"Do you have idea how sexy a bare pussy is?"

If she hadn't she did now. His face almost frightened her with its intensity, dark and hard, his eyes focused on her spread body as his hands gripped her hips and held them exactly where he wanted her. But a rush of excitement hit her as she watched the way he looked her open sex. Her clit pulsed with need as she watched his sharp gaze center on the little bud.

The bed moved as he left it, slipped over the edge and knelt on the floor. His hands pulled her toward him again as his shoulders forced her legs to continue spreading even further apart.

"A bare pussy just begs to be eaten."

Her breath caught in her chest as his head dipped and that hot mouth covered her mons. Her hips bucked away from the bed as pleasure shot straight up into her womb. Shane held her in place as he pressed another kiss over her spread body. The tip of his tongue probed the folds of her sex as she twisted with the wave of pleasure.

His hand released her hips and stroked firmly over her belly. His mouth caught the top of her sex and sucked it, making her whimper. Every inch of her body was too hot! Sweat beaded on her forehead as she flung her arms above her head and clawed at the bedding. Her torso twisted as his mouth continued its torment.

His hand touched her mons and spread the two folds apart uncovering her little nub. Cool air hit the bundle of nerve endings, making her shiver. Her eyes popped open to watch Shane's head as he lowered his mouth to suck on her clit.

She cried out as pleasure split her in two. It was too tight and hot, everything twisting and tightening under the tip of his tongue. He drove her toward climax again as she moaned in a low voice that didn't even sound human.

Just as she began to shatter, his hand moved. His tongue still worried the nub controlling her pleasure but two thick fingers thrust deeply into her passage. The climax speared through her body with the penetration. Her hips gave a desperate surge upwards as he worked his fingers in and out of her body with her shudders.

"That's it, honey, ride it out."

His cock was painful as Shane pressed his fingers into the wet pussy it craved. He penetrated her body again as she lay gasping for breath. Her body clung to his fingers making his erection twitch in anticipation of the tight embrace. Instead he stood up and walked toward the nightstand.

Her eyes flew open as he left her. She could smell his male skin all around her. It was carried into her lungs with her labored breaths and seemed to transfuse through the membranes of her lungs right into her bloodstream. He moved back toward the bed and her eyes found the thrust of his hard cock. Her hand reached for the weapon from pure need. The raw gasp from his lips made her roll over and slide her hand all the way up his length.

His cock was hot against her palm, the skin stretched over its width. Pulling her hand back down, she moved her fingers over the swollen head of it. Fluid crowned the tip and she sat up to taste him.

"Oh God, Christina!" His hand fisted in her hair as she relaxed her jaw to open her mouth even further. She wanted to taste him exactly like he'd tasted her. She needed to apply the same pleasure to her partner and listen to him moan with a satisfaction that she incited.

"Christ, baby, that feels so damn good!"

She smiled around his cock as his hand cupped her head. His hips thrust forward as she stroked the skin with her tongue. A harsh sound came from his chest making her bolder. Rising onto her elbows, she used her hands to stroke the length she couldn't get into her mouth. His hips began to thrust toward her as his breath hissed between his clenched teeth.

Every girl's locker room whisper rose into her memory as she used her tongue to circle the head in her mouth. Her fingers worked up and down his cock as she relaxed and opened her mouth wider. His fingers twisted in her hair almost brutally as his hips jerked and thrust toward her face. A hot blast of fluid hit her tongue as his body became rigid.

Christina licked every last drop of his climax away, and she purred around his staff as triumph filled her. His hand relaxed as he dropped onto the bed with her, and pulling her against his body, he placed her head against his laboring chest. Low cussing rolled out between his breaths as the moonlight showed her his cock still thrusting forward with need. A shiver went through her passage as she considered the next place he would relieve that swollen rod.

"Where in the hell did you learn to suck a man off?"

She laughed at his temper. Shane threaded his fingers through her hair but couldn't move beyond that. His body was still jerking with pulses of pleasure. No virgin alive should be able to do that to a man's cock with her mouth!

"Girls talk, you know, and I didn't ask where you learned to do it because I can figure that out all by myself. Just because I haven't let anyone have sex with me doesn't mean I didn't find out exactly what went on during the event."

And she was proud of herself too. Shane felt his jealousy bleed away as he listened to the ring of accomplishment in her voice. The idea that she'd ever touched another man's cock with her sweet lips made him want to kill. But the fact that she'd taken the time to study sex made his cock twitch with anticipation.

Rolling onto his side, he pressed her down onto her back. Gently cupping a breast, he rolled the nipple and listened to her breathing increase.

"You're an 'A' student, honey."

Her body responded to him so completely. His hand moved between her breasts igniting that same burning flash of heat again. This time it was a slow wave that moved from her breast to her passage and grew stronger with each touch. It settled into her womb where it twisted into an ache that throbbed and begged for true satisfaction.

"I haven't touched another woman since I met you, honey." She shivered in his embrace. Shane stroked her bare body with a firm hand. "All I think about is you. Maybe your dad should take out his shotgun and run me off."

"He likes you."

"It would have been better if he didn't." He caught her jaw and forced her to look at him while indecision crossed his face. "The last time our lives got mixed up you ended up in a pool of your own blood." His fingers stroked down her neck to the scar just below her collarbone.

"Roshelle seems to be doing just fine."

"Roshelle is a psychic. You saw what happens to psychics that aren't protected."

She didn't like the wall he was building with his words. Their bodies were bare and tangled together but he was laying a solid foundation for separating them. They hadn't shared enough of each other yet. Her body drew into a knot of tension as she considered the idea that he might leave her without completing what he'd started.

"Are you leaving now?"

His jaw tightened as she curled her fingers around his cock. The hard flesh twitched against her palm as her passage sent up a plea for the hard thrust of it within her.

"No, honey, I was just waiting for you to relax a little more. You won't be leaving this bed as a virgin."

His rose onto an elbow and pressed her back against the bed. His mouth landed on hers as he pushed her lips apart with a tongue that thrust deeply into her depths. Her body didn't seem to care about anything except the heat that flared between them.

So she wouldn't let her mind worry either.

Chapter Five

He was stealing time. Shane caught the renewed scent of her arousal and just didn't give a damn about anything else. He'd always known that his life wasn't one that a guy offered to share with a girl like Christina. Fate had dumped her in his lap and now he just couldn't let her go.

At least not yet. The last of his control was shredding as he looked over the body next to him. His senses were so full of her. He seemed aware of even the tempo of her heart rate. Her hips slowly gyrated as he found her slit and rubbed the little nub at the top of her mons.

The whimper that came from her lips set his blood pounding through his brain.

The condom he'd taken out of its foil was lying behind him on the bed. Grabbing the latex sheath, he applied it to his cock. The thin barrier was his only concession to the future.

He rolled over her body. Christina felt her thighs rise and grip his hips from some primitive instinct. Her pelvis tipped up as she felt the first blunt probing of her body. The hard head of his cock pressed past the folds protecting her passage but he held in place instead of giving her the deep penetration her body craved.

"Easy, baby, there's no hurry."

Her hips twitched but he wouldn't let her raise them to deepen their connection. Instead he reached between their bodies to gently stroke her little clit. Pleasure shot out from the touch making more fluid flow toward his entry.

The hard flesh stretching her body throbbed and twitched as her hips jerked with the deep need for friction. Her fingers had curled into claws on his biceps. She gasped as she felt the tiny seep of blood around her fingernails. His chest rumbled with amusement as his hips flexed and sent his rod further into her again.

"Claw me, honey. Let the pain loose." His hips flexed again and again as he deepened his penetration. "Just take me slow and easy."

Her body was twisting into a single flame that seemed to burn them both. She surged up to meet the thrust of his body and strained to take his length even deeper.

Sweat beaded on his forehead as her little moans tried to break the last bit of civilized thought in him. His hands fisted in the bedding as he slid his cock into her body. She was so wet he moved easily into her sheath, pushing his length back and forth within her. She thrashed beneath his body as her pussy suddenly gripped and milked his rod. Climax tightened her body so hard he exploded again and again as the muscles of her body pulled and contracted around his cock. Pleasure slammed into his brain as a harsh cry came from her lips.

Shane rolled onto his back taking her body with him. She lay completely on top of him as he tried to fill his lungs with enough oxygen to feed his pounding heart. The flutter of her heart hit his chest as he stroked the length of her back. They were still locked together. His cock still gripped within the tight walls of her pussy while her thighs still clung to his hips. Shane gently rubbed the cheeks of her bottom and the top of her bare thighs as he lifted her off him.

Pleasure rippled through her as she found herself listening to the beat of Shane's heart. The deep sound seemed almost hypnotic as her head began to emerge from the mist of sensation surrounding it. Every muscle she had was loose and relaxed. Sleep simmered like a shining reward. Shane rolled her over and gently controlled her descent to the mattress. His huge body surrounded and tangled with hers as her brain refused to function any further. One of those strong hands of his stroked along her hip and over her thigh making her skin hum with delight. The warm male scent of his skin lured her away into slumber as she felt truly protected for the first time since leaving his home.

Shane brushed the tangled hair back from her face and listened to her breathing lengthen and deepen. He softly cussed as his cock twitched and complained about her need for sleep. Rolling away from her sleeping body he stood up and walked silently to the bathroom. Tossing the used condom into the trash can Shane stepped into the shower for exactly three minutes. A quick swipe of a towel and he went back to his sleeping companion.

He wasn't tired, instead he was captivated by the delicate shape of her body next to his instead of just a dream. Pure enjoyment poured through his thoughts as he was able to stroke and touch her at will. Moonlight spilled over her body granting him the view of her feminine curves and mounds. Nothing intruded and he found himself listening to her breathing like the most peaceful sound his ears had ever heard.

* * * * *

Morning wasn't kind. Christina stretched and gasped as her body bitterly complained. Every muscle she had seemed to be strained so she simply froze in place as she lifted her eyelids.

Sunlight lit the room and the arm lying over her waist. She stared at the overly large and very obviously male hand as her face filled with heat. All the covers were kicked off but Shane's body heat was amazing. Just his body lying next to her was plenty of heat to keep her warm.

Her bed was filled to its capacity by her company. Only a double-sized mattress, Shane took up most of the bed and she was curled on her side just a few inches from the edge. Her bedside table caught her attention as she looked at the box of condoms sitting there. The thing was open and one foil package lay on the whitewashed wooden surface, empty of its product. The coal black butt of a pistol lay right next to it.

She stared at the blunt reminder of what Shane was, in the form of that weapon. It wasn't any small caliber handgun, instead the thing was oversized just like the hand of the man that owned it. It was polished to a blue-black shine and she would just bet there was a bullet in the chamber.

"Never touch my sidearm unless I'm dead."

"I wasn't planning on it."

The hand around her waist moved to cup her breast as Shane rolled over and his body curled along her back.

The blunt thrust of his cock made her breath lodge in her throat. His fingers began gently pinching her nipple as one of his legs nudged its way between her thighs. Heat flowed between her breast and her belly as he cupped her breast again. His mouth found the column of her neck and gently bit it.

"Hum… Good morning to you too."

He laughed against her neck and bit her again. The leg between her thighs moved and rose, parting her legs for the length of his cock. The hard head of his erection found the entrance to her body and slipped gently into her.

"I can smell you. Did you know that? Knowing your pussy is wet makes me a little crazy."

Her passage was flooding for him too, the fluid slipping down the walls of her body as he pressed his rod deeper into her. Her bottom lifted instinctively. The woman in her wanted to be exactly where she was.

No one ever talked to her with those kinds of words. She should have been mad to hear him call a part of her body a word like pussy. Instead it sent another jolt of fire shooting toward her passage and the hard intruder thrusting into her.

Maybe the language was just part of the difference between the boys she'd dated and the man who was lying in her bed.

"Am I hurting you too badly?"

Her bottom lifted toward his next thrust without conscious thought. Her body groaned but yearned for him at the same time. That knot of tension was twisting in her womb once again as she tried to move their pace faster.

His hands gripped her hips and kept them in place, her body screamed for the liberty to move but she was held still with his huge erection deeply inside her.

"Answer me."

Admitting her need in spoken words seemed almost too exposing. Her pride battled with her body as Shane refused to grant her any motion until she answered.

"I'm fine."

She snapped the words and it made him mad. Shane clapped his hands over her hips and denied his own desire. He wanted to hear her say it.

"And you want what, honey?" Shane nipped her ear before trailing soft kisses over her cheek. Her body trembled as he refused to release her hips. The walls of her pussy began to grip and tighten around his cock. It was a sweet torture that tested his will. Pulling out of her body, he thrust deeply into her and grinned at the little moan that escaped her lips. Lodged deeply inside her body, he once again held her hips solidly in place.

"I hear some women like to be the ones calling the shots in bed. Just tell me what your sweet little body would like or I could just wait right here for you to think about it."

Oh God, she couldn't survive that. The thick length of his rod was throbbing in her body. She needed it to move so badly. Every nerve ending seemed to be poised on that connection between their flesh.

"I just need you, Shane."

His hips jerked and thrust into her. She purred with delight as he stretched and deepened the penetration. One of his hands slipped over her hip and found the little nub at the top of her sex. Pleasure spiked through her as he rubbed that sensitive bud and thrust deeply into her body at the same time.

"That's it, isn't it, honey?" His hips flexed and his finger rubbed harder. Her hands clawed the sheets as his breath became harsh and cut with his approaching climax.

"Come for me! I want to feel that little pussy milking me again."

She didn't have any choice. Her body erupted into pleasure so tight it made her yell. A hard grunt hit her ear as his hand gripped her hip and held it in place for a deeper thrust. He shuddered inside her as she felt her body pulling on his length but the deepest desire wasn't fed. Her womb felt the climax and lamented the lack of his seed hitting it. She looked over her shoulder to see a second box of condoms on the other bedside table. She hadn't even noticed him slipping the thing on.

Turning her head slightly, she noticed there was a second box of condoms on the opposite bedside table. A hand stroked her face as he rose up onto an elbow to look into her eyes.

"I'll leave the damn things off but you have to accept one thing about that."

His face fell into a solid mask of stone as his eyes cut into hers.

"I fill your belly and you belong to me, forever."

Chapter Six

She was turning into a jellyfish. Christina gave in to the urge to snort with her frustration because the sound of her shower would cover it.

His? Forever? Sex had damaged her brain! A silly little thrill of excitement had raced through her at those barbarian words. She wasn't some cavewoman and shouldn't delight at the idea of being dragged home like a prize kill.

Relationships should be comfortable and open to discussion. She snorted again. Yeah, right! Shane Jacobs didn't have the word negotiation in his vocabulary.

Yes, but you liked the way he took over.

She didn't like that fact but couldn't exactly lie to herself. It was like he'd unlocked some secret door and found the control to her passion. Sex just wasn't that intense normally, it couldn't be. If it was, she'd have jumped into bed with half the boys who'd chased her. She had never felt her body erupt into lawless disorder, but it had last night.

Her face was flaming as she stepped out of the shower. Not sure where Shane had gone was making the hairs on the back of her neck stand up. He was not the sort of man you wanted sneaking up behind you.

A low whistle came from the hallway. Her lips twisted into a crooked grin as she turned to see Shane leaning against the top of the stairs. His face told her he'd been watching the doorway for her.

That same silly thrill crossed her mind as she noticed the fact that his duffel bag was still in the corner of her room. Somehow, the idea that he hadn't disappeared once he'd gotten what he wanted made her want to smile and think a little more about that forever idea he'd planted in her imagination.

Yup, brain damage for sure.

"Hungry?"

"A little."

He frowned at her response. Shane pushed his frame away from the wall and walked toward her. His eyes moved over her in a precise assessment of her body.

"You need to eat more. Are you on one of those stupid trend diets?"

"Excuse me, but my eating habits are just fine and there is nothing stupid about watching my weight."

His face told her otherwise. He reached for her hand and captured it. He pulled her behind him as he went down the stairs and headed toward the back of the store.

"You've lost weight since you were with me last." He pulled her out the back door and turned around to lock it. He pushed her ring of keys into his pocket before aiming his sharp eyes back at her. "You're thin and that is definitely my concern."

"Since when?"

That was a good question. One Shane wasn't sure he was ready to answer. Instead he pulled her after him as he moved to the place he'd parked his Hummer.

He sent her door closed with a slam as she raised an eyebrow at him. Communication definitely wasn't one of the man's charms. Her stomach grumbled, making her giggle. Lunch did sound good after all.

* * * * *

"You are a barbarian."

Shane grinned and displayed an even row of teeth in response. His eyebrow twitched up as he looked across the table at her. "Maybe I'm just a real bad boy."

"I think you're past the spanking stage."

A low rumble of amusement shook his chest before he leaned across the table and lowered his voice for his next comment. "Spanking does have its stages, you know. First when it's used to punish a child and then when it turns into a woman's bedtime fantasy. Maybe we should see if you've entered your second one yet."

"You are not going to spank me."

He pressed his lips together and sent her a kiss in response. "Then maybe you shouldn't look so excited by the idea."

Her cheeks were burning but it was temper. Christina glared at him but the waitress appeared to refill his coffee mug. Loving couples did not spank one another! Well, somehow she got the idea that Shane wasn't planning on being on the receiving ending of any paddling, but still! What kind of man spanked his girlfriend?

Her eyes went wide as she applied that word to them. She'd labeled him a barbarian because everyone in the diner was watching them and Shane made sure they had something to witness too. He caught her hand and sent her dark looks of longing that even a nun couldn't miss.

"My lucky day, two friends to have lunch with."

Sheriff Brice Campbell lowered his body into the booth right next to her as Christina stared at the man in shock. His brown eyes considered her with the same sharp movements that Shane always used. The waitress appeared with a lunch plate already cooked and sat it in front of him.

"Heard your folks were out of Benton for a spell. Any trouble around the shop?" Brice Campbell kept his eyes on her as he waited for a response. The question sounded so benign but it wasn't. The sheriff was part of that dark, shadow-breeding world that Shane belonged to. His wife was some kind of high-level psychic and Shane's father was her bodyguard.

The sheriff was just another reminder of the constant surveillance she was under but his face wasn't unkind. In fact, there was the firm authority of a parent lurking in his brown eyes. Her own father couldn't have done anything to protect her from a man like Shane, but Brice could.

"Everything's fine, thank you."

He nodded and looked across the table at Shane. "Nice to see you in town."

Shane lifted his mug and watched the sheriff over its rim. Christina got the impression that any other man would have been sent packing but Brice Campbell had the edge of respect from Shane. They glared at each other in a male battle of wills before the sheriff lifted his fork and pointed it at Shane.

"Relax, son, there are a few parts of my job I take seriously."

The protective manner of both men rubbed her pride. They both had just decided to look after her and nothing she had to say was going to change that fact. She pushed her half-eaten meal away because her stomach was suddenly too knotted to eat anything else.

Shane pushed it back in front of her. "Eat."

She would have laughed but the sheriff's eyes suddenly inspected her arm before he nodded his head with approval. "I hope you're not following this new fashion trend of looking half-starved."

"I don't stuff myself just to please some male idea of how much food is enough for me."

Brice inspected her, his eyes making her temper simmer.

"You've lost weight."

"All right! Fine, so what?"

Brice grinned at her before wiggling his eyebrows at her. "So, maybe you need a little more exercise to stimulate that appetite. Shane should have some good ideas for you."

She snorted and didn't care who heard the unladylike sound! Shane and Brice grinned like a pair of jackals before she borrowed one of Roshelle's favorite sayings.

Lifting her hand, she waved it in front of her face. "The testosterone fumes are nearing toxic levels."

* * * * *

"Wrong."

Most men never argued with that tone of his voice. Women normally retreated. Christina stood and folded her arms across her chest and faced off with him. Shane couldn't help but be impressed.

"You are the one who's wrong, Shane Jacobs."

She always used his surname when she was mad at him. Shane grinned as he recorded the detail and stored it in his brain.

"I told Mick I'd do the job, I'm going to work."

"My woman isn't serving in a bar."

"Who said I'm your woman?"

His eyes erupted with rage. Christina stood firmly in her place. Maybe she'd said that just to see what would happen. Shane stretched his hands out and looked ready to kill.

"I didn't ask you to break your word, Shane. Mick wouldn't have asked me if he didn't need the extra pair of hands. Besides, you didn't exactly tell me you were going to show up. I told him I'd be there." That brought him up short. His eyes turned somber as he considered the set look on her face.

"Besides, you're treating me like a toy. You can't just show up and play with me at your whim. I didn't ask you to toss that cell phone on your hip out the window so stop acting like my commitment isn't worth spit."

"All right, honey, you've got a point." His hand gripped her jaw as he placed a hard kiss over her mouth. He pushed right through her lips to stroke the length of her tongue. Her nipples tightened immediately as she kissed him back.

"But I'll be here when you get back."

* * * * *

She had to stop thinking about his promise. Actually, it had been more like an order but that just made her smile. Orders and Shane went together like a pair of shoes. That sneaky little voice in her head tried to suggest that she and Shane matched up like shoes as well.

Christina sighed and tried to drop her thoughts. Instead she found her eyes watching the clock because she had to know if he'd keep his word. Going home had never seemed so important before. Sure, she loved her parents and before her kidnapping, the end of the workday was met with joy, but this was vastly different. She wanted to go home to Shane. Details didn't seem to matter a bit as she felt the unmistakable rise of heat in her passage. She hadn't realized how much she'd missed him. Maybe that was why she hadn't really pushed for her independence back from her parents. She had been living in a haze of undefined emotions that still had strings running back to Shane.

Time suddenly became more precious than gold. The moments that you got to share with those you loved were the most valuable passions you could ever have. Her kidnapping had taught her that lesson. She and Roshelle had clung to life as they fought to live just one more day. She'd lain at Shane's feet in her own blood and made that bet with him just to make him think she was willing to fight to see the next sunrise.

So tonight he would be waiting for her and tomorrow he would be gone. Each minute remaining sparkled like a diamond as she looked at the harsh reality of their coming separation. Shane would return to his men and the worst part about that was the idea that he wouldn't even bother to ask her to go with him.

Turning on her heel she looked at the time. She would just worry about a broken heart later! Tonight she was going home to make some more memories to fuel her dreams.

* * * * *

She came home early. Shane watched her walk out of The Pit two full hours before she had the night before. People still milled around the pool tables but she sent Mick a wave and began her walk home.

She was coming to him. Shane couldn't suppress the emotion that filled his chest in response. He had no clue what he was doing coming after her like he was, only that he just couldn't resist the opening her parents' trip had provided him.

He wasn't sorry either, keeping pace with her he watched the little skirt bounce with her steps. His cock filled with raging need to get back into her tight pussy. It was a basic and maybe even crude reaction to her but it went deeper than just fucking. He wanted her, the sassy and soft civilian that was the very definition of off-limits to him.

* * * * *

A heavy step behind her made her spin around. Shane sent her a cocky grin and lifted his arm to defend against any punches she might launch at him.

"You didn't really think I'd let you walk home alone."

That was just a flat statement. The truth was, she hadn't even considered it but she should have. Shane didn't forget the details. His fingers stroked the side of her face as he considered her in the dark.

"You came home early." His expression was hidden but his voice was low and husky.

"Yes." Simple and straight, she didn't want to worry about words, all she wanted was to feel him once more. He stepped closer and the warm scent of his skin touched her senses. Her body instantly recognized it. Heat flowed over her skin and down to her belly.

"Why?"

In answer, Christina laid her hands on his wide chest. His breath turned harsh as she moved her hands over the ridges of his pectoral muscles and down over his abdomen. Her entire body seemed to hum with approval for his. It was more than prime conditioning, it included his stubborn commanding attitude and the blunt, frontal approach he always used to get what he wanted.

Shane pushed the door of her dad's shop open and pulled her inside with him. The door swung back shut and they both became shadows merging into a single form. His lips brushed her neck and as his fingers threaded through her hair, he leaned forward and inhaled the scent of her blonde curls before aiming his glittering eyes at her.

"Why, Christina?"

The man never gave up. Christina refused to listen to her pride as it ordered her to keep her feelings buried. "You said you'd be here."

Her words cut deep. Shane felt his own hands shake before catching her mouth in a hard kiss. He didn't want to hear anything that would give him a reason to hold onto her. Desperation drove him to deepen the kiss. Her mouth yielded and her body pressed toward his. That soft female form that soothed the hard edges of his own.

Hard little nipples dug into his chest as the scent of her pussy reached his nose. Need shot through him as restraint retreated at full force. She twisted in his embrace as one small hand boldly rubbed his cock.

Christina couldn't help herself and she didn't want to! What she wanted was him. She filled her hand with the swollen erection being held by his pants. Her body was already moist and wet in anticipation of being once again impaled on the weapon. Her fingers found a button and pulled on it. A little pop hit her ears making her search out another one to open.

His swollen cock fell out into her hand the second she opened the last button. The thing pulsed in her hands as she gripped its width. Shane lifted his head and sucked in a huge gasp of air between clenched teeth as she stroked his length.

His hands suddenly slipped up her thigh to the little elastic straps of her panties. One sharp tug and he snapped them at the hips. He dropped the ruined garment and cupped her bottom in his hands. Her feet left the floor as he lifted her up and placed her back against the wall. His hips spread her thighs as her body opened and the tip of his erection nudged its way toward her passage.

"Hold on to me, honey."

"Yes, Sir."

He growled at her response and thrust up into her body. She clung to his shoulders as her passage stretched and he lifted her even higher. His next thrust penetrated deeper, making her moan as pleasure shot into her womb. His movements were hard and deep. His hands held her in place for the deep penetrating thrust of his body.

He couldn't stop. She was too damn wet and his cock too hard to slow down. He felt the first twinge of climax nipping at his cock and slammed into her body harder. She moaned and dug her fingers into his shoulders. His next thrust was just as hard and she gasped as her pussy tried to grip his length.

"Come for me, baby. Now."

She did. Her body tumbled into climax as he slammed his length up into her with a force that shook the wall behind her. Pleasure exploded in her womb as the hot spurt of his seed hit her center. Her body clamped around him and greedily tried to extract even more.

He cussed low and hard as his brain managed to get a single thought through his skull. His climax had been so hard he was practically dizzy and grateful for the wall behind them. She lifted her head from his shoulder as his profanity hit her ears.

"If you become pregnant..."

"I'll have my baby." Her words were soft but firmly spoken. Her lips touched his with a gentle kiss as she wiggled her bottom against the hard surface behind her.

The length still lodged inside her body twitched in response. Shane glared at her but she refused to look away. "One of my reasons for waiting was the fact that no birth control is foolproof, Shane. A woman should think long and hard about a man before she takes the chance of having his child. So save your cussing for your men, I could have gone to my cousin's house for the night."

Instead she came to him. That humbled him. Her thighs wrapped around his hips made him shake his head with the pure gift she was giving him. Lifting her off his cock, he cradled her against his chest as he turned toward the stairs and her bed.

The night seemed far too short.

Chapter Seven

The bed was empty. Christine shoved the comforter away and looked around her room. Shane's gear was missing. She blinked her eyes and look at the corner where the army duffel bag had sat and found nothing but the wall staring back at her.

Jumping to her feet, she grabbed her clothing and jerked it on. She took the stairs at a breakneck speed on bare feet and slid to a halt as she found Shane standing by the back door. He was leaning against the doorframe watching the stairs and obviously waiting for her.

He looked so foreign to her. Head to toe he was dressed like the oversized action figure she'd first labeled him. Twin press marks went down his chest and his belt was buckled over his fatigue pants. His pistol was resting against his thigh. She searched his face for any hint of the man who had been her lover. His lips twitched up just slightly in response as he stood up and stepped forward.

His hands cupped her head, holding it in place. His mouth took a sip from her lips before slipping over their surface and parting them. He turned her head as his lips coaxed her to open her mouth for him. The tip of his tongue slipped in to join hers as she yielded and took the hot taste he offered her. Her hand lifted to his shoulders and smoothed over the fabric of his shirt. The green and brown camouflage garment seemed so foreign to hands that had spent an endless day free to roam over his skin.

She sighed as he lifted his head and ran his hands down her neck. Goose bumps rose all over her skin making her smile. Shane lifted one of her hands and gently bit the skin on the underside of her wrist. A little purr of delight came from her as another, deeper shiver traveled over her body. The sharp pressed lines running down his crisp shirt made her push her lip into a pout.

"I want to tell you something." His hand cupped the side of her head again. His eyes were somber as they looked into hers. "I want you to remember this one thing, honey. I love you."

Christina felt the blood drain from her face. The words weren't said in a joyful voice. Instead, his face had taken on its military mask of blankness as his voice became the steady firm commanding one she remembered too well.

"I don't live here, Christina. Not here in this world with you. It's time for me to go back."

He wasn't coming back to see her either! She saw it written in his eyes. The mask on his face was impenetrable. Not even the hint of an emotion rippled across it.

"Shane…"

His thumb closed her jaw. Her teeth snapped together as he held her jaw shut and her eyes locked with his. It was another one of those holds that just drove home how deadly he could be. His thumb applied just a small amount of pressure to an area that seemed completely vulnerable and she had never known it was.

"Remember that I loved you enough to walk away from you, honey."

Her head was suddenly free as he lifted one hand in his. There was a small click before he released her completely and turned toward the door. He grasped his duffel bag and was out the door in the same second he'd opened it. She surged forward to follow him but was jerked to a halt by her wrist. Looking behind her she saw the shine of a handcuff around her wrist. It bound her to the checkout counter as the door shut with a slam that shattered her heart.

He was leaving her.

It felt like half of her body was being torn away. Pain coursed through a body that only seconds earlier had rejoiced under his touch. His scent still clung to her skin, the taste of his kiss still lingering on her lips. She felt like screaming as she frantically jerked on the handcuffs. The metal bracelet cut into her wrist as an engine turned over and she listened to the Hummer drive away.

Shane wouldn't look back. She knew it in the center of her heart. He was a man who stuck to his decisions no matter the cost. But he had never lied to her.

Christina collapsed against the counter as her eyes refused to contain the tears that slipped down her cheeks. Shane had been painfully honest with her. He didn't live in her world and he had never intended to stay.

She wiped her tears away and straightened her back. Shane hadn't treated her like a child and she certainly wasn't going to stand there acting like one! Her parents were going to walk through the door in ten minutes and she didn't need them to witness her breakdown.

Her eyes looked at her wrist and tried to figure out how to get unhitched from the counter. It was a solid connection. Shane had cuffed the metal railing with one side of the manacles and the other was secure around her wrist. No cheap imitation handcuffs either, they looked like heavy-duty ones. Even the links between the cuffs were large and double-welded.

Great.

Her eyes moved over the counter looking for help in any form. A small brown box sat just within her reach, opposite the door. Reaching for it she pulled it across the counter to look at its lid. Her name was written on the top and it was simply tucked into itself.

Well, of course he'd made it easy to open. He'd planned to handcuff her to the counter. She lifted the lid. A small silver key lay over a single piece of paper. Lifting the key she fit it into the lock and ended her imprisonment. The note was curled from the weight of the key but she didn't have to lift it in order to read it.

"And if you love me enough, follow me."

The message didn't make any sense. She pulled it out of the box to look closer. She froze at what she found. In the bottom of the cardboard box was a small velvet jewelry box.

Her fingers shook as she picked it up. The soft velvet tickled her palm as she opened the lid. The white brilliance of a diamond flashed at her as she revealed a single stone, solitaire engagement ring. The stone had to be over two carats and was cut in a marquise-shape. A tiny note was taped under the ring.

Sunday 1400 hrs.

It's a one way trip, honey.

That was less than a week away! Oh God, it was almost forever! She pulled the ring from its velvet and pushed it down her finger. It fit her perfectly, making her smile. Shane certainly was a man who got the details right.

The front door suddenly swung in as her mother bustled into the room.

"There you are! Christina! Why didn't you tell me? Honestly! There is so much to do! One week? Who plans a wedding in one week?"

"Stop fussing at the girl, Terry. One week is plenty! Shane's a military man, he hasn't got time for nonsense. There's only one church in town and they already booked it. Go get the girl a dress and order some flowers. I'm sure Mick can handle the drinks."

Her mother ran off to the stairs as she continued to lament the lack of time. Her father stopped and pointed to his cheek. Christina gave him his kiss as she curled her fingers around her engagement ring.

One week was horribly too long!

* * * * *

Little girls fantasized about the wrong things. Christina stood in the open door that lead to the sanctuary of Benton's church and stared at the man waiting for her. Yes, little girls dreamed about their wedding dress and the flowers and the dresses they would insist their girlfriends wore.

What was really worth dreaming about was the man standing at the front of the aisle. Shane Jacobs wore his dress uniform. A smile covered her face as she realized that was exactly the most perfect thing he could ever wear. It defined him, almost looked like a refection of his soul.

Her dad looked ready to burst as he took her toward the man he fully approved of. Roshelle stood waiting to witness the wedding that would unite not only a couple in wedlock but a pair of friends separated by adulthood. Roshelle's new husband, Jared Campbell, stood behind Shane as her father handed her over.

The words spoken weren't really needed, the man standing there with her said everything she needed to know with his eyes. The message went straight to her heart and settled there.

Turning around she looked at the church. The faces that stared back at her were ones that most of Benton had rarely laid eyes on. Sheriff Campbell stood with a green-eyed woman that few knew was his wife. There were more uniforms in the pews than not. Rourke Campbell stood with his brother and winked at her.

It was a family. Their habits might be different but they were all bound by the common thread of love. Life could be carried out in so many different ways, right there civilian and military stood together for a single moment of life-changing action. A one-way trip? If she was lucky, Shane would keep that promise and never let her go.

The second the minister finished, Shane bent her over his arm to the delight of the men in the chapel. He winked at her as he took off down the aisle at a near run. Christina ran after her husband as his men leaned over the pews to swat her bottom.

She picked her feet up faster and doubled her pace. After all, life was too short to be slow!

About the Author

I write to reassure myself that reality really is survivable. Between traffic jams and children's sporting schedules, there is romance lurking for anyone with the imagination to find it.

I spend my days making corsets and petticoats as a historical costumer. If you send me an invitation marked formal dress, you'd better give a date or I just might show up wearing my bustle.

I love to read a good romance and with the completion of my first novel, I've discovered I am addicted to writing these stories as well.

Dream big or you might never get beyond your front yard.

I love to hear what you think of my writing: Talk2MaryWine@hotmail.com.

Mary welcomes comments from readers. You can find her website and email address on her author bio page at www.ellorascave.com.

Tell Us What You Think

We appreciate hearing reader opinions about our books. You can email us at Comments@EllorasCave.com.

Also by Mary Wine

Beyond Boundaries

Dream Shadow

Dream Specter

Ellora's Cavemen: Tales from the Temple III (*anthology*)

Alcandian Quest

Beyond Lust

Tortoise Tango

COWBOY AND THE THEIF

Lora Leigh

Dedication

The Ladies of the Forum.
Here's your Cowboy.

Chapter One

Sometimes, women just amazed him, Jack Riley thought pensively as he hid in the shadows of his ranch house and watched the cute, little bit of nothing slip through the opened living room window.

They shouldn't, not anymore, but he had to admit he hadn't really expected her to keep her very rash promise. Especially considering the fact that her daddy knew damned well what she would be getting herself into if he caught her.

Let your daughter even attempt to steal what's mine, Manning, and I'll show her a party she'll never fucking forget.

Manning hadn't appeared too worried.

A smiled slowly curved his lips as she pulled herself into the house, her long black hair secured in a tight braid, her rounded little body poised cautiously like a doe in hunting season. Damn, she made his cock hard. Even during a spot of breaking and entering, pissing him off in the worst way, she turned him on.

Angel Manning. Why anyone would name that bundle of fire and energy Angel, he had no idea. One look into those dark violet eyes, the first glimpse of wild, impetuous passion in her gaze, and it wasn't angels you were thinking about. It was wild steamy sex. Hot, naked, sweaty bodies tangled together as feminine cries of tortured pleasure echoed around your ears. That's what you thought about when you saw Angel. Hard, deep fucking. Watching her eyes widen, her body arch, the soft folds of her sweet little pussy stretching open as he impaled her with his steel-hard dick. That's what hit his mind.

He stood silent, motionless as she looked around the dimly lit room, obviously searching for the lights. Lights that weren't going to work for her. He had thrown the breaker the minute he realized someone was attempting to break in. God only knew who it could be. He had made several enemies over the past few years, none of whom he wanted to meet up with in a dark alley, or his normally well-lit home.

Now, he only shook his head mentally. He was going to have to remind her that cat burglars did not turn on the lights. It was an arrest waiting to be made.

He may not have been expecting Angel, but damned if he didn't know what to do with her now that she was here. Jack wasn't a fool, and he knew she wasn't averse to his touch. But how easily would she settle into the more perverted hungers he could unleash on her? It might not be easy for her, he thought in satisfaction, but she would do it. He knew her, and knew jail wasn't an option for her.

He watched as she pushed her hand into the small satchel she wore at her hip. A second later, he ducked as a beam of light swept across the room.

"Of course, he couldn't just make it easy for me. Dammit." Her voice was faintly accented, the soft Irish cadence stroking his flesh like a physical touch. He couldn't wait to hear her screaming his name.

No, he wasn't going to make anything easy for her. She had made certain of that the minute she attempted to steal from him. It didn't matter that she likely considered what he held hers. He had bought it in a fair deal and though it meant little to him, Jack kept what he considered his. It was a lesson he had learned during a particularly nasty episode years ago. When a man faced death, things changed inside him, whether he wanted them to or not.

He shifted carefully, staying hidden in the corner, moving a bit to the left as the beam of light came too close. His naturally blond hair was covered by a dark, woolen cap. Blond hair was like a beacon in the dark and he wanted to hide, not make a target of himself.

She checked the room carefully before proceeding through the rest of the house. Jack stood back quietly and let her have at it, knowing there wasn't a chance she was going to find what she was looking for. He would let her look, though. Sooner or later she would have to head upstairs. When she did, he would make certain he was right behind her.

He shook his head, though, thinking it shouldn't be so easy. He had actually been considering flying back to Ireland, his prized torque in hand to offer her, for the chance of bedding her. It wasn't as if prize Irish antiquities were his passion or anything. He had just particularly liked the piece when Manning had offered it to him. The gold and silver neckband had piqued his curiosity, but nothing more. Until Angel had demanded that he refuse it. Furious. Commanding. She had stared up at him with those raging violet eyes and informed him in no uncertain terms that he had no right to it. That he was in no way good enough to possess it.

He had bought it then and there without even haggling over the price.

Now, the pretty little sprite was out to steal it back. He would have chuckled if she weren't within hearing distance, cursing like a sailor and heaping insults on his ancestors. Damn, she had fire in her. A fire he was anticipating tapping quite soon.

Finally, he heard her near the stairs, her soft footfalls moving to the upper story before he moved. He stayed well behind her, moving up the staircase as she disappeared into the first bedroom. It would take her several minutes to check it well, which gave him plenty of time to slip past the closed door and to his own room.

It was in his room that the torque rested, still packed in his luggage, nearly forgotten amid the rush and bustle of ranch life after he returned home. His partner, Luc Jardin, had sold the last of the Clydesdale horses and taken up training mustangs for rodeos. The man was as mercurial as spring. The business seemed to change with the seasons where he and his new wife Melina were concerned. Not that they didn't make money. They did. But Jack never seemed to be certain if he was selling Clydesdales, mustangs, cattle or dry Texas dust.

"Men should be neutered." The soft voice approached his bedroom as Jack flattened himself against the wall. "Riley should be neutered. Too much testosterone making decisions for him."

Her soft mutterings were amusing, if insulting. He shook his head, watching as the bedroom door opened, the little penlight sweeping out in front of her as she stepped into the room.

Jack moved then. Silently, swiftly, he slid across the distance, coming behind her, his arms going around her, one hand locking at her throat as a frightened gasp left her lips.

"Testosterone can come in real handy at times, little girl." He pressed his hips against hers, grinding his erection against her lower back as his lips lowered to her ear, his teeth nipping at the silken lobe as he felt her tense in his hold. "Especially when it comes to punishing pesky little kitten burglars with smart mouths."

Oh hell! Angel stilled, tensed, feeling the thick wedge of Jack's erection pressing into the small of her back as his big hand circled her throat. And she should have been frightened. She should have been terrified and fighting for her life and she would have been, if she didn't know him so well. He was undoubtedly going to piss her off, but he wasn't going to hurt her. He wasn't going to let her go either—the snug hold he had on her assured her of that.

"You're a goon, Jack," she snapped as her hands rose to the fingers locked on her throat.

The position tilted her head back, angling her head on his shoulder as his teeth played at her ear, sending shivers of pleasure racing over her flesh. And the sensation wasn't one she wanted to feel right now. She didn't want to become aroused, weak with curious arousal when she knew the man holding her wasn't the keeping kind.

"Oh, it's goon now?" he purred at her ear. "Not nearly as brave as you were moments ago, are you, sweet thing? I think the last insult I heard in Ireland was much better. Stinking dirty cowboy with an attitude," he snorted. "I do not stink, Angel-mine."

Angel-mine. He had called her that every time he caught her away from her father on the Manning estate in Ireland. The possessive tone sent small flutters of pleasure attacking her stomach as an insidious weakness attacked her limbs. Just as it did now.

"I told you not to call me that," she retorted through gritted teeth as she strained against his hold. "Now let me go, dammit."

"Oh, I don't think I want to let you go, little Angel," he crooned at her ear, his tongue licking playfully at her lobe as an unbidden shudder raced through her body. "You've been a very bad girl. Stealing is against the law here, you know. Maybe we should give the sheriff a call."

Her eyes widened. He wouldn't. Surely, he wouldn't dare call the sheriff. If she was arrested for breaking and entering and attempted theft, it would ruin her father. Not to mention what it would do to her. She would lose everything she had worked for in the past six years.

"You wouldn't dare!" she gasped, unable to hold back the shocking thought that he would indeed.

"That's what we do in America, Angel-mine." His fingers stroked her throat as his teeth raked the sensitive flesh of her neck. "We put them in a cell and reporters crowd around for all those incriminating little pictures to flash in their trashy tabloids. It's all damned amusing while it's going on."

She heard the threat in his voice, but also a suggestiveness that had her eyes narrowing in suspicion.

"So what do you want in exchange for not calling the sheriff and the trashy tabloids, Riley?" Manipulating bastard, she knew he was up to something. And she knew she wasn't going to like it.

She felt his short beard rasp over her shoulder then, the prickly caress had her breathing in deep, fighting to maintain her composure as well as her sanity while pleasure threatened to swamp her.

"What do you have to bargain with?"

Bingo.

"You dirty bastard!" She twisted out of his hold, growing angrier at the thought that she had escaped him only because he allowed it.

Facing him in the dim light of the moon that pierced the thin curtains over the window, Angel clenched her fists at her side and stuck her chin out challengingly.

"I should have known you wouldn't play fair," she snapped. "Do you expect me to trade sex for your silence? To believe you would do anything so underhanded as to have me arrested for attempting to reclaim my own property."

"I bought it." He shrugged his broad shoulders, crossing his arms over his chest as his blue eyes gleamed from within his ruggedly dark face. "It's mine, Angel. Not yours."

"He had no right to sell that torque." She felt like throwing something at him. "It's mine."

"The papers he had said otherwise." He moved from the doorway, closing the door as he stepped over to the opposite wall.

Seconds later, the lamps on the bed tables glowed to life and she was certain the lights that were previously not working downstairs, were now blazing brilliantly just as they had been in the past two nights.

"His papers are a mockery." She faced him fully now, her lips thinning at the arrogance, the supreme male confidence that surrounded him like an aura.

His tilted grin was knowing, his stance—thumbs hooked in the pockets of his low riding jeans, his legs braced apart—was one of sexual assurance. He believed he had her exactly where he wanted her. Unfortunately, as much as she hated it, he might not be too far off the mark.

And as sad as it was to admit, he was turning her on. He had turned her on from the first moment she had met him, made her long for a touch she knew she shouldn't crave, a man she knew she couldn't hold.

He was like a wild wind, blowing in, ripping past defenses and tearing asunder denials, stroking with a devil's touch, only to blow away again, leaving what was left behind lost and broken. He would break her heart in just such a manner, if she allowed it.

"The papers are completely legal. I made certain of it, Angel-mine." His voice was a caress, stroking over her senses despite the male mockery in the tone. "They'll stand up in any court."

"You had no right to buy it, knowing it was to be left to me." And that hurt worse. That he had bought it, despite knowing that her father was selling it unfairly.

The gold and silver torque had been created centuries before for a warrior in her direct line. It was rumored to be blessed by an ancient druid and possessing a power that would always follow her family through the acceptance the first warrior had given it. One tall and strong, fearless in battle and gentle in bed. A man who had stolen the heart of the druid's favored daughter.

"If I hadn't bought it, someone else would have." Those wicked, wicked blue eyes stared back at her with a hint of laughter and a flame of arousal.

The very valid, logical argument did nothing to sway her.

"Then sell it back to me," she demanded roughly. "You've no need of it, Riley. The torque is nothin' to ya. It's everything to me."

She watched the frown that creased his brow as she faced him and prayed she was finally getting through to him. The man was such an enigma you could rarely tell what he was thinking. The most you could be certain of was that he was horny. She had rarely seen a time that the bulge in his pants wasn't fully engorged and stallion-hard.

"I doubt you would meet my price," he finally mused pensively. "And if you did, I'd more than upset to realize how easily you could be had. How easily can you be had, Angel-mine?"

She flew at him. Teeth bared, nails extended, she went for those damned laughing eyes. The bastard to dare think she would whore herself for him. For anything. And in doing so, block any desire she had to give in to him. Just as he had done when he bought the torque, he placed between them obstacles that her pride could never surmount.

His laughter echoed in her ears as he caught her, swinging her around and holding her nearly immobile as he pressed her into the wall, her cheek pressing into the cool dry wall as she screamed out in impotent rage.

"I'll cut your devil's heart out of your chest, Riley," she snarled furiously. "Black-hearted, evil wretch. I'll gut ye myself."

"Bloodthirsty little vixen," he growled at her ear rather than releasing her. "If you had been a little less confrontational and demanding you might have had the torque before I ever left Ireland. But you had to play the shrew instead."

He released her quickly, moving well away from her as she turned on him with blood in her eye.

"Ye say that now," she snapped heatedly. "But I know better. I did all but go to my knees and plead with you to not buy the piece."

She was breathing harshly, fighting not just her fury, but the unaccountable pleasure she had felt as he restrained her, held her immobile and pressed his hard body into her own.

Never had she known such weakening arousal and desire as she had each time he had done that.

"As I said, if I hadn't bought it, someone else would have. Your best chance was to convince me to sell it back to you before breaking into my home and attempting to steal from me. I don't like thieves, Angel."

"Ye should," she snarled. "Birds of a feather and so forth."

His eyes narrowed. "You're pushing your luck, baby."

"And I'm no your babe." Her hands were clenched at her side, her nails biting into her palms. "Go ahead, ye coward, call your precious sheriff and have me arrested. Do your worst. I'd expect nothing less from a bastard such as yourself."

"You think that's my worst?" His voice was a rough growl, proof that she had finally pierced that amused exterior. Let him get angry. Damn him, it wasn't possible for him to become any angrier than she was herself.

"I think you're a coward with no more honor than an alley cat skulking through the shadows," she charged, heedless of the darkening of his eyes, the way his expression tightened. "Only a man with no honor would steal such an heirloom for the paltry price you paid, despite my pleas," she accused him rashly.

"I'm going to tan your hide." He lifted his lip in a snarl, his body tense, his eyes narrowing on her dangerously.

"I've no doubt you'll try," she sniped. "It sounds like something you'd attempt to cover your own shortcomings. Does it make you feel like a big man, Jack Riley, to overpower the little women? To show them who you think is boss?"

She ignored the fact that it had turned her on like nothing she had ever known when he had done just that.

"Actually, it does." The smooth, dark tone should have warned her. She should have known better than to be taken in by his playboy image, his attitude of calculated disinterest. In that moment, she saw, and she knew she had made a grave tactical error, and now she would pay for it.

Chapter Two

"Now, there is a damned fine sight. Angel-mine, that has to be the prettiest little ass I've ever seen."

Angel screamed out furiously, the sound muffled by the black gag secured over her lips as she fought the strong hands that held her wrists behind her back as he stretched her over his lap.

She had fought him like a demon, attempting to rake his flesh with her nails, to kick out at him with her feet. He had laughed, a rough, sexy sound that she had liked entirely too much. And though fury raced hard and fast through her bloodstream, outrage that he would attempt to actually spank her rioting through her system, still, the flares of excitement were singing through her veins.

That didn't mean she had to let him live. No man would spank her and live to tell the tale. She was going to kill him. She was going to slice his heart out and feed it to the wolves. She would…

She screeched in humiliating surprise as his hand landed on her upturned rump with a stinging little slap that was more startling than painful. And much too pleasurable. It wasn't supposed to be pleasurable. It was supposed to be humiliating. Infuriating. Painful. It wasn't supposed to tear into her womb and leave it convulsing in erotic hunger.

"Stay still," he ordered lazily. "Let me at least admire my handiwork here. If you're going to go to the trouble to spank a spoiled little witch then you should at least have the pleasure of viewing the soft little ass you're getting to ready redden."

Her cheeks flamed in mortification as his hand smoothed over her nearly bare rump. What had possessed her to wear the silken little thong rather than the less-revealing panties she had packed as well? Sexy lingerie and playing cat burglar didn't go well together, but she realized, in one startling moment, that she had worn the softest, sexiest undergarments that she possessed.

Bits of silk and lace she had bought months before, imagining how they would tempt the shadowy lover she often dreamed would come into her life. The one who would make her feel courageous enough to be a woman, to take what she hungered for, to live out the fantasies she admitted to only in the darkness of the night.

This wasn't one of her fantasies, but it was making her hotter than anything she could have envisioned.

Jack had managed to not only wrestle her across his knees, but to lower her pants as well, leaving her nearly bare to his lust-filled gaze. And she knew it was lust-filled. She could feel the heat of it stroking her bottom even as his fingers smoothed over it.

"You have the most delightful little ass," he crooned, the sound striking a bolt of pleasure straight to her cunt.

How she hated that response to him. Hated the knowledge that what he was doing to her was unlike anything she had known in her life, yet was likely commonplace to him. A ragged whimper of shameful need escaped her lips at the admiring tone of his voice. She had never considered herself particularly pretty. She had rarely felt sexy or as sexual as she did at this moment.

She struggled against him again, fighting his hold, determined to break free before the dampness leaking from her pussy began to wet the dark silk of her panties. Before he realized the erotic pleasure she was gaining from her helplessness. Who could have known? Surely she hadn't imagined that such dominant extremes could destroy her defenses in such a way.

"Bad girl." He smacked her bare rump again, causing a throttled scream to tear from her chest. One she prayed he thought was no more than fury.

Velvet heat rushed through the warmed cheek of her ass and struck her pussy like a sword of erotic fire. Mercy, she screamed silently. Have mercy on the helpless pleasure tearing through her.

She wasn't a bad girl, but at his accusation she realized how much she wanted to be one. To be a wicked, wanton. To take him as she had only dreamed of taking a man before.

"Soft and sweet." His hand smoothed over the curves again. "Do you know what I'd like to do, Angel-mine? I'd like to put you on your knees, part these pretty curves and watch my dick slide deep inside that tight little entrance to your ass."

Her eyes widened in shock as his words tore through her at the same time he delivered another heated strike to her ass. Her anus clenched, her pussy began to drench her panties. Black silk panties that she knew would show the proof of her arousal.

Her breasts swelled instantly, her nipples hardening to the point of pain as he delivered another slap to the opposite side, heating her backside repeatedly as she began to shudder, to writhe in his grip.

She would not enjoy this, she screamed to herself as he continued to redden her rear, making it blush, making her entire body heat with the forbidden pleasure. And each second of it reminded her of his words, the image of him behind her, parting the cheeks of her ass and forcing his cock into the dark hole there.

She screamed as another blow landed, the sensations spearing deep inside her pussy, rioting through her clit until it became engorged with the need for release. Each heated strike to her rear had her twisting on his lap, common sense and sanity retreating further into the ether of lust as she began to moan in compliance, in desperate pleasure.

"Fuck!" She could hear the rough tone, almost awed, definitely surprised as he halted the erotic spanking, causing her to arch her back to lift her ass to him for more. She was so close, didn't he understand how close she was to attaining that final pleasure?

"Angel?" His voice was almost guttural as his fingers slid between her thighs, rasping against the black silk of her panties as she shuddered in ecstasy at the touch. "Oh, baby, you're so wet. So fucking hot and wet."

He moved then, lifting her from his lap, tearing the gag from her lips as he stood her before him.

Her legs were so unsteady she swayed, staring down at him, shocked by her own body, by the weakness assailing her. If it wasn't for his hands steadying her, she wondered if she would have melted into a puddle at his feet.

Dazed, she stared down into gaze, wondering at the near blackness of his once blue eyes as she felt the fingers of one hand move once again between her thighs.

"Jack," she whispered his name, unable hold back the shudder that racked her limbs as his fingers smoothed over the sodden crotch of her panties once again. "Jack, please."

She pressed her hips forward, tilting them, gasping at the fiery sensations as his hand cupped her mound, his upper palm rasping against her clit and sending it rioting in extreme ecstasy.

"Such a naughty, wet little Angel," he whispered again, causing her pussy to spasm in greedy hunger as she felt his fingers move beneath the elastic leg band. "So wet..."

Like an erotic whisper, the pads of his fingers smoothed over the drenched curls as Angel felt the breath rush from her body. It wasn't hard enough, the touch was too soft, barely there. She needed more. Needed something harder, something hotter.

A second later, her hands flew to his shoulders, gripping them in desperation as he began to part the tender, sensitive folds, his fingertips rubbing against nerve-laden flesh as she trembled violently. Waiting. Oh God, the waiting was killing her. She wanted him to rip the silk away from her body, feel his fingers plunging inside her, hard, fast, ripping away her sanity and throwing her into the endless abyss of pleasure that she could feel waiting just out of reach.

It was this that had drawn her to him during the weeks he had spent in Dublin. The naughty, wicked sexuality. The knowing glint in his eyes that assured her that she would find delights in his arms she had never known in another's. He was like a flame, and she was the moth, desperate to be burned.

Her lips parted, her mouth opening as she fought for breath, fought to keep her eyes open, her gaze locked with his as she felt his fingers, broad and calloused, nearing the spasming entrance to her burning pussy. So close. She wanted them inside her, filling her…

"Jack…" The low keening cry echoed around them as her hips jerked, pressed closer, the honeyed, slick juices spilling from her cunt as his fingers paused, holding rapture just out of reach as she gasped in lust-crazed desperation.

"Fuck, this is insane!" His sudden curse was followed by the removal of his fingers from her burning flesh as he bent, grabbed the waist of her pants and jerked them quickly back to her hips.

"No. Damn you! What are you doing?" She pushed at his hands, only to have him grip her hips as he rose, turning and pushing her to the bed.

"Not like this," he growled, breathing roughly as she steadied herself, staring up at him in shock. "Shit." He raked his fingers through his hair, watching her with a shocked expression she felt must mirror her own.

Angel blinked back, fighting to breathe, to make sense of the sudden shift from hungry passion, greedy lust, to being bereft of his touch.

"Stay put, damn you!" he ordered, his tone guttural as she moved to rise.

She shook her head, her eyes lowering, only to widen again as she realized how very close she was to the instrument of pleasure she needed so desperately. The bulge of his cock was only inches in front of her face, pressing against his jeans, the thick length clearly discernible beneath the material.

Dazed. Uncertain where her daring originated from, she reached out, her hand running over the hard ridge as his body tensed violently. A sizzling curse escaped his lips as his hand caught her wrist, the other gripping her chin to raise her head.

"Think about it," he snarled heatedly. "I'll fuck your mouth until you can't scream, can't whimper because you're so full of my dick. And when you think it will never stop I'll bury myself between those sweet lips and shoot every drop of my come down your throat. And it won't stop there, girl. I'll strip you down and fuck you so hard and deep you'll never forget the feel of me. Ever. Think about it, damn you, because once I have you. Once I taste that sweet pussy or bury my dick inside you, I won't let you go until I own you. Body and soul, little witch. I'll own you. Make certain, very damned certain you can accept that, before you try to accept me."

He had lost his mind. Jack raked his fingers roughly through his hair as he stalked down the stairs, ignoring Angel's furious screams as she pounded on the locked bedroom door, her enraged threats almost amusing.

There was no room for amusement inside him at the moment. His guts were ripped in half, every bone and muscle in his body hurting with the need to fuck the tempting little witch, to hear her screams of pleasure rather than those of fury.

What the hell had happened? He had meant only to teach her a lesson, to spank that tempting little ass hard enough to teach her a measure of respect. Instead, what he had meant to be a disciplinary action had turned into an erotic lesson in his own self-control. Something so fucking hot he felt blistered from head to toe.

What had she done to him? Jack paused at the foot of the stairs, raking his fingers through his hair as he realized his hands were trembling. He could still smell the sweet, hot scent of her body. She smelled like honey, warm and slick, tempting the senses and reminding him of why he hadn't pushed the sexually boundary she had placed between them in Ireland. Because he knew, one taste—taste, nothing—one touch and he was addicted.

He could feel it, that compulsion for more. The driving need to lay her on that bed and taste every creamy inch of her.

"Damn." He paced into the living room, twisting his head and shoulders as the furious screams above began to abate.

Walking away from her had been next to impossible. Turning away from the fiery, hot feel of her body had torn something apart deep inside him. He wanted to go back. He wanted to stalk into that bedroom, throw her to the bed and drive his dick so hard and deep inside her that he couldn't tell where he ended and she began.

He grimaced painfully, one hand dropping to the heavy bulge beneath his jeans as the material bit at the sensitive flesh of his cock. A groan tore from his throat as pleasure whipped through his body.

"Son of a bitch," he cursed, throwing himself into the wide, heavily cushioned chair that sat beside the picture window.

He leaned his head against the back of the chair, breathing out roughly as he fought the nearly overwhelming impulse to go back upstairs. To finish what he had started. To take her, to hear her cries, her pleas, to feel her tight and hot around him. To let loose the control he fought so hard to maintain, and for the first time in his life, to immerse himself in the woman he would have beneath him.

It was that damned torque's fault. Had he not bought it, had he ignored the stubborn challenge in Angel's eyes and left the piece be, then he wouldn't be in this situation, he reminded himself. Hell, he didn't even like the damned thing.

But he was also honest enough to admit that there wasn't a chance in hell he was going to walk away from it. He had probed at Angel's guard the full two weeks he had stayed at her father's estate. Teasing her, tempting her, growing unreasonably aggravated by her cool demeanor of unresponsiveness. No other woman had ever tempted him as she had. He had known that even then and he had fought it. Angel was different, and he didn't want her to be. He wanted her to be like every other woman he had known in his life. Easy to walk away from. Easy to maintain his control with. There was going to be nothing easy about the confrontation rising between them now.

He should stalk upstairs, pull the bit of jewelry from his luggage and just give the damned thing to her. It would belong to her then. She would possess sole ownership to it, and he could then have some peace.

And he would have, if she hadn't tried to steal from him. No, it wasn't even that. He stared at the ceiling in furious realization that he wouldn't return it to her simply because he knew if he did, she would walk away. There would be no further reason for her to stay. And he had no desire to have her leave.

"Jack Riley, you dirty, black-hearted bastard." Something crashed against the bedroom door as his lips kicked up in a grin.

Damn, she was a hellcat. And hotter than anything he had touched in his life.

He breathed out roughly, wearily.

Something inside him warned that if he took her, if he let himself touch her again then it would be the greatest mistake of his life. But Jack knew himself well enough to know that he wouldn't leave her alone long.

Chapter Three

Dawn was nearing when Jack finally made his way from the guest room he had slept in through the early hours of the morning. He unlocked the door quietly, opening it slowly as he stepped into the room.

He throttled the groan that threatened to escape his chest at the sight that met his eyes. This was not a sight designed to aid a man in keeping his control. To the contrary, it was like adding fuel to the flames.

She was stretched out in his bed, wearing nothing but the little black thong and a silk and lace bra that cupped the full, creamy mounds of her breasts in a wicked, erotic frame. Long, slender legs were slightly parted, a graceful hand lay on her slightly rounded abdomen. Long, black curls framed her sleeping face and her soft pink lips parted as she breathed in and out in relaxed slumber.

His cock hadn't abated through the night, despite the hour he had spent jacking off before he got out of his bed. A frown creased his brow as he felt a spurt of anger rising inside him. She had taunted him with a cool façade, teased him with her haughtiness while in Ireland and then attempted to steal from him. She had kept him erect, hot and out of sorts for weeks, and he was trying to be a gentleman?

His fears of the night before, his knowledge that taking her would somehow change him receded beneath the arousal twisting his guts in knots. God, he wanted her. He could see clearly, imagine with a realism that shocked him, the sight of her on her knees, dressed in nothing but silk and lace, her lips surrounding his cock, sucking him to her throat, creating a fire inside him that would burn out of control.

He shook his head, fighting it, fighting his own arousal.

"Rise and shine, Angel-mine." He moved to the bed, gripping her slender ankle and pulling at it firmly as she jackknifed in the bed.

A frown pulled immediately at her brows as fire shot through her gaze.

"Take your hands off me, toad," she snapped, jerking her ankle from his grip as she pushed the thick strands of black hair away from her face.

"Such a sweet disposition," he chastised her mockingly as he stood by the bed, staring down at her. "Get out of bed." He bent, picking up her clothing and tucking it beneath his arm as he grinned down at her. "You can wear one of my T-shirts while I wash your clothes. I'll see about having you a few things delivered today to wear. Be a good girl now, and get cleaned up for breakfast."

"Excuse me?" she snapped, scrambling across the bed as she attempted to jerk her clothing from him. "Give those to me. I won't be staying here so I'll no need you to get me anything."

"Tsk tsk, Angel-mine." He shook his head in reprimand as he held her clothing out of reach. "Remember the sheriff? The pesky tabloids? We'll discuss this over coffee and food. But I think you might want to reconsider your position here. Jail can be a very bad place."

She pulled back, wondering how serious he was. The one thing she had learned about him while he was in Ireland was that he could be counted on to keep his word. If he set his mind to having her arrested, she had no doubt he would.

The fury of the night before had receded beneath not just her normal common sense, but also the arousal he had fired inside her the night before. But that didn't mean she would immediately bow beneath whatever his arbitrary rules would be. There were other ways of fighting this battle. Jack Riley did not hold all the cards as he believed he did. She wasn't the only one who had been caught in the web of lust and pleasure the night before. He too had burned, and she knew it.

Narrowing her eyes, she allowed her gaze to rake over him. From the darkened blue eyes, lower to the heavy bulge beneath his jeans. She could feel her pussy throbbing, her breasts swelling as the memory of the night before whipped through her head. His touch, his fingers parting the folds of her cunt, rubbing against the entrance to her weeping vagina. There had been a lesson to be learned in those all too brief moments that he had touched her. Some pleasure was so extreme that it wasn't worth losing. Never had she known such intensity of pleasure. Such promise of more to come. She wanted, needed more. As though his kiss, his touch was a drug that was rapidly becoming addictive.

She leaned back then, propping her weight on her elbows as she watched his gaze flare at the way it pushed her breasts forward prominently. She loved that look in his eyes, and even though she highly distrusted him emotionally, she had been unable to stem the arousal he could spark inside her.

"Very well." She shrugged. "Rather than buying me clothing, ye could just have my things collected from the motel in town. I'm sure that would much easier on ye."

His eyelids lowered, his gaze raking over her body, centering on her thighs. The rapidly moistening folds beneath the silk began to pulse in excitement. Her clit was like a living flame, burning out of control with her hunger to feel his mouth suckling at it, his tongue moving around it. She had a feeling she had never truly known lustful pleasure, but that this man could teach her much about it.

"You're playing with fire, Angel," he told her then, his voice deepening, roughening. "You may find that what you're asking for is much more than you can handle."

She rolled her eyes. "Americans are so dramatic," she sighed. "Do you delight in the warnings? Do they bring you some measure of heightened pleasure? Or do you just enjoy the theatrics?"

His blue eyes flared at the challenge. Sensuality covered his face, giving him a darker, more wicked demeanor than ever before. She had never known an American lover, she admitted. The few men she had allowed in her bed were cool, well-bred Englishmen who performed between the sheets in the same manner that they performed in public. Cool. With dignity. With very little excitement. Were all American men like her captor?

"You're asking for trouble," he growled.

Her fingers played, with all apparent nonchalance, against the flesh of her abdomen, mere inches from the elastic band of the thong as she sighed with mocking patience.

"Very well, Jack. I will don your pitiful excuse for clothing and come down for breakfast." She rose on the bed, moving slowly as she swung her legs over the side and stood up, watching him, her gaze locked with his as he stood silent, merely staring back at her.

The move placed her much closer to him, mere inches from the heat of his body as his eyes darkened, heated sensually. The look had her breathing accelerating, her mouth drying out in anticipation. There was a message in that look, one that backed up his previous warning that she was playing with fire.

"Any particular shirt I should wear?" She tilted her head, kept her voice soft, suggestive as she moved away from him, deliberately turning to give him a view of her naked buttocks as she walked to the chest across the room.

She made it, perhaps a few feet before his hand wrapped around her upper arm, bringing her to a stop.

She turned, staring at him over her shoulder, her brow lifting in a haughty demand despite the dark sexuality that covered him like an aura.

"Tell me, Angel-mine," he whispered then. "Do you have an idea of the dirty little games men can play with soft flesh like yours?"

She licked her dry lips. No, she had no idea, but she was curious about the games he could play.

"You wouldn't hurt me," she finally whispered. "Others might, but you wouldn't."

His expression was almost savage now. His cheekbones seemed higher, sharper, his lips fuller, more sensual than before as he watched her broodingly.

"And you know this how?" His fingers tightened on her arm as his expression darkened with some undefined emotion. It was gone so quickly, that she couldn't analyze nor decipher it, but the shadow of it ran deep.

"If you were going to hurt me, you would have finished what you started last night, Jack," she whispered then. "I trust you with my body. I would trust you in what you call your dirty little games." She gave a sad smile then. "But I would know better than to ever trust you with my heart."

It was there again, that shadow of emotion. For a moment, bleak, almost overwhelming pain flashed in his eyes before it disappeared once again.

Angel felt her heart trip in dread, felt something in her chest expand and ache with the need to soothe something she was certain he would never let her see. Why would her declaration that she could never trust him with her heart hurt him? It was apparent it had.

"And you think your heart is so safe, little Angel?" he asked her, the curve of his lips mocking, almost a sneer as he stared down at her. "What makes you think I couldn't make you love me?"

She turned to him, moving her hands until they were braced against the warmth of his cloth-covered chest, feeling the hard thump of his heart as it battered against the flesh there.

"Would you want me to love you, Jack Riley?" she asked him then, a wry smile tilting her lips. "If I would risk your ire, and your justice system to steal back a mere torque I feel is mine, what more would I do to punish one who stole my heart and broke it heedlessly?" Her hands caressed him subtly, moving against him with slow, sensual strokes. "Were you not the one who called me a black-hearted witch with no more sense than to cut my nose off to spite my face? Trust me, Jack, I would cut off the cock of any man stupid enough to steal my emotions and toss them away as though they were no more than trash from the day before. Believe that one well before you make the mistake of taking up a challenge I have not yet offered."

One hand still retained its grip on her other arm, and it was joined then by his hand at her opposite hip, his fingers cupping it, drawing her closer as his head began to lower.

Angel felt her heart slam in her chest, her mouth watering with the sudden need, the anticipation of the kiss she was so longing to taste. Her tongue flicked out to dampen her lips, her eyes widening as a throttled growl of hunger left his chest.

"You just have me shaking in my boots," he whispered, no more than a breath from her lips as she fought to hold her eyes open, to catch the flash of emotions that flared in the dark centers of his gaze. "Trust me, baby, it's not your heart I want. So if you lose it, you do so at your own risk. Now, that sweet, hot little pussy is another matter... After breakfast."

* * * * *

Angel was beginning to believe that American men were all tease and no true intent. Twice. Twice Jack had pulled away from her. Was it her willingness to have him that made him draw back? Her mother had always said that men wanted a challenge, not a willing sacrifice.

She brooded over that thought through breakfast in the large kitchen, sitting at the table and staring outside the window to the bleak Texas landscape beyond and sipping the after-breakfast coffee Jack had provided.

She had no time for games. She was never a game player, especially not in any relationship she had ever conducted. She pouted silently. She was now ready to merely go home. It was evident Jack was not going to give up the torque, no matter how she pleaded. And what proof would he truly have that she had broken into his home with the intent to steal it? There was little he could truly do unless she was honest with the law enforcement officials. Who said she had to be honest?

She sighed in disgust. She hated liars. Of course, as insane as she was, she would have to be honest. Besides, she was a lousy liar. Her father had always known when she was attempting to cover the truth with him.

"My coffee doesn't taste that bad." His rumbling voice drew her from her thoughts as she turned her head and watched him sit once again in the chair across from her.

"It could stand to be a bit stronger, but it's fair." She shrugged her shoulders. The coffee really didn't matter.

He leaned back in his chair, his expression thoughtful then.

"You're too quiet," he said. "What are you up to?"

She rolled her eyes at this. Why did men always think that silence from a woman was a direct insult or possible threat to them?

"Nothing." She lifted her cup to her lips, sipping the dark liquid before returning it to the table. "I was merely wondering how long you intend to force my presence here in your home."

He lifted a dark blond brow mockingly.

"I didn't invite you here, or force you here, darlin'," he drawled. "You arrived of your own free will."

"And I am now ready to leave," she informed him coolly. "I came, I failed. The torque, as you say, is fairly yours. I should have heeded my better sense rather than my emotions in coming here."

It was a bitter disappointment, losing that torque. Legend held that as long as it stayed within the bloodlines it was created for, then happiness and true love would come to that family. Her mother had known such a marriage. Her parents had loved each other deeply, so deeply there was little left for the child who had lived in their shadow.

"Maybe I'm not ready to let you go." His expression was once again shuttered, brooding.

Mockery twisted her smile then. "You can't keep me here forever, Jack. I have a life and a job to return to soon. I'm certain that matters little to you, but other than the torque you purchased from my father, it's all that matters to me."

A smile quirked his lips. "You need to widen your horizons, darlin'. A woman needs more than just a career to keep her warm at night."

"I have an electric blanket. It works quite well and bitches much less," she responded drolly. "What more could a woman want?"

"An orgasm?" he questioned in amusement.

"My vibrator does the job." She lifted her shoulders in a shrug.

Men were so insane.

"Hmm," he murmured. "Well, we'll let you get back to your vibrator and your blanket eventually. Until then, I think it's my duty to punish you for your criminal activities. I mean, hell, I let you get away with this, only God knows what you'll attempt next. Bank robberies, assault, the list goes on and on. I think someone needs to teach you the error of your ways."

She would have laughed if his high-handed mocking attitude didn't spark a flame to a temper already out of sorts.

"Excuse me?" She drew herself rigidly erect as offended fury began to fill her. "And what makes you think I'll allow you to be my judge and jury in this matter? You know what that torque means to me, Jack."

He grimaced with mocking sobriety. "Sorry, sweetheart. It's me or jail."

"It's your word against mine," she reminded him furiously.

"Yeah, but the sheriff is a real good friend of mine," he pointed out. "Hell, we're almost family. I think he'll believe me over you."

This was a nightmare.

He looked entirely too confident, too superior for her to doubt his word. Of course the sheriff would believe him over her. Small towns in America would be no different than in Ireland. It would make no sense if it were.

"So much for American justice," she harrumphed. "So how much longer do you intend to hold me prisoner here?"

He tilted his head, watching her with a thoughtful, considering expression.

"Oh, I don't know. How long do you think it would take you to learn your lesson?"

Angel snorted. As though she would attempt to deal with an American again. "Five minutes after I realized you were aware of my presence?"

The expression on his face assured her he wasn't falling for that one.

"Fine, Jack, you're going to punish me." She waved her hands dramatically. "So what exactly do you have in mind? Scrubbing floors? I can do it well enough. Where should I start, my lord?"

She allowed her accent to thicken, her expression to become disdainful. Damn man.

"You'll definitely be on your knees," he growled then, his gaze filling with infuriating male arrogance. "But it's not the floors you'll have your attention on woman. Rather, my dick. So open wide and get ready to suck."

Before Jack was even aware of his own intentions he was out of his chair and pulling Angel into his arms. That smart mouth and haughty air made him crazy. It made his cock so damned hard he wondered how he managed to contain it beneath his jeans. It should have been bursting through the material and aiming directly at that hot little pussy between her thighs.

"Jack, you wouldn't dare..."

He broke the exclamation by the simple means of covering her lips with his own. His head tilted, slanting over those pouty curves as he pressed home his advantage and speared his tongue between her lips.

She was one of the most infuriating, aggravatingly smart-assed women he knew. She was also the softest, sweetest bit of female he had ever taken in his arms. Her gasp against his lips inflamed his lust, the way her body tensed, shuddered, the obvious fight to hold back the response he could feel trembling through her.

Her hips jerked against his, the soft pad of her pussy tilting to accept the pressure of his cock as he bent his knees to drive it against her.

There was that little gasp again. Shock and pleasure as her tongue tangled tentatively with his, as though she were wary of her response to him. But he could feel the flames burning inside her, reaching out to him, heating his own hunger.

What was it about this woman? His little thief. If he wasn't careful she would attempt to steal more than just the torque she came looking for, she would steal a part of him he had sworn no other person would ever hold.

His arms wrapped around her, one going around her shoulders as his fingers tangled in the soft weight of her witchy black hair. A fine payment for the slender fingers clenched in his own now, holding him still against her as she allowed him to eat at her lips.

She was as sweet as sugar, as hot and spicy as a ripe cayenne. He had always been partial to the little fire-hot peppers, and even more so now. She was a temptation, a challenge, everything about her dared a man to tame her, to take her, to find the nasty, sexual creature lurking behind that innocent, too-cool gaze.

He would find that woman.

He lifted his head, staring down at her, feeling some emotion clench his chest as she stared up at him in equal parts dismay and arousal.

"On your knees," he whispered then, dying inside, craving the feel of her lips around his tortured cock in a way he couldn't explain, even to himself.

She stared back at him, her expression such a challenge it had every bone and muscle in his body clenching.

"And if I don't?" she whispered, obviously, deliberately pushing him.

"Then I tie you down and see just how long I can tease and tempt that pretty little body. And how long it takes you to beg me to let you on your knees before I put out the fires both of us know I can stoke inside you, baby."

She seemed to think about that one for a moment before a mocking little smile of submission crossed her lips.

He got more than he bargained for.

Standing in the middle of the Mexican-tiled kitchen, the rays of the sun sending shafts of fire washing over his body, he watched as slender, graceful fingers began to loosen the buttons of his shirt.

"Straight to my knees?" she asked him then as her violet eyes darkened in response to his warning growl. "Or may I play in between?"

What was that little warning at the back of his brain? The one screaming at him to get her the hell away from him, out of his home, out of his life?

Whatever it was, he didn't want to hear it.

He didn't want to hear anything but that pleased little murmur that escaped her lips as she spread his opened shirt back from his chest. Her face flushed, her eyes nearly black as she lowered her head to lick at the skin teasingly.

Jack had to grit his teeth to keep back the groan that would have escaped. He allowed his hands to hang loosely at his sides, wondering how far she would go. How brave she would get.

She licked her way across the expanse of suntanned flesh to a hard, flat male nipple. He expected no more than a perfunctory little lick. What he got instead had his fingers clenching into fists as he fought for control.

Those sharp little teeth of hers raked against it slowly as her hot, wicked tongue licked over it, and flickering flames danced across his skin, scouring his nerve endings and causing his cock to jerk in painful need.

He stared down at her, entranced by the apparent enjoyment she was receiving from touching him. One hand moved lower along his side to the tense flesh of his abdomen as the other tweaked and caressed the mate to the one she was tormenting with slow strokes of her tongue and gentle nips of her teeth.

He had never known how sensitive his own nipples could be. It was a vaguely disconcerting feeling, feeling that tingle of awareness that shot straight to his balls and tightened them painfully.

Then those wicked, mischievous lips moved across his chest to the small nipple her fingers had tormented with such insidious heat. He was going to explode, he thought in surprise. Surprise, because he had never known a time when a woman hadn't gone straight for his dick, or hadn't demanded a romantic, deeply involved kiss before going down.

Women were strange creatures, but he could always count on those two rules to remain steadfast and true. Until now. Now, one small bit of Irish fluff was blowing all he had known straight to hell and burning him alive in the bargain.

She licked, kissed and stroked his chest. Her tongue painted circles around his nipples as her teeth scraped erotically against the hair-spattered flesh. Sweet heaven, her mouth was hot. If she managed to make it to his cock he would burn in the inferno.

"You're so hard, so warm," she whispered as her lips began to ghost along his tense stomach. "I can feel your muscles just under the skin. They feel so powerful. So strong."

She bit into the hard flesh of his upper stomach and his head fell back with a groan. Son of a bitch, his knees were even growing weak.

He reached out, his fingers burying in her hair, intending to halt her play, until he felt her fingers at the buckle of his belt. He had to fight to keep from trembling like a weak-kneed greenhorn. Damn it to hell, she was destroying him, her fingers moving at a snail's pace as she tracked each corded muscle of his abdomen with her destructive mouth and heated tongue.

And for all the protests his mind was throwing out in allowing her to continue, she was delaying his pleasure—hell, no, she was accelerating it to a depth he could have never imagined. He had demanded a blowjob, not a damned map made with her tongue across his flesh, but what pleasure that seemingly aimless journey was creating.

He stared down at her, seeing her on her knees now, just as he demanded, her hands parting his jeans, pulling them lower, revealing, inch by thick hard inch, the erection straining beneath it.

He expected her to devour it. To take it in her mouth and begin the hard, fast suckling that would have the event quickly finished. Hell, this was one time he wanted nothing more than to release the pressure building in his balls.

But did she know that?

Was she kind enough to do as any other of her sex would have done?

No.

"Fuck!" Thighs were not supposed to be fucking sensitive. Son of a bitch.

Her teeth raked over the inner flesh before her lips opened, pulling a bit of the skin into her mouth for a heated caress.

Once again, her mouth was an aimless destroyer, moving from one thigh to the other, licking and stroking, destroying him as he felt his legs shake. Yes, his fucking legs were shaking. So what? What man's legs wouldn't shake with such beauty worshipping something so seemingly undeserving as the sensitive flesh of his thighs?

"Witch!" His strangled groan surprised him, but the liquid heat washing over his balls shocked him more.

Almost timid now, searching, learning, her tongue moved over the tight sac, probing at it, circling the hard spheres beneath the flesh before she gently, tenderly sucked one into her mouth, tonguing it like a favorite treat.

Pre-come spurted from the tip of his cock, running in a silken trail down the throbbing shaft as she tortured him with her mouth. And it was fucking torture. Lightning bolts, whipping fingers of white-hot heat shot through his body, searing nerve endings and curling his toes inside his boots as she began to lick at the creamy trail of liquid that had escaped the pulsing crest of his erection.

She moaned in pleasure, as though his taste pleased her.

The woman was fucking crazy.

His hands tightened in her hair as he watched her unman him. Bit by bit she was ripping away his preconceived notions of a head job and replacing them with pure, undiluted ecstasy.

"So hard and hot." The thick Irish accent had to be the sexiest sound he had ever heard in his life. "Throbbing as though it has a heartbeat all its own."

He would have replied. He was certain he could have found some kind of smart-assed mocking comment drifting around in his mush-head if she hadn't chosen that moment to envelop him in the dark, lava-hot depths of her silken mouth.

His abdomen convulsed. He could feel his balls tightening further, drawing close to the base of his cock as warning fingers of impending release scraped up his spine. Her mouth… God help him if he thought another man had known such pleasure from that mouth…it was making him crazy. He felt like howling with the sensations.

Instead, a broken groan tore from his chest as he thrust in deeper, feeling her tongue caress the sensitive underside, her lips tightening on him, her mouth drawing on him.

Hell, yes! A rebel cry was building in his head. "Fuck, yeah. Suck me, baby. Suck my cock…"

His hands held her head in place as he stared down her, meeting the pitch-black of her eyes as he watched his cock shuttle between her stretched, reddened lips. Her cheeks were flushed bright, her eyes glowing, his dick glistening with the moisture from her mouth.

She sucked him, all right. Her tongue twisted around the head, probed at the underside, flattened and stroked while she moaned. The sounds of her pleasure vibrated against the crest as he pushed it nearly to her throat, feeling her fingers caress the rest of the shaft as her honeyed mouth sucked him to his destruction.

Then the fingers of her hand became a devilish instrument of erotic devastation. They began to play with the tight sac below, cupping and caressing, nails raking as he fucked against her lips with a hunger he knew he would never forget, no matter how long or how hard he might try. Her mouth, lips, tongue, played in harmony, drawing on the tortured flesh of his cock as her fingers tortured other areas. He could feel the warning tingles of impending release. Knew there were only seconds, no more, before he erupted.

"Angel…" he groaned her name. He couldn't, wouldn't spill his seed into her mouth without her permission, without her knowledge. "I'm going to come, dammit. Stop now, or you're going to get something you might not want."

"Mmm…" Her mouth tightened, her stroking fingers moved faster, as her mouth sucked at him harder.

Destruction.

He gritted his teeth as his head fell back and he felt his release explode through his system. The white-hot flares of pleasure exploded through his body, tightening his muscles, his bones, sending a cry of near pain past his lips as he felt the semen shoot from the tip of his cock to the depths of her mouth. The stroking, swallowing, taking-every-damned-drop-of-his-come, mouth.

He could feel her cries, echoing from her throat to his erection. Aroused, hot little sounds that sent his blood pressure soaring back to the boiling point.

Not yet, he cursed viciously, his head lowering, his eyes opening to stare down at her as he eased his still hard flesh from her lips.

"Jack?" She whispered his name, the sound echoing with her own arousal, her own needs.

Hell. What had he done? What had she released inside him? He could feel an unnamed, unknown emotion riding on the back of the pleasure still pulsing through him, one that intensified not just his lust, but his pleasure as well.

"Witch," he whispered again. "Hot, seductive little witch. I'm going to fuck you until you scream for mercy…"

Chapter Four

Angel gasped breathlessly, anticipation rising hot and hard inside her as Jack pulled her ruthlessly to her feet. Staggering, she cursed her weak knees and the arousal blistering through her body. She wanted to climb him, to wrap her arms around his neck, her legs around his hips and ride. What was that saying? Save a horse, ride a cowboy? Oh yeah, she could definitely adopt that sentiment as her own.

Never had she done anything so erotic in her life. The sheer sensual sexuality of the act she had just performed left her dazed, her body throbbing in agonized arousal. Every nerve ending, every cell was screaming out for relief, for release.

"Come on." He took only the briefest moment to secure the snap of his jeans before he impossibly, surprisingly, lifted her into his arms and headed for the stairs. The world tilted on its axis as her arms wrapped around his neck, her lips moving for the strong, tanned column of his neck. She needed the taste of him, any part of him. Strong, heated, all male, it was an aphrodisiac she wondered if she was now addicted to.

"Little witch," he growled as he started up the stairs. "Keep that up and we'll never make it to the bedroom."

Who the hell cared? The stairs suited her fine.

Her teeth scraped his neck, her tongue stroking the tough skin as her hands buried in his hair to hold his head in place. She wanted more of him, now. She gripped the flesh between shoulder and neck, gripping the tough muscle there with her teeth as she began to draw on it erotically. God, he just tasted too damned good.

"Son of a bitch!" He stumbled against the wall, breathing in harshly as a hard shudder racked his body. "Woman, I'm going to fuck you on the stairs if you don't stop that."

Good. She wasn't alone. She was horny and ready, now. Readier than she had been for the tough American who had invaded her life, possessed her torque, and now possessed the very essence of her pleasure.

"I'm game if you are," she whispered the words against his ear as her lips lifted from his neck, her tongue curling over the lobe of his ear.

"I'm going to paddle your ass," he grunted as he continued to the bedroom. "And not in a good way, Angel-mine."

Her womb clenched at the very thought of another of those erotic spankings. As though he could do anything more sinister. The sound of his voice did not lend itself to a painful beating, but rather to a sensual firestorm of pleasure.

"Any paddlin' you gave, Cowboy, would be not less than pleasure." She smiled up at him as he placed her on the bed, staring down at her intently.

Her breasts were swollen, pressing against the T-shirt demandingly as her nipples rasped against the material. Below, her pussy was a rioting, gluttonous heat that pulsed and wept in hunger.

She licked at her suddenly dry lips as he began to strip. First, the white shirt, revealing the powerful muscles of his chest and shoulders. Sitting on the bed, he pulled his boots from his feet, tossing them carelessly to the floor with his socks before rising again and jerking his jeans loose. Seconds later he stood before her, completely naked, a sun-bronzed warrior, a sensual conqueror.

His rampant erection stood straight out from his body, a heavy, sensual weapon intent on impalement.

"Take off the shirt."

His voice was a rough growl, sending tingles of sensation rioting over her flesh.

She sat up on the bed, removing the shirt slowly, watching him from beneath lowered lids as one broad hand circled the shaft of his cock and began stroking it lazily.

It was a mouthwatering sight. That lovely, pleasure-giving cock, the dark stalk, the purplish crested head, the pre-come glistening at the tip. She licked her lips slowly.

"Now the bra."

She unclipped the bra, discarding it slowly, panting for breath.

"Lay back." He moved closer to the bed, his eyes heavy-lidded, his lips heavy with lust. He looked like a dark, lustful warrior. A man determined and willing to take what he wanted. To give what he knew she craved.

How could he know what she craved? How had he tapped into a hunger, a need that even she had been unaware of until now?

Angel lay back on the bed, her breath rough, ragged as he stopped at the mattress.

"Take off the panties," he whispered. "Slowly."

Slowly. She smoothed her hands over her abdomen, allowing them to meet at the silken bank below her navel. Her thumbs hooked in the elastic as she peeled the material over her hips with excruciating hesitancy.

Tension thickened the air, burning her lungs with the incredible, sexual heat.

Jack watched every move, his gaze intent as the panties passed over the swollen folds of her aching pussy, down her thighs, until she was able to move her legs to aid in discarding the last shield between her and his eyes.

She lay still beneath his regard then, fighting back the whimpers of anticipation as he watched her.

"How pretty." His voice was a hard rumble. "Spread your legs for me, Angel. Let me see paradise."

Angel shuddered, the sensual blow to her womb nearly kicking her into climax. A man should not have such power over a woman, that his voice and his look alone could cause such a response.

She opened her thighs slowly, her hands smoothing up them, framing the mound of her pussy as he placed one knee on the bed, his cheeks flushed a brick red as he watched her hands.

She watched, entranced, as his head lowered.

"Open yourself for me," he demanded roughly. "Part that pretty pussy for me, Angel-mine."

She whimpered, shocked that the hungry mewl had actually come from her throat. Her fingers moved, parting the swollen, sensitive folds as he hovered over her.

"Oh God, Jack..." She breathed the small prayer for mercy as he blew a waft of breath over her throbbing clit, sending the hot juices flowing freely from her vagina.

He bent over her as she watched, her eyes widening, the breath halting in her throat until she felt the rapid, fierce strike against her aching clit. The sweep of his tongue was like wildfire, sending her hips arching closer to his mouth as a strangled scream erupted from her throat. Another hot lash and she was twisting beneath him, her knees bending, feet pressing into the mattress as she lifted closer.

"Stay still." His hand landed on the open flesh of her cunt.

Shock resounded through her. She felt the explosion trigger in her clit, setting off fireworks in her pussy then in her womb as her orgasm took her by surprise. A strangled scream of rapture tore past her throat as she pressed her head into the pillow, her eyes closing as she shuddered through the extraordinary pleasure.

"Jack..." She still ached. She was empty, burning.

"Oh, baby, how greedy that little pussy is."

She realized then that she was still holding herself open for him, giving him a clear view into the spasming opening to her vagina.

He moved slowly between her thighs.

"We can play later." He lifted her hands, holding her by the wrists as he lay them by her head. "Stay there. Stay real still, baby, and I'll see about feeding that hungry little cunt."

God, he looked so wicked. With his long hair hanging around his face, those dark blue eyes glittering beneath the lowered eyelids, his lips fuller, more sensual than before. He resembled the wicked, sexual dream vision she had lusted after for so many years. The one that came to her only in the dead of night, his features hidden, only the gold torque encircling his neck a familiar sight to her.

And how she longed to see that torque there now. Gleaming dully against his sun-rich flesh as he made a place for himself between her legs.

Her gaze went lower, her mouth drying at the thick length of his cock as he paused, kneeling between her thighs, watching her, driving her insane with the wait.

"Lift to me," he growled. "Raise your hips for me."

She did as he commanded, bracing her feet against the blankets and lifting her drenched pussy for the stretching she knew was coming. Her previous lovers hadn't been exactly endowed, but she wondered if somehow Jack had taken more than his fair portion in that department.

He gripped the steel-hard flesh, running the thickly crested head through the honey-rich slit before it.

"Fuck, you're hot," he groaned as he tucked it at her opening. "Hot and wet and so very, very greedy."

"Oh God, Jack, have mercy." Her hands fisted in the blankets beneath her head as the head began to press into her. Her head thrashed, stars glittering behind her closed eyelids as she felt him separating her, slowly, so very slowly she thought she would die from it.

"You're so tight, Angel-mine," he whispered as he gripped her behind the thighs, holding her in place as the smooth flesh of his cock began to pierce her. "So tight and sweet, it's enough to make a grown man cry in pleasure."

Her head tossed, her eyes fluttering as she fought to keep them open, fought to watch the slow impalement of her cunt.

She couldn't watch. She could only feel. Her eyes dazed and lifted to his, her body bowed, tension tightening it to a near breaking point as she felt him slowly, oh-so very slowly, working his cock past the tight, tender tissue of her pussy.

"You'll kill me…" She was aware of the thickening of her accent, but could do nothing for it.

"Fuck. Stay still, woman," he growled as she twisted against him. "You're so fucking tight I'm going to lose control any minute."

Yes, she wanted that. Needed it.

"I'll never survive this pace," she cried out, frustration eating her alive. "For pity's sake, Jack. Fuck me. Fuck me or kill me, whichever ye've decided to do. But do it right quick. No this slow."

"But I like slow, baby." His hands tightened beneath her legs. "Slow and tight, feeling every sweet muscle in that tight little pussy gripping my cock."

His expression was a grimace of pleasure and arousal.

A frustrated, agonized moan slipped past her throat as he filled her more. Mere inches, stretching her so deliciously, heating her, sending her blood pressure to the boiling point as she endured a pleasure never before imagined.

She couldn't take it. She needed more. Needed him deep and hard inside her.

She clenched around the portion of his cock that was there. Stroking it with her inner muscles as she fought for an anchor in the tumultuous storm overtaking her. There had to be something, some way to at least hold on to her sanity. What minute portion of it he had left her to this point.

She knew the slow, fierce digs into her cunt were driving her past sanity. She needed to be filled, not teased to death.

"You're a demon, Jack Riley," she accused him harshly as he kept his hesitant, teasing pace. "A torturous, arrogant demon."

"And you're a witch. A black-haired, violet-eyed, hottest fucking pussy I've been in witch," he groaned, sinking in deeper as she gritted her teeth and fought to hold back the cry that escaped against her will.

"Son of a bitch, Angel..." The desperate curse heralded a sudden hard push that gave her more. Then more.

"Yes. Oh yes, Jack. All of it. I need it all." She was gasping, fighting to press closer, to feel every inch stretching her wide.

Until he pulled back.

Baring her teeth in a snarl, Angel arched then forced herself forward, her hands gripping his shoulders as she came astraddle his hard thighs, then forced herself onto the hard wedge of male muscle tormenting her.

Her keening cry echoed in the air around her as she felt him fill her, the head butting into her very cervix as her teeth gripped his shoulder like an animal in heat. His hard hands now gripped her buttocks, clenching in the soft flesh there as she felt his cock throbbing hard and heavy inside her.

Her knees clasped his thighs, her feet pressing into the mattress as she began to ride her cowboy. Moving up until only the crest remained inside her hungry pussy before sliding back down in an erotic dance that had the breath slamming from her throat and pleasure overwhelming her.

"Save a horse, ride a cowboy," she whispered before nipping his ear and clenching on the invader with a tight, caressing grip.

She wasn't anticipating his reaction.

Before she could do more than gasp he was moving. He slammed her back on the bed at the same time his cock slammed into her pussy and he gave her what she had been pleading for. Hard, driving, fierce strokes that drove her headlong into the storm swirling within her body.

He fucked her like the demon she had sworn he was. Holding on to her, his cock shuttling in and out in a rapid, destructive pace that had her tightening, clenching, rapidly ascending a peak that alternately terrified and exhilarated her.

She stared up at him, dazed, feeling the fires swirling in her veins as her legs lifted, clasping his hips, opening herself further for the tumultuous invasion.

"Harder," she panted, feeling it, the orgasm she knew would change her forever. "Harder, Jack. Fuck me harder…harder…"

He gave her harder. He gave her deeper. Shafting her with a ferocity that had her screaming, exploding, dying in his arms as the flames consumed her.

Angel was only distantly aware of his release, the feel of his semen shooting inside her, prolonging the orgasm tearing her apart as she shuddered beneath him. Her arms and legs surrounded him, refusing to let him go as he finally stilled against her. Glowing aftershocks repeatedly shook her frame, leaving her breathless, astounded.

Such pleasure should not exist. It was destructive to the mind. It was destructive to the heart. The one part of herself she swore she wouldn't lose, she feared was the first part to go.

"My warrior…" she whispered the words at his ear as he moved from her grip, falling to his side and pulling her against him. "My warrior…"

* * * * *

It had to be a dream, but Jack knew that if it was, it was the most intense dream of his life.

He stood in the bedroom of the ancient castle that lay in ruins behind the Manning estate. A castle fully restored and teeming with activity. He walked purposely up the stairs, knowing where he was going, knowing that what awaited him would be a daunting chore…

How did he, an English warlord, unused to gentleness or to fond play ever hope to tame the wild heart of the one he knew he must conquer? He knew she had the oddest habit of making his calloused, rough hands tremble in fear of bruising her delicate, creamy flesh.

What was a man to do? With any other woman he would merely stomp into their room and take what had been bequeathed him. These were desperate times, a man had to hold on to what was his, by strength and by force. Doing so had never bothered him before.

But this Irish lass, this delicate, somber-eyed young woman did things to him that no other ever had. She made him want her tenderness, her willing touch. He wanted no tears in her eyes, no recriminations. Nor did he wish to hear her frightened pleas. He had heard too many of those in years past from those young girls claimed by his brethren. He had no desire to hear it from the woman who was now his own.

He paused at the landing, his hand rising to the torque that now circled his neck. What had he done there? He was sworn to destroy the Celtic druids, especially the priests who practiced their devil's magic. But somehow, he had been unable to lay hands to the kindly man who came to him on the girl's behalf.

The same who had given him the Wolves' Head Torque and the warning that only his heart could conquer the proud Irish maid his King had sent him to conquer. This castle, these lands and all it held were bequeathed to him. But he knew that the people would only follow him willingly if their Lady did as well. How odd that a land would hold such love for a mere slip of a girl, beautiful though she was.

Breathing in roughly, he moved to the door of her rooms, lowering his head for a moment as he willed himself to open the door. Just open it, man. Go in and take what is rightfully deeded to you, *a part of himself raged.*

This was his future, the future of any sons he might have. The land was rife with conflict, with war, and only the best of alliances would save it. If he could gain her willingness, then he could rule the land and the people, and with it, gain prosperity.

He breathed in deeply before gripping the latch and swinging the door wide before stepping inside. She stood, her back to him, skeins of long, silk black hair flowed past her hips, rippling like midnight down her back.

Slamming the door closed, he watched as she stiffened, a tremor shaking through her.

"The priest has blessed this union, our King has decreed it. I'll have none of your objections m'lady." He kept his voice firm, authoritative, when he wanted nothing more than to ease the fears he knew she must feel.

She had seen the degradation and rape of her female relatives before his arrival. Had witnessed her parents' deaths and the blood of defeat. Only the King's decree that she did indeed belong to him, had saved her from the rutting of the army that preceded him. She would not come easily to him, he feared. And though the thought of her rape was a sour stench in his nostrils, he knew he would do what he must this night to preserve his hold on the land.

He watched as she straightened her shoulders then turned to him slowly.

Her gaze landed on the torque, her eyes widening in startled surprise as her lips trembled.

"Does he still live?" she breathed roughly.

"Who?" A frown creased his brow at her odd question.

"The old one who gave you the Wolves' Torque," she whispered. "The priest whose death our king has decreed?"

He heard the fear in her voice, the grief that rose inside her.

"The old man lives." He shrugged. "His days are not many, his body frail. He will not die by my hand."

She stepped forward then stopped, licking her lips with an unconsciously sensual flick of her tongue.

"He gave you the torque?" she asked him then, her voice tremulous.

"Well, I am no thief, if this is what you mean," he snorted. "He brought it to my room after the blessing of the union. What does it mean to you?"

Her reaction was far too curious to mean nothing.

She drew in a shaky breath, her breasts rising beneath the night rail that covered her from head to toe.

"The Wolves' Torque has been only a legend. That it would be worn by a warrior strong and true. One who will bring prosperity, who will bring happiness. A stranger to our land and a warrior who will bring peace rather than blood, and prosperity rather than starvation."

He lifted a brow in mockery, though the words seemed to resound within his soul.

"Interesting legend," he responded quietly, though his body was wreaking havoc with his mind. He wanted nothing more than to possess her. To move between her thighs and slide into the bounty that awaited him there. She was tempting, incomparable beauty and grace.

She came closer, a step or two before stopping.

"He is an ancient priest," she whispered the words fearfully. "If you lie, his power is enough to bring your death, to wipe you from this Earth as though you never were. Do not play me false, warrior."

He frowned at that. "None but God holds such power, m'lady. Remember that always. But I do not play you false. He was an old one, I give you this. With flowing silver hair and eyes that spoke of the many years he has known. This is all I know. He entered my room and gifted me with this torque, advising me that only in wearing it will this land ascend to its rightful owner. I am weary enough of our battles to give it its due should it achieve that."

A smile quirked her lips, mocking, bitter. "You will do whatever it takes then to lie within my bed and to fill my belly with your sons, you mean. Odd. I would have expected a man such as yourself to reach much higher than an Irish estate of little value."

"There is much value here," he told her then, stepping closer, his fingers reaching out to touch her silken cheek. "The least of which is this estate. I would work with you, m'lady. To see not just my dreams of prosperity, but yours as well. Our alliance can bring this end, but only with your willingness." He gestured outside the door. "Even now, the servants' ears are lifted for the sounds of your pain and horror as I force you beneath me. Rumors come to my ears of those who lie in wait, to spill the blood of any who would force from you what is yours to rightfully give. Your people will not lay down beneath the foot of one who would take this land by force, or its women. I will do what I must to bring peace."

She lifted her head proudly then.

"Even bed a priestess to the gods ye have sworn to wipe from this planet," she whispered the words, as though other ears might hear her bleak confession.

It was no more than he had expected.

"Such a woman would have to show great care," he said then. "Were I to know such a woman, I would expect her to keep this secret deep within herself, and to remember the game at play here. Such a woman would have to remember times have changed. And she will hold not just her own life in her hand by practicing such beliefs, but the lives of her husband, her children, and perhaps more importantly to her, her people, in the palm of her hand. Such a woman would be a weighty burden for she could never, ever practice what she believes so deeply within. Not and expect my protection to cover her."

A tremor racked her once again as her eyes closed in painful acknowledgement. Then her hands lifted to the shoulders of her gown, trembling fingers releasing the tie that opened it, allowing it to fall from her flesh and pool at her small feet.

"A willing sacrifice," she whispered then, raising her eyes to his, the violet depths whispering of dreams despite her fatalistic tone. "I will try, m'lord, very hard, not to scream."

Fear marked her expression, her eyes, as he went to her then.

"And I will try, m'lady, very hard, to give you no cause..."

Jack came awake in a rush. He sat up in the bed, staring directly into Angel's eyes as she moved slowly from the doorway to the bathroom.

It was her. A near identical replica of the woman in his dream. His eyes narrowed as he watched her come toward him, a frown on her face as she held the towel tight around her body.

"Damn, I hope you don't wake up like that on a regular basis," she snorted, irritation flashing in her eyes. "You nearly scared me to death, jumping like that."

He blinked, feeling his chest clench as he watched her. He wasn't a man much given to fanciful imaginings or dreams such as the one he had just escaped. But damn if that dream hadn't been one like none he had ever known.

He snorted at her comment, moving from the bed as he checked the time on the clock.

Nearly four. How long had he slept anyway?

"I'm surprised you're still here." He moved from the bed, scratching his chest before stretching the sleep from his limbs.

She tilted her head and shrugged. "Beats jail."

Jack shot her a sharp look. Did she mean it? Hell, no, she didn't. He wasn't falling for that shit. She had met the heat, the wildness that reared inside him perfectly. That was not an unwilling lover, giving in to a fate little better than another that could await her.

She smiled. An all-too innocent smile that didn't cover the feminine knowledge in her eyes. Damn her. She had been making him crazy for much too long. The time he had spent between her thighs earlier wasn't near enough to make up for the many weeks she had been making him crazy at her father's estate.

That dream was messing with his head. But damn, if it hadn't been a dream that should have messed with a man's head.

"Tell me about the torque." He moved to the dresser, pulling out clean clothes as he glanced over his shoulder.

She shrugged her bare shoulders. "As I told you, it was gift from an ancient Celtic priest to an English warrior who had wed a child of his line. As long as the torque remains within my line, it's promised that we'll always know happiness and love in the marriage bed. Should it ever be taken away, then the blessing placed upon us goes away as well."

He shifted uncomfortably. Marriage he could do without. He didn't want marriage. Then he looked at her again, remembered her in his bed and frowned at the unfamiliar surge of longing that struck his chest.

Hell, no. No marriage.

Besides, he doubted she would give up her nice cushy life in Ireland to be a rancher's wife. He had decided while on the Manning estate that his days of traveling, buying and selling were coming to an end. Luc needed him on the ranch, to make it profitable rather than just the hobby they both played at. He should feel relieved at that thought. Shouldn't he?

"A piece of jewelry doesn't make a good marriage," he finally grumbled. "It's the people."

"I agree." She shrugged, her voice quiet. "But the blessing could make certain those two meant to be together, come together. Whichever. Fact or legend. It's the one piece that we have left from centuries of history. A piece that has passed from mother to daughter since it was given to the first warrior."

"Then why mother to daughter?" His tone was a shade mocking, and he knew it.

"Because it was given to the husband of the female of that land. Not the son. But as I said, that is beside the fact. Father had no rights to sell it. Mother's early death prevented the will she had planned to make, leaving the torque to me upon her death. Though their joint will leaves the remaining estate to me upon Father's death."

"The estate is worth plenty," he pointed out.

"The torque is worth just as much to me, if not more." She stared back at him, her violet eyes filled with emotion. "I'll let it go eventually, Jack. There's no sense in rubbing salt into the wound now. Perhaps, as you say, it is only legend."

"The Wolves' Torque has been only a legend..." The words from the dream haunted him now.

He grunted, moving for the shower rather than replying to her comment.

"Don't bother dressing," he warned her as he passed. "I won't be long."

Chapter Five

Arrogant ass. As though she had any of her clothing to dress into. Though if she did have anything clean, she would have definitely dressed into it just to spite him, she thought nearly twenty minutes later as she stood in the kitchen, dressed only in another of his T-shirts.

She was hungry. And she refused to cook naked. It just wasn't going to happen.

As she pulled eggs and omelet ingredients from the refrigerator, she frowned, wondering at his strange behavior before he disappeared into the shower. What would it matter to him where the torque came from, or the legends behind it?

It mattered to her. She had trusted in the legends, perhaps too much, to lead her to the man who would complete her, body and soul. At first, she had believed it could be Jack. The dreams had become more vivid, more sensual with his arrival at the estate. But with each word out of his mouth he had done nothing but sought to spark her temper.

But he had grown on her. She had enjoyed sparring with him, rebuffing him only to see what new game he would come back with. It was exciting, titillating, it had kept her arousal and her intellect challenged as no other man ever could.

But he had taken the torque. Despite her furious pleas, he had bought something that was priceless to her and taken it from her. He had taken the one thing left of the glorious past her ancestors had lived and loved through.

"You dressed." His voice was dark, forbidding as he stepped into the kitchen.

Angel placed the first omelet in its place and poured the second in.

"So I did." She glanced at him over her shoulder, once again seeing his features in the fuzzy image of her dream lover.

He was going to break her heart and she knew it. She could feel it in the vague, hollow ache in her chest and she hated it. Despite her determination to hold her heart from him, he had taken it as easily as he had the torque.

How was that, she wondered? He had stolen the torque. Had purchased it. It had been no gift, it had not come to him through their marriage…

Yet, neither had it come to its first wearer in such a way. She remembered the legend of the first bearer of the torque. The English warrior who had been gifted the emblem by the grandfather of a conquered maid. The daughter of the landholder. A peace offering. A promise…

She shook the thought away. This wasn't centuries past, this was here and now, and Jack wasn't an English lord, nor was he a conqueror or a warrior. He was a cowboy, one with a gift for acquiring things that should have never been his. Things such as her torque…and her heart.

She slid the second omelet to a plate and then placed both on the small round kitchen table along with silverware. Turning back to the counter, she poured two large mugs of coffee and set them by the plates before taking her seat.

The feel of the cool wood against her bare rear was a shock. She drew in a deep breath, sighed at the distraction then picked up her fork.

"You can eat or you can fume because I'm flashing body parts for your pleasure. Doesn't make a difference to me, I'm going to eat," she informed him coolly, refusing to turn to look at him.

"You're a stubborn woman." He made it sound like a curse.

"I consider it one of my better qualities." She lifted a bite to her lips, inhaled the aroma then devoured it. Sex with Jack made her hungry.

Another of those male snorts sounded behind her before he moved around her to the opposite seat and the plate awaiting him.

He looked more amused than displeased with her.

Silence reigned as they both ate, though Angel could feel the tension growing between them.

"I have to return tomorrow," she finally announced as she stood and collected the empty plates.

"You mean if the sheriff lets you?" He lifted a brow mockingly.

"Sheriff or no, I have no choice." She shrugged indifferently. "I haven't moved to America, Jack, I was only visiting."

She turned back, her gaze moving to the window and the land outside it. It appeared barren, scruffy, but there was a beauty within it that she hadn't expected to see, a beauty she feared she would miss when she returned to Ireland.

He leaned back in his chair, a frown crossing his face. "Forget it. I'm not ready for you to leave yet."

She smiled at his stubbornness, shaking her head as his arrogance reared its head. He was really quite charming, even when he frowned like that.

"Then in the morning, I suggest you notify of the sheriff of my attempted theft of your property. Because by afternoon, I will be gone. This isn't my home."

So why then was regret eating at her soul?

"And you think two nights is enough to make up for the near month of hell you put me through while I was trapped on that estate of yours?" he growled, rising to his feet. "I don't think so, little witch."

"Angel," she corrected him, her smile mockingly innocent. "Remember?"

He crossed his arms over his bare chest. "I want a month."

"You're a big boy, Jack. Your wants won't hurt you." But some of hers did. Because she didn't want to leave. She wanted to stay with a strength that actually made her chest ache.

He made her ache. Just staring at him, seeing not just the incredibly sexy male body, but the man as well. The one who made her laugh, made her scream in frustration and made her hotter, wetter than any man ever had, than she knew any other man ever would.

"You're not leaving."

His declaration was a surprise. The frustrated look on his face was even more so, as though he had surprised himself with the words as much as he had surprised her.

She adopted his stance, crossing her arms beneath her breasts and watching him with curious amusement. He rather looked like a little boy not getting his way. It was oddly cute, exasperating, but cute nonetheless.

"Tomorrow I leave, Jack," she reiterated. "Unless you are proposing more than a fly-by-night affair?" She lifted a brow suggestively.

His frown, if possible, became darker.

"I didn't say that." His response was immediate. A second later a thoughtful glimmer entered his blue gaze as he shifted uncomfortably. "Why, do you want more?"

She arched her brow. That bit of confusion, of ill ease, would have been endearing if it wasn't her heart he was playing with.

"I'm merely pointing out we both have lives," she finally answered coolly. "The sex is incredible, Jack, but I have a life. Sex, no matter how incredible, is not the be-all and end-all to life. I have to return to my life."

"So take a vacation," he snapped impatiently.

"Ireland isn't America." She rolled her eyes at the demand. "I can't just vacation whenever the mood hits me. The matter isn't up for argument. Tomorrow…"

"I won't let you leave."

Arrogance, pure and simple. There was nothing uncomfortable about that statement.

"Kidnapping is illegal in America as well," she pointed out.

"I didn't kidnap you. I'm just keeping you." It was obvious he wasn't seeing the complications here.

"You, and whose army?" She mocked his declaration then.

"Who needs an army, sweetheart?" He smiled then, a sensual wicked curve of his lips that made her want to groan. "I have handcuffs. Velvet-lined and soft as sin. They'll keep you in place. I promise."

Why couldn't he let her leave? Jack moved slowly across the kitchen, his cock aching like a wound as he stared into her confused, amused expression. She had no idea how very serious he was. Hell, even he was unaware of how serious he was until she mentioned leaving.

Everything inside him screamed at him to keep her there, in his bed, in his life. He couldn't imagine not having her there, the sweet heat of her pussy gripping his cock, her kiss making him hot and hard. Her laughter filling the house.

For so many years this place had been a silent tomb, a place to sleep, but nothing more. In the last two days, it had become that something more. It seemed lighter, brighter, it echoed with life. Just as she had lit something within him during his stay in Ireland. Something he had been unaware of until now.

But she was entirely too serious about leaving him.

He backed her into the counter, his arms braced on each side of her as he stared down at her, his eyes narrowed, everything inside him rejecting her announcement.

Her hands flattened on his chest, delicate fingers trembling against his bare flesh as her gaze lowered.

"Don't." She said that hated word. Dammit, he hated it when she did that.

"Don't what?" He lowered his head, nudging her chin up before allowing his lips to whisper across hers. "Don't tempt you into spending more time with me? What would it hurt, Angel? A week, maybe two?"

Something flashed in her gaze, a glimmer of pain, a shadow of fear as her lips parted before the soft stroke of his tongue.

She was soft and heated, her tongue flickering against his as it licked over her lips. Damn. His muscles clenched at the deliberate temptation of the caress. She made him so damned horny he forgot what patience was. He wanted nothing more than to lift her to the counter and fuck her like an animal in heat. The nearly overwhelming urge to do just that sent a shudder up his spine.

"Jack." Her hand lifted, her fingers smoothing over the stubble roughness of his cheek. "If I stay, you'll break my heart. Is this what you truly want? Let me go now, while I can still retain the memory of what we had, without the pain of losing it forever. Leave me something for the future."

Her eyes were like large, bruised violets, dark with emotion, with a feminine plea for mercy.

A frown pulled at his brows as once again the dream from that morning swept through him, the emotions that had pulled at him then, pulling at him now.

"No." He shook his head, not clearly understanding why the word came so naturally to his lips.

"No?" she questioned him roughly. "Jack, you can't make me stay. Handcuffs and sheriff aside, you can't force it on me."

Her accent thickened with her anger. The smooth, soft lilt of her voice became a thick brogue that had his cock hardening further, every instinct in his body screaming out that he take her, bind her to him, never let her go.

"Son of a bitch." He pushed his fingers roughly through his hair as he let her go, turning away from her and the erratic, erotic temptation of her slender body. "Fine. Tomorrow you can leave. But that still leaves tonight, in my fucking bed." He turned on her swiftly, catching her swift intake of air, the pain that flashed across her face. "And my bed is not in this kitchen, Angel. Get up there."

She wasn't going to cry, Angel promised herself. He was giving her what she asked for, no more, no less. He would let her go and leave her something for the future. But what?

She moved up the stairs, aware of him stalking slowly behind her, his gaze never leaving her back, heating the air around them. She had never seen him like this, determined, almost savage, the playboy exterior eroded away to show the steel core of the man beneath. A man who aroused her, fascinated her, and threatened every part of her woman's soul. This was a man who could destroy every dream she had for her life.

And still she was moving up the stairs, heading for his bedroom, every cell in her body screaming out for him, her pussy drenching with the hunger rising in her body. She entered the doorway, stepping slowly into the room before turning to face him.

He was stepping out of the sweatpants he had worn downstairs, his cock a rampant impaler standing out from his body, engorged with lust. His expression was one of fierce determination.

Before Angel could do more than breathe in sharply, he was pulling her to him, his lips coming down on hers, slanting across them as he sent his tongue pressing firmly between her lips.

Her head fell back on her shoulders as a weak moan of submission left her lips. She couldn't fight him. She didn't want to fight him. She wanted nothing more than to be held in his hard, muscular arms, to feel him, dominant and powerful, overtaking her.

She heard the material of his shirt ripping from her body. The sound sent a surge of excitement powering through her veins as a rush of heated juices ran from her pussy. God, he made her wild. Too wild. He took too much of her, made her feel too much. It wouldn't matter when she left, she knew she was leaving her heart behind.

Her hands moved, unable to keep still, to keep from touching him, holding him. She needed to feel his flesh, to memorize the texture of it, the warmth and power of the muscles beneath the hair-sprinkled, suntanned skin.

They roamed over his chest, his shoulders, finally sinking into the silken texture of the overly long blond hair. Who would believe that she had fallen in love with a cowboy? A devil-may-care charmer who cared nothing for her heart, only the relief he found in her sexually. It made no sense to her, but she knew that forever her heart would linger in this dry, rough land, always longing for him.

"God, you feel good." His voice was as rough as his breathing, as intent as the cry that slipped past her lips.

His hands smoothed over her breasts, cupping, his fingers rasping her nipples as his mouth followed suit. His tongue licked over one as his hands moved lower. His lips covered the hard tip, his tongue licking with all apparent enjoyment as the fingers of one hand slid between her thighs.

Heated fingers of lightning crashed inside her as sparks dazzled her vision. The pleasure was so intense she wondered if she would survive it this time.

"You're wet, Angel-mine," he growled, his fingers caressing, sliding through the cream flowing from her vagina as she arched against him.

"So fix it," she panted, feeling his lips stroking her nipple as he spoke, causing tiny shards of sensation to travel from the hard tip to her womb, convulsing it with pleasure.

"Is it fixable?" he drawled, his voice sexy and dark as his lips moved to her neck.

Hell, no, it wasn't.

"I'm sure you can find a way if you think about it a second." She arched closer, feeling his cock against her stomach, a hard, hot, living stalk of pleasure.

A rough laugh vibrated from his throat as he smiled against her neck.

"There's no cure," he warned her. Something she was well aware of. "Only intense therapy. Lots and lots of this…"

His hands cupped her buttocks as he lifted her against him, his cock sliding between her thighs to notch at the tender opening of her pussy.

Angel's eyes opened wide as she gasped, her legs automatically lifting, her knees clasping his hips.

"There you go, baby," he nipped at her neck erotically. "Ride your cowboy now."

She felt him brace himself, holding her close as he began to work his erection inside her. Sliding in, pulling back, shafting the sensitive channel with burning thrusts, sending him deeper with each stroke, stretching her further as she began to keen in pleasure.

God, she had never imagined being taken like this. He held her weight confidently, his legs braced apart, his cock spearing inside her, stretching her when she was certain she could take no more, stroking nerve endings still sensitized from the morning's previous play.

She was shuddering, needing him, aching.

"God no. Don't you stop…" she demanded fiercely as he slid from her, his soft laugh one of strained control as he moved to the bed, dropping her to it as he followed her down.

But he wasn't moving to reclaim the territory he had possessed moments before, instead, he spread her thighs wide, lowered his head, and used his tongue to still any protest she would have voiced.

Shock held her rigid for long moments, but the pleasure was more than she could have imagined denying. Her hands clenched in his hair as a long, low moan passed her lips and she gave in to the pleasure building inside her.

His tongue was like a whip of burning pleasure. Licking…licking as though he was devouring a favored treat as his tongue slid through the thick, heavy juices of her pussy.

The sounds of his enjoyment vibrated from his lips to the folds of her cunt, the cries of her pleasure pierced the air as his lips wrapped around her clit and his tongue probed at the nerve-laden knot.

He was making her insane. She was going to die of the pleasure.

Angel writhed beneath him, lost in the dark storm of excessive sensation, reaching, climbing higher with each diabolical stroke of his tongue. She was close. So very close to an orgasm that she knew would steal her soul and she fought it with every breath.

Until two hard, broad fingers slid inside her clenching pussy, opening her, fucking her with smooth strokes as his mouth and tongue licked and sucked and threw her headlong over the precipice she had fought so desperately.

Her hips bucked, arched. The orgasm tore through her, taking her breath, tightening her muscles to near breaking point as it exploded through each nerve ending.

Wicked, lustful demon that he was, Jack chose that moment to move to his knees, position the thick head of his cock and push inside the contracting, gripping tissue of her cunt.

She screamed with her last breath. She bucked against him, seeing stars in front of her vision as his cock surged inside her, beginning a hard, fast rhythm she couldn't fight, couldn't deny. There was no time to save herself. No time to pull her defenses around her before he stripped the last of her fragile control.

She was a creature of pleasure. One long, rapidly exploding, melting orgasm that refused to stop. She dissolved around him, shuddering helplessly, going from one pinnacle to another, only to be driven higher, higher, until the gripping, destructive, final release sent her juices pouring around his cock as it spurted inside her, filling her with the heat and strength of his seed.

She collapsed. There was barely the energy left to breathe, to remain conscious as she drifted in a sea of bliss unlike anything she had heard or read about. She was only distantly aware of the fact that he had covered her, that her hands were locked around his neck, her fingers buried in his hair. She couldn't release him. She had a death grip on him, or was it a soul grip, for surely she still lived?

When he moved to take his weight from her, his arms wrapped around her, pulling her with him as her head fell naturally against his shoulder.

"Don't forget me, Angel-mine..." he whispered against her ear as she began to drift between sleep and wakefulness. "Never forget me..."

"I will not let you go, woman." Jack was surprised to find himself once again in the ancient castle, Angel standing before him, her long hair flowing around her as she faced him, dressed in a gown of rich fabric that fell to her feet, and covered her creamy arms.

A robe was thrown over her shoulders, its hood folded back, and it was more than apparent she was preparing to leave the castle.

"What do ye care, English?" she fairly sneered, but he could see the tears that glittered in her eyes. "Ye've no love for me. Yur heart is stone-cold, only ye body warms for me."

Well, some things never changed. He fought to escape the dream, but he couldn't leave her, not with the pain he could see in her face, not with the knowledge that she was going to leave him.

What the hell was up with these damned dreams? He shook his head, but the words that came from his mouth were nothing he meant to say.

"You are my wife!" he snarled back at her. "You will not leave me, Lady."

She turned from him, her shoulders heaving.

"Ye steal all that I am," she whispered. "My heart, my verra soul. Ye steal it like a thief, and cast it aside as the fodder ye feel it is. I am naught to you..."

"My wife..."

"'Tis not enough." He heard the tears as she spoke and his chest clenched with pain. Why was he hurting? Love wasn't what he wanted. "Ye wear the Wolves' Head Torque, a symbol of legend of the heart that would unite with this land. With me..." She turned back, her violet eyes blazing fiercely. "Ye were to love me. To hold me not just with yur lust. To hold me with yur heart, with all that ye are, the same I have held ye. Rather, ye hold yourself bleak and cold, believin' to find yur strength in things other than the one who has given ye her soul."

"I asked not..."

"Ye had not to ask..." Tears ran freely down her cheeks. "Ye had not to ask, warrior. 'Twas yurs the moment ye rode into this land. 'Twas always yurs. But ye've nothin' ta give in return but a cold, unfeelin' sword, and the bitter dregs of dreams fallin' at yur feet."

"No..."

"Aye." She nodded, sobs shaking her shoulders. "Ye're a warrior. A fine, fine warrior ye are, English. Ye're King should be well proud of ye. For ye've held yerself distant, ruled this land, brought profit and conquered the heathens as ye were bid. Conquered even my heart with yur cold English ways. But ye have no heart. And I'll no lie beneath a man not mine."

"I'm your husband." Confusion swamped him. "You are mine. By law, by King and by God."

"If yur God is as cold and unfeeling as ye are, then perhaps 'tis better our people have our own," she whispered bleakly. "A merciful God such as the one ye speak of to me would no leave ma life this barren, ma heart achin' in despair."

She went to her knees, her cries tearing from her throat, ripping through his chest. What had he done? How had he brought his proud Irish lass to her knees?

"What would you have of me?" he gritted out, his fists clenching with the frustration rising inside him, the pain building in his chest. "What more can I give you?"

Her head raised, her face was so pale it sent a spurt of fear through him, her eyes dark with misery, with a pain he could not bear to look upon.

"Yur heart," she cried, sobbing, her hand trembling as it reached out to him. "Only yur heart can save any of us. The one thing ye do not possess, my fine English warrior… Love."

Jack shook himself awake, jerking upright in the bed, his body coated with a cold sweat as he felt the agony resounding through him.

Okay, this was enough, he told himself silently, fiercely, as his head swung around to stare at Angel as she slept. There were no tears. No recriminations. At least, not coming from her.

But she was leaving. Dawn was only hours away, and he was going to have to watch her dress, watch her walk out of his life forever.

He reached out, touched the silk of her hair, and felt something he had never known at any other time when he acknowledged the fact that he may never see a particular woman again.

Regret.

Pain.

Grief.

And he had no idea why… Or did he?

Chapter Six

There were tears in her eyes. He saw them, even though she was careful to keep from looking him in the eye as she finished dressing in the black jeans and black shirt. She looked like the dark angel she was, flitting about the room to hide the trembling of her lips, her hands.

He sat on the edge of the bed watching her, the torque clenched in his hand, hidden by the blanket at his side.

"The cab will be here soon." She lowered her head again as she faced him. "I'll miss you, Jack."

The words tore through his chest.

Fuck. Fuck. What had she done to him? Letting a woman go, no matter how hot and sweet her pussy was, had never hurt.

He rose to his feet, stepping before her and taking her hands. Slowly he placed her precious torque across them, watching the dull gleam of the gold as she held it.

Her gaze flew to his.

"I would have brought it back to you," he told her then. He had denied it at the time, but he had known he was only buying the damned thing because of her.

He had wanted to please her. To bring a smile, some glimmer of joy to her face. Instead, a tear slipped down her cheek as a bitter smile crossed her lips.

She lifted her hands, spreading open the neckband until she clasped it around his neck, allowing the wolves' heads to lay at the center of his collarbone.

The weight of it was odd, the heat from it warming his flesh.

"It's yours," she whispered then. "Not only fairly bought, but fairly earned. Remember me, Jack," she repeated his words from the night before. "Just as I'll always remember you."

He stood still, frowning down at her as she placed a quick, tearful kiss on his lips before rushing from the room.

He could feel himself fighting for breath, feel the urge to go after her, sling her over his shoulder and force her to stay. But he knew it wouldn't be enough. Force would never work with his proud Irish lass. But what would?

"Yur heart." The words she had spoken in a dream haunted him now. *"Only yur heart can save any of us. The one thing ye do not possess, my fine English warrior… Love."*

Love?

Love did not exist. Not for him. Not in this world. He had admitted it to himself years before. No matter how much he had longed to find that perfect woman and make a home in the land he loved, he had been unable to. He couldn't feel. Not that intense overriding emotion he heard love was.

He had given up.

He had traveled the world more than once, searching for priceless treasure, for that one great adventure, but the search had begun with the search for love.

He sat back down on the bed, feeling the torque like a weight of incrimination.

At twenty-two he had realized what he searched for didn't exist in Madison, or the small towns that surrounded it. It wasn't in Dallas, or in Fort Worth. It hadn't been found in New Orleans, Fort Smith, or any of the other cities he had traveled and worked his way through.

Eventually, he had stopped looking for elusive emotion and concentrated instead on profit. On prosperity. On making the land he loved something he could find pride in, something worth fighting for.

The emptiness of the house mocked him now.

Outside he heard the cab pull into the drive. Less than a minute later it left. And he was alone.

Alone in the house he had built from the money he had made as he traveled the world conquering adventure. And losing himself.

"Fuck!" He rose to his feet, pacing to the window to stare into the dry heat of another Texas morning.

Damn, he loved it here. This was home, but honest to God, the only time he had found peace here, felt fulfilled, were the hours Angel had filled it with her presence. Just as she had her father's estate.

Her laughter. Her irate voice. Her soft sighs.

She haunted him, and she was no more than a few miles from the driveway he was certain.

He lifted his hand, releasing the torque from his neck before staring at it, holding it in the sunlight, staring down at it with a frown.

He hadn't even wanted the damned thing, so why had he really bought it?

Because she claimed it.

It was the one thing he could possess that would anchor her to him. It was the only thing she truly loved, her father had claimed.

In that moment, he realized that he had wanted it. From the moment he saw it, held it, it had been familiar, felt comfortable in his grip. Just as it felt comfortable around his neck.

He clasped it around his neck once again, his eyes narrowing as he stared into the vivid blue of the sky.

He told her she wasn't leaving him, and by God, he meant it.

He showered, dressed quickly, then walked to the dresser, opening the middle drawer. Staring at the assortment of adult articles there, he decided quickly which ones to take along.

Handcuffs were a must. The black silk kerchief. Couldn't have her screaming too hard at a hotel, someone might call the sheriff. A few toys. Definitely the small tube of lubrication, just in case he decided to get adventurous.

He threw them all into a small bag, pulled his boots on, grabbed his keys and headed for the front door. It was time to bring his woman home.

Angel held back her tears as she rode into town. She kept her head turned away from the rearview mirror. She didn't want the cabbie to see the tears swimming in her eyes, or the pain that raged through her.

Walking away from Jack was the hardest thing she had ever done. Watching the Texas landscape pass by, the flat valley filled with grass, the rolling hills beyond thick with trees and a hardy wildness that called to something in the very depths of her soul.

She didn't want to leave. She wanted to stay, if only for the few weeks he had suggested. But if it hurt this horribly now, how much more would it hurt weeks, or even days from now? It would destroy her.

She closed her eyes and let the image of him form in her mind. His crooked smile. His brilliant blue eyes. His broad, calloused hands. Every inch of his body was adored by her inner vision as she silently forced herself to say goodbye.

The old writings that had passed through the ages with the torque, told of its first owner. A proud English warrior who had wed the daughter of the fallen Celtic landowner so many centuries before. The MacTaidhg family lands had fallen beneath the sword of the one called the Hewn Wolf. A blond-haired warrior who had found favor with the English King and given the Irish lands and the order to conquer the wild hearts that fought against the crown so fiercely.

He had moved to the very heart of the land, wedding the granddaughter of its hidden priest, and protecting the secret that would have seen her beheaded. It was said he was a scourge of the people, until she tamed him. That she had bewitched the wolf and brought him to her feet. Though the tales Angel's mother had told hinted that both warrior and proud Irish lass bowed to each other.

The torque will bring the warrior destined to tame your wild heart, Angel, her mother had told her countless times. Before Megan Manning had died, she had spoken often to her daughter about the legends. Those that assured love and happiness for the female ancestors of that first blessed marriage. As long as the ancient neckband stayed within the family it had been given to, then its power would remain true.

And now it was gone. Sold by her father to the man who had stolen Angel's heart and would be lost to her forever.

She would begin the legacy of discontent now, rather than one of happiness.

She blinked back her tears, raised her chin and stared into the hazy reflection the window provided. She looked as broken as she felt. And that just wouldn't do. She wouldn't give others the knowledge of her pain, for surely if she did, news of it would reach Jack. It wasn't his fault he couldn't love her, and she wanted no guilt to be heaped on him. Loving him had been her choice.

"Here we are." The cabbie stopped in front of the small hotel in the center of town. The three-story building had all the quaint charm of the west on the outside, though the inside was fully modern.

"Thank you." She pulled several bills from the pocket of her jeans as she stepped from the cab.

"Thank you, ma'am. I hope your stay at the J.R. Ranch was a good one. Ole Jack's not home often, so not many get to stay in that nice new house he built a few years ago."

"It's a beautiful house." She fought the burning tears behind her eyes. "Thank you again. Good day, sir."

She moved away from him quickly, heading inside the hotel and to her room. The dark wood lobby was decorated in the style of the old west. Heavy brocades and large pieces of furniture.

She passed through it, for once taking no time to admire the unique decorations. Her room was on the third floor, and if she hurried, she would have time to shower and pack before heading to the airport and the late flight she had booked back to Ireland.

Entering the elevator, she moved to the back corner, wrapping her arms around her as she lowered her head to stare at the rust brown carpeting beneath her feet.

She missed him.

She ached for him.

Leaving him was ripping her soul apart…

* * * * *

Hotel security in Madison, Texas could really suck. Jack slid the stolen key card through its computerized pad, waited for the green light then eased it slowly open. Few people thought to use the metal latch on the other side to prevent access. He wondered if Angel had been diligent enough to use hers.

Nope. The door eased fully open, not even a squeak of the hinges to give away his presence.

The bathroom door at the side of the entrance was closed, the sound of the shower running assuring him that Angel was suitably busy. A slow, wicked grin crossed his lips as he closed the door behind him, sliding the latch over onto its metal peg to assure privacy. He didn't want one of the housekeepers coming in at the wrong time in the morning.

Moving further into the room, he set the duffel bag on the bed, quickly opened it and began preparations for Angel's final fall. She might think she was leaving him, but he was going to show her differently.

Soft, padded cuffs attached to long chains came first. Looping the ends of the small chains to the bed legs, he clipped them in place before laying the padded cuffs on the pillows. Next were the ankle cuffs, which he arranged at the lower corners after securing them.

The tube of lubrication was laid on the table along with nipple clips, a dildo and a butt plug. Finally, he undressed, folding his clothing neatly before sliding them into one of the empty drawers of the dresser by the bed. He was going to play, and Angel was going to be his personal little toy in the games he had planned.

The shower shut off.

Smiling in anticipation, Jack moved to hide along the wall, waiting until she walked through the short hallway.

It didn't take long. A few short minutes later, he heard the bathroom door open and watched as her shadow neared. Emotions swamped him in those fragile seconds. Possessiveness, love, love unlike anything he could have imagined, and tenderness.

She stepped past him.

Moving quickly he came behind her, his arms sweeping around her, pulling her around, giving her only a second to glimpse his face before his lips lowered to hers. But he had glimpsed hers as well. Her eyes reddened, tear-drenched, her cheeks pale, her expression miserable.

"Shh," he whispered against her lips as her lips opened to cry out. "It's okay, baby. It's all okay now…"

One hand cupped her cheek as his chest clenched at the dampness he felt there. He had made her cry. Pain streaked through him at the thought of that.

"Don't cry, Angel-mine," he whispered, sipping at her lips, his tongue stroking over the swollen curves as her breath hitched, a small, strangled sob coming from her as her hands gripped his arms, her nails biting into the flesh. "No more tears, baby. Only this. Only this."

His lips swallowed the words parting her lips, his tongue driving deep as he maneuvered her slowly to the bed, holding her to him as he lifted her to the center before laying her back.

He ignored the gasping little moans that left her throat. Rather than allowing her voice to her questions, he snapped the cuffs on one wrist. She jerked beneath him as he did the same to the other.

Then he released her lips, staring at the kiss-reddened flesh with a sense of satisfaction.

"What are you doing?" Her voice was hoarse as she tested the strength of the chains.

Jack moved back, going to her ankles, chuckling as she kicked out at him.

"Jack, have you lost your mind?" She struggled furiously as he restrained her ankles, testing the length of the chain for enough freedom of movement to allow him his play. She could bend her knees, but she wasn't going anyplace. She couldn't turn from him, nor would she be able to writhe from his grip.

"Let me go!" she snarled up at him, her violet eyes still damp with tears as she fought against the restraints. "Do you think this will solve anything? That it will make it better?" Her voice trembled. "For God's sake. Don't hurt me like this, Jack."

He sighed, shaking his head in chastisement as he watched her.

"Shame on you, Angel, thinking I would just let you walk away," he said gently, amazed at how free he suddenly felt, at the joy that rose inside him.

He had no idea how much he did love her, how much he had loved her before he ever left Ireland. Until now, staring into her pain-ridden gaze and seeing a reflection of the pain he couldn't explain within himself, he hadn't a clue how much she meant to him.

She opened her lips to berate him further when her gaze fell on the torque circling his neck. Her eyes widened then, a gasp leaving her lips as shock filled her eyes.

"I won't let you go," he whispered then. "Not ever, Angel-mine."

Then he lowered his head, taking her lips in a kiss that swamped him with pleasure, with emotion, with a sense of coming home.

He was the dream.

Angel moaned beneath his kiss, her lips parting for him, her tongue tangling with him as he began to sip at her lips, to nibble and stroke as he inflamed every cell in her body with the pleasure.

He was the dream. The one who had tormented her for so many years. And now she knew why she had never been able to look beyond the torque to see his face. Why she had been filled with such a sense of wonder and overpowering emotions. Because she had given up on the dream, just as she had given up on the torque. Only to learn that the man and the neckband went hand in hand.

"Jack." She moaned his name as his head lifted, his eyes, brilliant blue and filled with arrogant assurance meeting hers.

"I love you." He whispered the words she had felt certain she would never hear from him. "I've waited a lifetime to say those words, Angel. Searched until my soul grew weary with disappointment. I'll not let you leave me."

She wanted to wrap her arms around him. Wanted to hold him to her and laugh aloud in overwhelming relief.

"Let me go." She jerked at the restraints. "I want to hold you, Jack."

He grinned. A devilish, wicked curve of his lips that had her lips parting in excitement.

"Not yet, baby," he growled. "We're going to play tonight. For hours and hours and hours. And when morning comes, you're going to be too damned tired to even consider leaving. You won't remember your name let alone any desire to walk away from me."

She wasn't going anywhere now. She nearly whispered those words then held them back at the last second. What had he said about playing? Would her pleasure be better served in allowing him his way?

Well, duh, as the American students said. Of course it would be.

She relaxed back upon the pillows.

"Do your worst," she whispered, smiling herself as his eyes narrowed at her challenge. "But I bet I still remember my name well."

Chapter Seven

"What's your name, baby?" Jack's voice was tight, hoarse, as she twisted beneath him, writhing beneath the steady penetration of the dildo filling her pussy as the plug in her rear stretched her unbearably.

She was on fire. She could feel the flames burning through her body more than an hour later as she begged, pleaded for release. He was killing her. He had been steadily killing her since the first kiss, making her beg for more when she swore she could take no more of the blistering torment.

She was panting, perspiration covered her, dampened her hair, her flesh, and the comforter beneath her body. Still, Jack lay between her thighs, fucking her slow and easy with the fake cock as she fought to get closer to him.

His tongue was a demon. It was evil. No pleasure such as this should be possible.

He licked his way around the straining nub of her clit, flickering over it with devilish disregard for her hoarse cries as she arched closer to him, only to have him pull back.

"Please," she panted. "For mercy's sake, please…please…"

"What's your name?" he whispered again, pushing the dildo deeper inside her, forcing her take it to the very depths of her pussy as her muscles spasmed around it, her juices flowing, her cunt weeping with the overwhelming need to orgasm.

She had held out as long as she could.

She tried to scream as one hand moved up, fingers tugging at the clips attached to her swollen nipples and sending pulsing fingers of sensation raking along her nerve endings to the overly sensitive depths of her cunt.

Her back arched, her head shaking as he sucked her clit into his mouth once again, never truly touching it, merely surrounding the swollen knot of nerves with moist heat.

It was almost enough. But in this game, almost counted for nothing.

"This is unfair," she wailed, a moan tearing from her throat as the dildo moved with slow precision until only the head rested inside her once again, stretching her opening, burning her before sliding back once again.

"Harder, damn you. Fuck me properly." She nearly screamed the words. She would have screamed them if she had the breath to do so.

"What's your name?" he whispered again, licking over her clit as every muscle in her body clenched at the nearness of release. "Tell me, baby. Do you remember your name?"

"Yes." She stared down at him then, her eyes dazed. "Jack's. I'm Jack's. Whatever he wishes to call me, whenever… For pity's sake, Jack… Please…"

He moved before the words were out of her mouth. The dildo pulled free of her body, causing her to arch, her feet bracing on the bed as she lifted, attempting to follow it.

Oh God, she was so empty. Too empty. She was dying…

"There, baby," he whispered as he came over, the head and steel-hard perfection of his swollen cock nudging against the opening of her pussy. "Feel how much better this is."

He pushed inside her.

Better? It was nirvana. It was ecstasy, rapture, it was fucking incredible.

She shook, trembling so hard her teeth nearly chattered as she stared up at him, feeling him push into the tightened channel of her pussy, passing the heavy weight of the plug still anchored in her rear, making her muscles grip him so snugly she wondered that there was room for him.

But he made room, working his cock inside her like a knife through melting butter as he penetrated the syrup-slick confines of her cunt.

Electricity whipped around her. It sizzled in the air, crackled along her flesh, preparing her for the explosion building with her. One she wasn't certain she would survive.

"Look at me, Angel," he whispered when her eyes began to drift closed. "Look at me, baby, let me so those pretty eyes when you come around my cock. Watch me, sweetheart…"

And he began to move.

Each powerful, straining thrust had his pelvis raking against her clit as his erection burrowed hard and deep inside her. The thick length stretched her, burned her, sent her senses careening as her cry tore from her throat.

Her eyes widened as his strokes increased in speed, his hips slamming against hers as his face twisted into a mask of pleasure.

"God, I love you," he growled as his head lowered, his teeth tugging at the nipple clip as the fingers of one hand tugged at the other.

The additional flare of sensation, the destructive pleasure ripping through her undid her.

Angel arched, her breath catching in her throat as she began to shudder, feeling the tension exploding within her as her pussy seemed to melt around him. Her clit pulsed, throbbed, then followed in the wake, sending brilliant arcs of fire to burn through her senses as she burned beneath him, only distantly aware of his release as well.

She was flying, soaring in a world of dark pleasure unlike anything she had ever known, feeling her body as though it were an alien creature, erupting again, then again, as her orgasm ripped through her soul and rather than tearing her asunder, making her whole.

For the first time in her life, she was whole.

She didn't know how long she lay there, her body convulsing in the aftershocks of the pleasure, but she knew Jack was with her. His arms enfolded her, holding her tight, his face buried at her neck as his body shuddered atop hers.

Then his head turned, his lips ghosting over her ear.

"Angel-mine," he whispered. "I love you."

A smile tugged at her lips as she drifted sleepily within the waves of pleasure that still surged through her.

"I love you, Jack," she whispered in turn then. "Now remove these chains before I'm forced to kill you."

She tugged tiredly at the restraints. There wasn't a chance in hell she could sleep like this, and now, she wanted nothing more than to sleep.

A rough chuckle sounded at her, but he moved, hurriedly releasing her wrists and ankles before dragging his nude body back up the bed.

"Let me catch my breath and we'll try that again." He yawned as Angel brushed the nipple clips that had fallen beside them on the bed out of her way.

"Sure." She snuggled against him. "In the morning."

He sighed deeply.

"We're going home in the morning," he said, his arms tightening around her. "To my ranch. Where you belong."

"Home." Her eyes closed, a smile tilting her lips.

Yes, she was going to go home.

Epilogue

Joseph Manning hung up the phone and stared at the portrait that hung over the fireplace of the family room his wife had so loved.

"I did it, my love," he whispered, smiling at the laughing green eyes that showed the wit and charm that had been so much a part of her. "Just as you said I would. I found our daughter her American warrior."

At first, no one could have ever imagined Jack Riley was a warrior. A charmer. A playboy. Not a warrior. But the weeks he had spent at the estate had given Joseph another insight into the young man. A loner because he believed what he sought didn't exist. A man who feared love was an illusion.

And, ahhh, the sparks that had flown whenever his Angel was in the cowboy's company. She had lit up like a grand light, her eyes sparkling, her cheeks flushing as she fought against the attraction that was so very apparent.

In those weeks Jack had stayed with them, he had watched them seek each other's company, only to bicker like children fighting for supremacy.

He had known Jack for many years, but he had never seen him react so to a woman. And he knew his daughter better than she imagined. She had fallen in love so easily, yet had fought it so hard.

"Well, love, I was looking forward to returning to your loving arms," he sighed, though without regret. "But I think when we meet again you would like to know of the grandchildren that will soon be coming. Perhaps a fine granddaughter looking like yourself that the torque will bless as well."

He lifted the glass of wine that sat at his elbow and toasted the portrait.

"I miss ya, love," he whispered, his chest aching with the loss. "But I was blessed in you."

He sipped at the wine.

It had been many years since he had visited America. Perhaps it was time to return. To see the fine ranch Jack spoke of and to share in the happiness he could hear in his daughter's voice.

"Just a short visit, love," he whispered, glancing at the portrait once again. "Shall we go?"

She was gone these many years, but he knew she traveled with him, no matter where he went. She was his heart.

Just as Angel was now Jack's heart. As Jack was Angel's.

A generation for the torque to bless.

About the Author

Lora Leigh is a wife and mother living in Kentucky. She dreams in bright, vivid images of the characters intent on taking over her writing life, and fights a constant battle to put them on the hard drive of her computer before they can disappear as fast as they appeared.

Lora's family, and her writing life co-exist, if not in harmony, in relative peace with each other. An understanding husband is the key to late nights with difficult scenes and stubborn characters. His insights into human nature and the workings of the male psyche provide her hours of laughter, and innumerable romantic ideas that she works tirelessly to put into effect.

Lora welcomes comments from readers. You can find her website and email address on her author bio page at www.ellorascave.com.

Tell Us What You Think

We appreciate hearing reader opinions about our books. You can email us at Comments@EllorasCave.com.

Also by LoraLeigh

B.O.B.'s Fall *with Veronica Chadwick*
Bound Hearts 1: Surrender
Bound Hearts 2: Submission
Bound Hearts 3: Seduction
Bound Hearts 4: Wicked Intent
Bound Hearts 5: Sacrifice
Bound Hearts 6: Embraced
Bound Hearts7: Shameless
Cowboy & the Captive
Dragon Prime
Elemental Desires (*Anthology*)
Ellora's Cavemen: Tales for the Temple I (*Anthology*)
Feline Breeds 1: Tempting the Beast
Feline Breeds 2: The Man Within
Feline Breeds 3: Kiss of Heat
Legacies 1: Shattered Legacy
Legacies 2: Shadowed Legacy
Legacies 3: Savage Legacy
Manaconda (*Anthology*)
Men of August 1: Marly's Choice
Men of August 2: Sarah's Seduction
Men of August 3: Heather's Gift
Men of August 4: August Heat
Ménage a Magick
Moving Violations *with Veronica Chadwick*
Soul Deep
When Wizards Rule
Wolf Breeds 1: Wolfe's Hope
Wolf Breeds 2: Jacob's Faith
Wolf Breeds 3: Aiden's Charity
Wolf Breeds 4: Elizabeth's Wolf

Why an electronic book?

We live in the Information Age—an exciting time in the history of human civilization, in which technology rules supreme and continues to progress in leaps and bounds every minute of every day. For a multitude of reasons, more and more avid literary fans are opting to purchase e-books instead of paper books. The question from those not yet initiated into the world of electronic reading is simply: *Why?*

1. ***Price.*** An electronic title at Ellora's Cave Publishing and Cerridwen Press runs anywhere from 40% to 75% less than the cover price of the exact same title in paperback format. Why? Basic mathematics and cost. It is less expensive to publish an e-book (no paper and printing, no warehousing and shipping) than it is to publish a paperback, so the savings are passed along to the consumer.
2. ***Space.*** Running out of room in your house for your books? That is one worry you will never have with electronic books. For a low one-time cost, you can purchase a handheld device specifically designed for e-reading. Many e-readers have large, convenient screens for viewing. Better yet, hundreds of titles can be stored within your new library—on a single microchip. There are a variety of e-readers from different manufacturers. You can also read e-books on your PC or laptop computer. (Please note that

Ellora's Cave does not endorse any specific brands. You can check our websites at www.ellorascave.com or www.cerridwenpress.com for information we make available to new consumers.)

3. ***Mobility.*** Because your new e-library consists of only a microchip within a small, easily transportable e-reader, your entire cache of books can be taken with you wherever you go.
4. ***Personal Viewing Preferences.*** Are the words you are currently reading too small? Too large? Too... ANNOYING? Paperback books cannot be modified according to personal preferences, but e-books can.
5. ***Instant Gratification.*** Is it the middle of the night and all the bookstores near you are closed? Are you tired of waiting days, sometimes weeks, for bookstores to ship the novels you bought? Ellora's Cave Publishing sells instantaneous downloads twenty-four hours a day, seven days a week, every day of the year. Our webstore is never closed. Our e-book delivery system is 100% automated, meaning your order is filled as soon as you pay for it.

Those are a few of the top reasons why electronic books are replacing paperbacks for many avid readers.

As always, Ellora's Cave and Cerridwen Press welcome your questions and comments. We invite you to email us at Comments@ellorascave.com or write to us directly at Ellora's Cave Publishing Inc., 1056 Home Avenue, Akron, OH 44310-3502.

Breinigsville, PA USA
30 June 2010
240966BV00001B/75/P

9 781419 952326